Folkloric Ruse

Book Three of the Folkloric Series

Karenza Grant

L'Ours

A L'OURS BOOKS ebook

Ebook first published in 2024 by L'Ours Books

Copyright © Karenza Grant

Cover: Deranged Doctor Design

Copyediting: Toby Selwyn

ISBN (ebook) 978-1-915737-09-0

ISBN (paperback) 978-1-915737-10-6

www.karenzagrant.com

To Rillian

FOLKLORIC RUSE

BOOK THREE OF THE FOLKLORIC SERIES

Written in British English

www.karenzagrant.com

CHAPTER 1

WHAT I WANTED MOST OF ALL WAS TO LOSE MYSELF FOR the night, then all my problems would disappear.

Yes, it was a temporary solution. Actually, it wasn't a solution at all, but it would mean I could forget the raw emotion surging deep within me, just for a little while.

My plan was working. Eliot made the perfect distraction. He stood only inches away in Castle Rock, the crowded medieval-style bar. His combination of intense gaze, swept-back dark waves and pensive, sensuous lips was so damned hot.

"I have to admit, I'm intrigued, Camille," he drawled, his voice low and melodious. "The folklore you've studied in the region is fascinating, and it ties in with my field of history. I'd love to hear more."

Our electric eye contact was enough to ease away eighties night and Vanessa Paradis blaring out. It was almost enough to make me forget Alice standing at the far end of the bar beyond the tables, chatting with Raphaël and some of our old friends. Thinking of her submerged me under a fresh wave of despair. She couldn't understand why I was against her engagement to Raphaël, and we'd fallen out about it. Majorly.

But Eliot was saying all the right things. We both knew we weren't here for folklore. Every part of his fit body under his black V-neck T-shirt was attuned to mine. And dang, his scent. Honestly, it reminded me of old churches—myrrh, perhaps—though churches really shouldn't be a turn-on, and there was nothing holy about this guy. Whatever. I wanted more.

"I'd like to tell you about it," I said, my voice slow and suggestive. "Where to start?" I tipped back the last of my awful non-alcoholic wine, my shoulders stiff from the constant bouts of Keeper training over the last couple of weeks since midsummer.

Eliot's lips blossomed into a smile. Oh my god, that smile. Playful, a little mischievous, utterly delicious. "Hold that thought." He took my glass. "What will it be?"

"Uh, mineral water would be great."

With a scorching backward glance, Eliot eased through the crowd to the bar.

Boy, did I need something stronger than water to alleviate the turmoil, but I'd already drunk one glass of real wine, and I had hand-to-hand combat with Grampi in the morning. He was lethal, despite his age, and I was taking training seriously. It was the least I could do to ease his worries about me being a Keeper. Plus, the instruction was top notch. I was also sparring with Lucas every evening after work. The sessions were gruelling, but I was improving quickly.

All that aside, ever since the drunken night when I'd slept with Lucas, I was being a good girl. Well, not too good— my sights were set on Eliot—but I wasn't going to make any more drunken mistakes. Sober mistakes, on the other hand, were perfectly acceptable.

I leant against a pillar as I waited, the sultry heat of the place pressing in, the track changing to something I didn't recognise. Unbidden, my gaze drifted to the other side of the bar. Alice. All my frustration and anguish rushed back. Not knowing what to do with myself, I folded my arms across my chiffon top as I looked around for someone nearby that I knew. No one, damn it. I'd join Eliot at the bar if it wasn't so packed.

My gaze returned to Alice. Her arms were wrapped around Raphaël's neck, a suit of armour on the wall to one side of them, a shield to the other. I missed her so much. She was my confidante, my stalwart supporter. We just sort of fitted together, and life was so much better that way. She was more than a friend—she was everything to me. She leant toward Raphaël and drew him into a deep kiss.

Ugh. If only she could see his grey leathery skin, his pot belly, his wrinkles and those jagged goblin teeth. He was a complete and utter fraudster. I narrowed my eyes so I could see the glamour he was projecting. With brown curls, long eyelashes and strong shoulders, he was dishy. If only she knew. But Alice had no idea about the hidden world, and she'd think I was mad if I told her.

They were already talking about a date for their wedding. Never one for tradition, Alice was opting for tying the knot as soon as possible at the town hall. I picked up all the details, working with her at the café.

I'd tried to justify them being together so many times. Perhaps Raphaël really did love her. It definitely looked as though he did. Maybe he would make a good husband. But how could they have a relationship based on lies? I drew in a shaky breath, the air sticking in my throat.

Alice's gaze flicked to mine. In an instant, she turned away.

Fine cracks split my heart. Shit. I didn't need this right now. I scanned the room. Where was Eliot? I couldn't see him through the crowd, but I needed to get out of here. I shouldn't even be in the same room as Alice at the moment, but Guy had dragged me to Foix, our French county town, pleading that he'd needed someone to go with him to eighties night. He'd purposefully not told me that Alice was going to be here. A sweet but naïve plan to get us back together, Castle Rock being our favourite bar. If only Guy knew half of what was really going on.

Eliot pushed back through the throng and passed my mineral water. Sweetly, he'd opted for the same. "Where were we?"

His gaze locked on mine, his eyes dark—possibly more impenetrable than Lucas's, which was saying something, but I really didn't need to think of *him* right now. "History, was it? Or folklore. And before that, you were saying that you've just moved into the area."

"Yeah, I can't get enough of the town. Foix is stunning. I've explored the chateau repeatedly. Troubadours, chivalry, honourable gentry who cared for their people. The place is amazing."

Caught by the intensity in his gaze, I shifted closer. Even if Eliot hadn't been so fine, he would've had all my attention with those sentiments. I'd worked in the Chateau de Foix on and off as a volunteer a few years ago and loved the place. What was this man doing to me? He was certainly a distraction from Alice. All the same, I couldn't stand much more of her ignoring me.

Eliot took a lock of my hair and wrapped it around his finger. I'd worn it loose for a change. It was so often tied up whilst training or working. My lips parted as I watched him. "Maybe history could wait for another time," I murmured close to his cheek, his warmth intoxicating.

"I really would like to know more." His breath tickled my skin.

"We could talk a little... at your place." Like that was going to happen. I vaguely noticed "You Give Love a Bad Name" by Bon Jovi coming on.

Eliot's mouth quirked. "I'd like that very much."

That was it. I couldn't resist any longer. Tilting my head, I drew my lips to his. As my eyelids fell in expectation, I caught a commotion in the crowd—people jumping aside as a figure charged through.

Before I could make sense of what was going on, the figure slammed into Eliot, our drinks flying, glass shattering. The two of them hurtled through the throng and hit the bar.

The figure pinned Eliot against the top and drove his fist into the side of his head again and again.

Panic streaked through me. I could only see the attacker's back, but the dishevelled hair and sturdy physique were unmistakable.

Lucas.

CHAPTER 2

I stormed through the startled crowd, my alarm edged with fury.

"I can't believe it," I yelled at Lucas, who was still laying into Eliot. Blood was trickling from the poor guy's nose. "Let him go!"

"Get back, Camille." Lucas continued his barrage without glancing up. Eliot, flat against the bar, wriggled in his grip, trying to escape. The whole place was gazing on in agitated fascination.

"I'm not going anywhere," I shouted. "That's my goddamned hookup."

Outrage twisted Lucas's broad mouth and angular cheeks.

Was that a smirk on Eliot's battered face? I had to be mistaken. "My hookup," he managed.

Lucas thrust the punch to end all punches into the side of his face. I grabbed his waist and tried to pull him off, avoiding his elbow as he drew his arm back repeatedly, but he was too strong.

"Is this some sort of possessive drac behaviour?" I growled. There had been signs of it before with Pascale. "What have you been doing, watching me?" I honestly didn't think it was possible to feel angrier than I did right now.

Lucas ignored me. If I didn't do something, he was going to kill Eliot. I needed help. I glanced up at the bar staff. The nearest girl was staring at the spectacle, her mouth open.

"Where's Big Boris?" I called. He would sort this out. Though I doubted even his brawn was a match for Lucas.

"Stuck on the loo," she said. "Tummy trouble. I'll go see if he's done."

I tugged at Lucas again, to no effect. Eliot's head was lolling to one side. Nothing for it. I balled my fist, drew back my arm and drove it into the only vulnerable part of Lucas I could reach, his left kidney.

It was like striking granite. Lucas shot me a side glare, and it was enough to give Eliot the advantage. Dazed, his face a mess, he reached along the bar, grabbed a bottle of wine and thrust it toward Lucas's head. But Lucas was too quick. He slammed his fist into the bottle. It exploded in Eliot's hand, wine splattering over them. Eliot mustered himself, pushed forward and shoved them both away from the bar, then drove a series of punches and kicks into Lucas. Lucas could do nothing but defend himself, stepping backward.

I stared, my jaw slack. There was no way Eliot, primary

school teacher and history buff, should know how to fight like that. And he was fast... a little too fast for a human.

I swallowed. Eliot was fae.

Eliot smashed his knuckles into Lucas's face so hard that he was thrown back onto a table, the inhabitants diving out the way, coq au vin and pieces of baguette scattering everywhere, glasses and cutlery crashing to the ground.

In a split-second, Lucas recovered. He ran at Eliot and drove him through the open double doors of the fire exit into the dark side street. They tumbled over, breaking apart. I dashed out after them. Eliot scampered to his feet, glaring at Lucas. Hauling ragged breaths, he stepped backward into the street-lit square at the front of Castle Rock. "Enough," he said with impressive dignity, considering how smashed up he was.

Lucas returned a death stare as he strutted forward. His cheek was split and sweat soaked through his shirt, mingling with wine and blood that was probably Eliot's. He wasn't going to let it drop.

I followed them into the square, a load of patrons behind me. Castle Rock's tables sprawled from its open front onto the pavement, diners watching with curiosity. Tall townhouses rose around us, most of the windows shuttered for the night. The drone of Bon Jovi was quieter here, but still audible, mingling with the bubbling of the fountain in the square's centre.

Lucas and Eliot faced each other in a Western standoff, two perfect specimens, chests heaving, clothes torn.

Eliot made to walk away, shaking his head, then he

turned, and before I knew what was happening, he swung around and thrust his foot into Lucas's temple. Lucas didn't have a chance to react. He stumbled back and fell to the cobbles. With a look that could have razed Foix to the ground, Eliot sprang on Lucas, pinned him down and gripped his throat. I had no idea what was going on, but this had to stop. I dove forward, this time trying to pull Eliot off.

"Keep out of this, Camille," Lucas slurred as Eliot squeezed. Was he drunk?

"Yes," Eliot replied. "Keep out of this. We need to keep you in one piece for when I'm finished and we go back to my place. I'm going to do you so hard."

"Way to charm, Eliot. And I really thought you were a nice guy." Yep, this had been one hell of a sober mistake.

If Lucas had appeared evil before, he looked worse now. With a battle cry, he forced himself up, threw Eliot off and jumped on him. Eliot's head struck the edge of the fountain. The impact would've knocked out a human, but he was merely dazed.

"You can't kill me," Eliot spat.

"Want to bet?" Lucas pummelled him afresh.

Sirens wailed.

These two weren't playing by normal rules. But the onlookers that by now constituted the majority of the bar plus residents peering from their windows were totally aghast. Alice and Raphaël stood in the crowd, Alice shaking her head. Lucas was pummelling Eliot in a way that would mean death to most folk. If he wasn't careful, he was going to be in serious trouble. He changed tactic and slammed Eliot's head repeatedly against the fountain rim.

I knelt down at Lucas's side, blanching at the waft of alcohol on his breath. "Lucas, listen to me." A police car drew up, the lights casting blazing clarity on the mangled state of both men.

Fury contorted Lucas's face, his gaze laser-focussed on Eliot. He wasn't on this planet—he was in some kind of kill mode. He'd clearly drunk a lot, and no doubt that wasn't helping.

"Lucas, we're partners." I placed my hand on his back. "You have to listen."

His eyes flicked to mine.

"I don't know what the hell is going on here, but to everyone else, it looks bad. Very bad. You need to stop now because people are watching. You don't want to lose all the trust you've built as a doctor."

He lowered his fist and gripped Eliot around the neck. With a last thrust, he stood up and stepped away, his eyes burning.

Eliot sprang up and raised his gashed chin in an expression I recognised from Lucas. "As you're unlikely to deal with the police, dear brother"—he spat blood onto the ground —"I guess I'll have to." He shook his head and laughed as he turned to meet the two gendarmes.

Brothers.

I gaped, my gaze switching from one to the other. How could I have been so stupid? I could see it now in Eliot—no, Elivorn. He had to be Elivorn—the line of his battered cheeks was similar to Lucas's. His nose was a close match too, but his face was rounder, his features softer, and he was a little shorter.

How had I found him so attractive? He was gorgeous in one way, but it was the soul that lay beneath outer appearances that gave a person their true beauty, and I could tell by the menace in Elivorn's eyes that his soul was black. For heaven's sake, only two weeks ago, he'd tried to kill Lucas and tear the realms apart, albeit indirectly through Anthras.

But then, of course, he was a drac, which meant he was an incubus like Lucas. Dismay filled me. I'd been seduced.

CHAPTER 3

CONFUSION TORE THROUGH ME, MY STOMACH WEAK. IT was just like the time when Lucas had shown me what it felt like to be under the sway of an incubus. Elivorn had done the same, but I'd had no idea. It left me reeling, much too open, way too vulnerable. A flare of fierce indignation blazed inside. I wasn't going to let myself feel used. Elivorn was absolute ground slime. He could go to hell.

The crowd gaped at us, their concerned gazes switching from Elivorn, who couldn't keep the mirth off his face, to Lucas, who was swaying precariously.

"Come on," Lucas slurred. "Let's get out of here. My car is by the chateau."

"What? We can't walk away from the police. They'll want to have a word, if not more."

"You heard Elivorn. He's dealing with it."

"How?"

"The same way he dealt with you." Lucas's split lip

curled, causing him to wince. "He's highly skilled in coercion, and he's happy to use his influence whenever he can."

Anger needled me. I couldn't believe I'd been such an easy target.

Guy stepped out of the crowd, blond hair bouncing, bright eyes concerned. "Hey, is there something I can do to help? A lift home?" He was talking to me but staring at Lucas. "You're totally wrecked, Doc."

Lucas flicked gore off his hand. "I'm fine."

"Doesn't look like it, bro."

"I'm going to take him back," I said. "I won't be needing a ride. Thanks for trying to help with Alice."

Guy shook his head, his gaze not leaving Lucas. "Sure thing."

Elivorn was still talking to the police. I grabbed Lucas's hand and tugged him toward the street that led to the chateau. Time to get them as far apart as possible. I could feel Alice's eyes burning into me. I didn't look back. There wasn't any point. But even as we rounded the corner out of sight of the square, the burning remained, so much worse than Elivorn or my anger.

"I have healing potion in the car," Lucas said. "I need some."

"You don't say." Those beautiful features were swollen, his cheek and chin split, both eyes rimmed with blue and swelling fast. On top of it all, there was a green tinge to his skin. He was so completely battered. It took a lot to injure Lucas, but I supposed the dracs were evenly matched.

"But how did you know Elivorn was at Castle Rock?" I

asked. "I thought you'd been stalking me or something." And my reaction just went to show how much I was still struggling to trust him. How many times did he have to prove he had my back?

He bumped into me, laughed at his lack of coordination, then groaned. "Stalking you?" He heaved a little and thrust his hand over his mouth.

"It was the most likely explanation. I didn't know the details." The Chateau de Foix, perched on a huge outcrop of rock, rose high above the roofs of the townhouses as we walked closer—or in Lucas's case, swayed closer. The medieval castle's three massive turrets were floodlit. Beacons in the balmy summer night.

"Yes, I was stalking. Stalking Elivorn, not you." He glowered in the direction of the square. "That absolute..." He made to head back.

"Police, remember. Let's get home."

Lucas tottered sideways, narrowly missing a lamp post. "One day, I'll tear him limb from limb." He heaved again, then yelled, "You hear that, Elivorn? Tear you limb from limb!"

I glared at the mess that was Lucas. "You're so completely plastered, and if you're not careful, you're going to wake up everyone in Foix."

"Don't be silly, Camille," he said, holding his head high. "I'm absolutely, one hundred percent compos mentis." He stumbled into a doorway, fell onto his knees and vomited.

"And this is my partner?" I turned the other way as the acrid stench of sick wafted over. But I couldn't deny he'd saved me from Elivorn's charms. When I turned back, Lucas was lying on the cobbles, groaning.

I walked over and nudged him with my foot. "The quicker we get you out of here, the better, and there's no way I can carry you."

"I'm fine, Camille. Just leave me to my beauty sleep."

"Not here. You'll attract the police or end up in hospital with a face like yours." And definitely not with Elivorn close by.

"Well, if you insist." He hiccupped then said, "Men."

Slaughter and a large band of pint-sized prehistoric warriors popped out of a doorway behind us and marched over. The Men of Bédeilhac. And for once they weren't holding weapons.

Slaughter tutted, his wild beard shaking. "Honestly, Camille. Look at the state Lucas has gotten himself into. You can see why he needs us, can't you? We shouldn't really let him out of our sight. Look what happens when we do."

Lucas groaned some more.

As one, the Men shifted into formation around his body, tucking their shoulders under him. "Heave ho," Slaughter ordered. With Lucas still flat on his back, they levered him into the air, positioned themselves underneath, and set off.

Lucas glided down the street. Grinning, he stretched his arms out to the sides. "It's the only way to ride!"

"For crying out loud," I muttered. What if someone saw? But at least I didn't have to carry him. The Arget river was nearby. Perhaps if I got Slaughter to tip him in, he might sober up. But first things first. "Elivorn—"

Lucas shifted his weight to one side, his ripped shirt falling open, revealing his sculpted chest splattered with red.

"Support his left," Slaughter commanded. Staggering, the Men altered their positions, the whole caboodle of fae and prostrate drunken drac swaying to the other side of the street. Lucas shifted once more, and they swayed back again.

"Whooooaaaa," Lucas yelled.

I closed my eyes for a couple of seconds then followed. I did not need this on top of Alice. Lucas laughed to himself as he soared along. He raised his hands toward the chateau looming above us. "Raymond Roger," he cried. "The most honourable of men. I miss you, my friend."

"What?" My jaw dropped. "You knew Raymond Roger, the sixth count of Foix?" I had to check because a number of the Trencavels shared that name in the twelfth century. Clearly a favourite. Anyway, Lucas was out-of-his-mind drunk. Not exactly a reliable source.

"Raymond," Lucas bellowed as he flew along the street. "I'm sworn to your allegiance. I will fight eternally at your side."

"Will you shut up!" a voice roared from one of the houses.

I couldn't help myself. "You really knew him?" I was fascinated by the history of that time. It was the reason I'd helped out at the chateau. But I could barely believe it all the same. I still hadn't asked Lucas when he was born because I had an inkling the answer would fry my brain, but I was sure it wasn't in the common era.

He turned his head, the Men underneath diving to

support his weight. "I was his loyal, undying servant." Undying was true. "His most trusted knight."

I snorted. "I hadn't really pegged you for chivalrous on account of your penchant for trickery. But I guess if I put that aside... maybe. And that's a definite maybe." This plus my lovely introduction to Elivorn only highlighted how little I knew of Lucas's past.

But he'd known Raymond Roger. He'd been here when the Trencavels had shaped the future of the Western world with their noble beliefs—equality of gender and race, and the extolling of faith, courage, loyalty, generosity and, above all, love. Chivalry had emerged here, back then, right in this very spot. I eyed the drunken, battered mess that floated along the street under the struggling band of fae, unable to believe it.

"Come on, Camille, even the most committed knight has to have a laugh once in a while. A little trickery helps lighten the mood, especially before battle." Lucas hiccupped again. "Raymond Roger was more of a brother than Elivorn will ever be." He slumped back, almost crushing a cluster of Men, who cussed heartily.

"Keep still, gov," Slaughter hollered. "You're heavy enough as it is."

"And anyway," Lucas continued, pointing a finger at me, "those principles are still alive in Fae courts—the ones I prefer to associate with—although there are plenty of fae that operate by their own standards."

A couple, arm in arm, emerged from a side street a little way ahead. In the blink of an eye, the Men deposited Lucas flat on the cobbles and disappeared.

"Hey," Lucas called. "Come back."

The couple eyed him as they walked past, wincing at his injuries. He just grinned inanely. But hell, he was a bloody mess. Not knowing what else to do, I plastered on my best I-have-everything-under-control smile.

"You look like you could use a hand." one of the guys said, his brow furrowed.

"Uh, no, it's fine. Our ride isn't far." I glanced at Lucas. "He'll be up in a moment." Up in the sense of soaring upon a load of miniature prehistoric Men, but they didn't need to know that.

They headed onward. When they were out of sight, the Men appeared from an alley and raised Lucas aloft. "We're off," he cried, and broke into hysterics.

"But Elivorn," I said, hurrying after them. "What's going on? He knew who I was, so why did he hit on me?" One thing was for sure, I needed to raise some inner defences against his incubus crap.

"No idea what that shithead is up to. He moved into the area not long after midsummer. The Men have been watching him. Slaughter raised the alarm tonight, and I got here as quickly as I could. See...? Knight in shining armour." He shifted his weight once more, the Men groaning.

I snorted. "Today you get knight points, although I'm deducting some for throwing up in the street, not to mention the tricks you've pulled in training lately."

"Not all fae play fair in combat. You need to know what you're up against."

We swung a right and headed up the incline around the

base of the massive prominence on which the Chateau de
Foix stood. The street opened into a small tree-lined square,
Lucas's SUV parked in the far corner. To our side, the
chateau entrance and the museum were cordoned off with
yellow police incident tape, the scene long abandoned by the
gendarmerie.

"I wonder what's going on," I said. Old Herbert, the security guard, walked along the battlements above. He'd always
been so sweet when I'd worked there.

"I hope you're not asking me." Lucas and the Men
slowed to a halt by his car. "Because nothing is making sense
at the moment."

The Men lowered Lucas to the ground. "There you go,
gov," Slaughter said. The whole troop disappeared under the
chassis.

Lucas staggered up, fished in his pocket for his keys and
pulled the boot open with a groan. He really did look a mess.
He grabbed a leather case, undid the buckle and drew out a
vial. Lifting his brow, his smile slightly manic, he waved it in
front of me. "Sobering potion. I really don't want a clear head
right now, but if I don't take it, I'm going to be sick again." He
narrowed his gaze, swore under his breath, then chugged the
bottle.

Immediately, his eyes focussed and his skin returned to a
healthy colour. He inclined his head to the police cordon.
"Another break-in, maybe?" His voice was steady, all hilarity
gone. "But that would be the second here in a week. There
have also been thefts at the Musée Saint-Raymond in
Toulouse, the Biblothèque Nationale in Paris and a number

of private collections." He wiped his mouth with the back of his hand. "The police think they're all linked."

I stared at him, unable to believe the transformation. "Yeah, I read about it. A load of medieval manuscripts were taken at each place. But... you're back to your normal self, just like that?" Well, apart from his completely battered face. "No more 'Wheeeeee, this is the way to ride'?" I mimicked him vomiting.

"What?" He shrugged. "Sobering potion. I told you. I always have some handy. Unfortunately, I'll still get something of a hangover in the morning. Anyway, I wasn't that bad."

I shook my head. "Next time, keep the vial on you, then the Men and I won't have to carry you home."

Ignoring me, he pulled another vial from the case and downed it. "Healing potion..." No doubt he'd be alright in a few minutes. The stuff got to work right away. "But that asshole of a brother of mine..." His face closed over.

"Let's get you home." Ideally before he took it upon himself to hunt Elivorn down again.

Scowling, he hobbled around to the driver's side. I held out my palm. "You were plastered a second ago. I'm not comfortable with you driving. Anyway, you don't look up to it."

With a shake of his head, he passed me the keys and limped to the passenger door. I climbed in and pushed the ignition. As we drew away, Lucas gazed up at the chateau, and for an instant, a hint of vulnerability flickered in his eyes.

CHAPTER 4

I DREW UP BEFORE LUCAS'S ELEGANT HOUSE, THE headlights illuminating the mansard roof and painted woodwork. Alice was still heavily on my mind, but right now, Lucas was my primary concern. It was difficult to see in the dim light, but he looked just as bad as he had when we left Foix, his face swollen, his wounds open. When I'd called for a cab home, he hadn't even argued that he'd drive me. My ride wouldn't get here for a while, so I'd have enough time to make sure he was alright.

"I thought you would've begun healing by now," I said as we got out. "The potion usually works immediately."

I followed a hobbling Lucas to the back door, crickets singing. The stars shimmered above the outline of the mountains, the scent of evening primrose heady in the warm air.

"It's a drac thing," he replied, "especially between brothers. If we injure each other, the damage doesn't heal easily.

It's one of a few age-old caveats to prevent siblings using lethal means to gain land and status."

"Gives a new dimension to sibling rivalry." We stepped into the kitchen. The floral fragrance was replaced by a hint of rosemary, bringing back the scent of Lucas's skin.

He clicked on the lamp by the window, the glow suffusing the wooden cupboards and worktops, the range a homely centrepiece. Bundles of herbs hung from the beams, casting long shadows. With a groan, Lucas pulled out a chair at the old farmhouse table and slumped down. He'd developed a permanent glower on the way home, but now it was even darker.

"Where's your first-aid equipment?" If he wasn't going to heal super fast, his wounds would have to be dealt with.

"My lab. The cupboard behind the door." Lucas's eyes were closed and there wasn't a hint of objection. "And grab the small blue bottle there too."

I put the kettle on, then headed into the lab and found the bottle, gauze swabs and a dish. Once I'd carried everything in and placed it on the table, I filled the dish with warm water, grabbed a towel, then paused to examine the damage, wincing at Lucas. He scowled back at me. One of his eyelids was painfully swollen, the other not much better, and there was a lot of blood—from his nose mainly but also from cuts on his cheek, chin, forehead and lip.

He met my gaze, his glower not shifting. "Handsome as always."

Right at this moment, he was far from it, though the state of him did nothing to diminish the sense of something feral beneath the surface, which only made me want to fathom him—to truly understand who he was. "Seeing you injured makes me realise how indestructible you are most of the time."

He pulled the bowl over and tipped the contents of the bottle into the water. "With wounds slow to mend because of the drac caveat, I've found that mayweed potion speeds healing. It's not fast acting, but it's something." He dunked the gauze and dabbed at his chin, wincing painfully.

I shook my head, took the gauze and slid onto the table before him, my legs either side of his. "Let me."

"I'm fine, Camille," he snapped.

I let out a sharp laugh. "You didn't even flinch when the dwarf king knifed you. This time you're drac-mangle. And unless you want to stand in front of a mirror, which you don't look up to, you're going to struggle."

He opened his mouth to argue, then sighed.

I wrapped the towel around his neck to catch the drops, then dipped the gauze in the water. Starting at his hairline, I followed the curve of his forehead, wiping off excess blood.

Lucas shifted restlessly, the sinews of his neck tightening. "Really, Camille, I know how to clean my own wounds."

Sitting back, I studied him, a little of his blood dropping from the gauze onto my jeans. "Really? Do you really not want me to help?" Every part of his face was rigid. But I had an inkling that his glower wasn't about his wounds or me. "It's Elivorn, isn't it?"

His gaze darkened. "He almost..." The words grated in his throat.

He'd almost what? Had his way with me, or would it have been worse? I had no idea, but I got the general impression. "He almost, but he didn't."

"I'd like to think he only did it to wind me up," Lucas growled. "It wouldn't surprise me. But as he just moved into the area and the bounds cracks are widening by the day, there's a chance he's up to something else, especially if his collaboration with Anthras was anything to go by."

The bounds cracks had been Lucas and Roux's prime concern since Anthras's escapades. The fae and human realms balanced each other. Humans needed the emotion and inspiration of fae, and fae needed the materiality and structure of the human realm. "I don't understand why anyone would want to split the bounds, seeing as the consequences are so dire." Widespread sickness, insanity, environmental cataclysm and the end of humanity had been mentioned.

Lucas's fingers tensed and released. "Some think that humans are a burden to the world, that this realm isn't vital, and that without it, tremendous power would be released for the benefit of Fae. Elivorn is one of them, and it's likely he's after information of some kind, probably concerning yours truly as he thinks I'll oppose him. I doubt he'd harm you directly. As you're a Keeper, there would be consequences, and he'd bring the assembly's attention on himself."

But coaxing me to sleep with him was just fine? I wasn't going to say it out loud, though. Lucas was tense enough already.

"With me being Elivorn's brother," he continued, "being

a Keeper doesn't mean as much. The assembly would never interfere in drac affairs."

"Just how much power does he have?" I asked, restraining a shudder.

"The usual incubus coercion, engendering desire in another. But he's good at it. He's had plenty of practice. Although it only works when he's close to his victims."

I'd better keep well away, then. The hair by Lucas's ear was caked with dried blood. I softened it with water and brushed it back gently.

Lucas studied my face and swallowed. "It's past time I went into Fae to find out what Elivorn is up to. Being hammered did a great job of making me forget it for all of about five minutes, but I shouldn't have put it off this long, and my reticence placed you in danger. I'll arrange a locum and head there tomorrow, first thing."

I began working on his nose. "I'll come with you—"

"No," he shot out, the word hard and final.

I raised my brow. "Partners, right?"

"Yes, but not this. Grimmere is no place for you."

"What do you mean by that?" I straightened up. "You're the one so desperate for me to gain experience in Fae."

"This is different. You don't want to go anywhere near Grimmere. Trust me. I'll go home for a few days, suss out what's going on, then return to update you fully."

"Trust?" I leant forward, wiping the blood from his chin in soft sweeps. Tonight he'd proven once again that he was loyal, yet a part of me wasn't convinced. I drew the gauze over his top lip, the graceful line enticing me despite the swelling and the split.

"Camille"—there was gravity in his gaze—"we're partners. I need you to trust me. Our relationship depends on it."

I scowled. "Way to build a relationship, spiking my drink, playing jokes on me and being a complete..." I was going to say ass, but that wasn't it exactly.

"A complete what?" A glint lit his eye, and with it, his shoulders relaxed a little.

"A complete fae, that's what." He really was the epitome of a trickster. It was his nature, but it didn't exactly help. And now he wasn't willing to share about his family. It was his life, though, and if he didn't want me to accompany him, there wasn't much I could do about it. "But Grimmere..." I couldn't stop myself laughing as I pulled the towel from his neck and dabbed his reasonably clean skin. "What a name. It's so storybook and... dark."

"Are you being judgemental about my birthplace?" The decent side of his mouth curved up as he wrapped his hands around mine, his touch sending shivers through me. The caves near Les Profondeurs came to mind. The taste of him. His body pressed against mine. He studied my fingers for a moment. "But yes, it's a dark place."

"I'll have to take your word for it." I scoured his face. The swelling had eased a bit, although the cuts were still as evident. "You're looking a little better already. What about the rest of you?"

"I should be good by the morning. No need to undress me." He smirked, releasing my fingers.

Shaking my head, I got up and gathered the gauze. With my concerns for Lucas dwindling, Alice returned to the fore, the all too familiar wave of despair hitting me anew. I missed her so damned much. There had to be something I could do about her and Raphaël—

"Camille?"

"What?" I turned to Lucas.

"Something's bothering you. Is it Elivorn? I can't believe I let—"

"No." All of Lucas's rigidity had returned. He really didn't need to get worked up. "It's not him." Yes, Elivorn had completely creeped me out, and I hated to think what might have happened, but what lay between me and Alice was far deeper, and it hurt so badly.

By the flush spreading up his neck, Lucas needed convincing. "It's Alice and Raphaël," I said, my voice rough. "I still don't know how to handle it."

He nodded, his shoulders sinking again. "Relationships where the fae isn't open about their true nature happen sometimes." There were plenty of accounts of that sort of thing in folklore. He adjusted his shirt. "Keepers don't usually get involved—not that I'm condoning it. It's just uncommon for the human to find out, and both parties generally lead normal lives, all things considered. I have to say, it's curious that Raphaël is managing to hold down a job and a fiancé."

"Oh?"

"You know what goblins are like. They're pranksters who see the world in their own way. A few make it work in the human realm, though, and I guess Raphaël is one of them. But your friendship with Alice is important. Maybe you should do something about it."

"You don't say?" I bit out. Shaking my head, I leant against the table. "But what? I can't tell her the truth. There's nothing I can do."

"There is something. Give me a moment." He pushed himself up carefully, rolled his shoulders, then strode out of the kitchen, not a limp in sight.

A thread of hope twisted through me. Perhaps there *was* some way around the situation. I dropped the gauze in the bin and tidied up everything else. Lucas returned with a vial. He placed it on the table.

I stepped over, an eyebrow raised.

"Verity," he said. "One drop should be enough for Alice."

"What?" Every shred of hope fell away as I gazed at the potion that revealed the hidden world.

"You'll need to be careful. Humans are fascinated by the stuff—drawn to it. When I put it in your tea, I had no doubt you'd drink it."

"I really can't believe you're offering this to me again." I gritted my teeth, anger roiling in my chest. He'd brought up the idea when we'd been dealing with Anthras. I thought I'd made it clear where I stood on the matter, and I wasn't just furious with his reminder of that oh-so-lovely day when he spiked my drink, it was his nonchalance. He was oblivious to the implications. "You don't get it, do you? I'd be altering Alice's reality, stripping away everything she knows and loves in one fell swoop, denying her any chance of an ordinary existence." Which was exactly what had happened to me. My world had come crashing down, and here I was, spanning the bridge between two realms, unable to talk to my best friend about my life. "I would never put her in that position."

"But Camille," he said softly. I might have been mistaken, but those dark eyes appeared to hold a glimmer of compassion. "You would be showing her reality."

"And what right do I have to make that decision for her?" My voice rose, my heart pounding. "Absolutely no right at all."

Tyres crunched outside, an engine purring. The cab.

My breath grew shallow. I wanted to help Alice. I wanted everything to go back to normal. I needed her. But what Lucas was proposing... It was impossible. I watched the cab reverse, then met Lucas's eye. "I have to go. Good luck in Grimmere."

He nodded. "I'll need it."

But my gaze returned to the vial. The glass bottle held so much within. I turned to the door then paused, glancing at the verity again. With a trembling hand, I stepped back, grabbed the vial and headed out to the cab.

CHAPTER 5

As I cleared Shroom-Jean's table, I tried to ignore the vial of verity that lay in the pocket of my chinos. All day it had felt as if it was burning a hole in my leg. To take my mind off it, I glanced out to the parking area through the array of open windows along the front of the café. Alice had mentioned to Guy that Raphaël would be dropping by soon to force her to have a break from the accounts. Perfect timing because there *was* something I could do other than give Alice verity. I could have it out with that sleezeball goblin.

It should've happened long before now, but I'd never gotten the creep alone. He was avoiding me on purpose. He wouldn't be able to today, though. Alice was always super absorbed with the accounts. She wouldn't notice Raphaël was here until he headed into the office, which meant if I caught him in the car park, I had my chance.

"Lovely, Camille," Shroom-Jean said as I wiped the table.

His bright eyes twinkled behind glasses, his narrow face framed by long grey hair. "I much prefer a clean table."

He'd certainly stockpiled the empties. We'd supplied him with plates of patisserie on the house. One thing everyone at the café agreed upon was that Shroom-Jean needed feeding up. None of us could bear to see him so skinny. He was only managing sporadic shepherding work this year, and he was struggling with his bills, food his lowest priority.

"I have to say, I really am very full now." He sat back with a satisfied grin and rubbed his non-existent tummy.

"All part of the service. And don't leave it so long before you come back next time." I slid the vase of golden cone-flowers back to the centre of the table. They were part of Inès's latest floral scheme, along with large displays of sunflowers here and there that complemented the cosy wooden interior. With another glance outside, I picked up the tray and headed over to the D&D nook.

Félix sat facing Hugo and Zach, his longstanding D&D friends who had helped deliver healing potion to the towns-folk during the hantaumo attack. The three of them were in full after-school campaign mode, their more recently recruited comrades in arms missing.

I set my tray down and piled up the plates. "What happened to the other guys doing the campaign?"

Félix glanced up, his caramel curls bobbing. "They couldn't hack the long-term commitment, the lightweights."

Something caught his attention on the other side of the café. I craned my neck to see. Gabe and Nora were heading in, their conversation lively as they gestured and laughed, Gabe's cloak swirling, a contrast to Nora's skinny jeans. It was great that they had each other to share the hidden world with now, and Gabe was definitely enjoying the company if his flushed face and permanent grin were anything to go by. Nora was so absorbed in their conversation that she bumped into Shroom-Jean heading out. His wallet flew from his hand.

"Oh, so sorry!" She bent down to pick it up, swishing her dark, shoulder-length bob to the side. A smile lit her perfectly made-up features. That was unusual in itself, but it was even stranger that she hadn't uttered a snarky comment.

"Not at all, nothing to worry about." Jean shot her a warm grin as she passed his wallet.

I piled the last of the plates onto the tray, Hugo and Zach thanking me as they rearranged game cards and paraphernalia ready to continue.

Félix's gaze was still on Gabe, who had joined the queue at the counter. "I just can't believe it," he muttered, his puppy-dog brow wrinkled. That and his soft nose made him look younger than sixteen. "Gabe has only gotten the most popular, most beautiful girl in school."

"The biggest bitch in school, don't you mean?" Hugo murmured as he rifled through a rule book, his bulk filling a good amount of the bench, leaving Zach only a little room.

"He's not *gotten* her," I replied. "They're just friends."

Félix shook his head. "Even so, I don't get how he managed it. I mean, he dresses as an elf, ears and all. Maybe that's what girls want. Legolas *was* pretty cool."

Zach smirked at Félix. "Maybe you should try it."

I laughed. "That I'd like to see."

Félix's gaze lowered to my leg. He studied my chinos with a frown. The corked top of the verity was poking out of my pocket. I shoved it in deeper and turned away to clear the next table, scanning the car park as I piled on cups. No sign of that devious phony.

My tray full, I hauled it up and crashed into Félix. Everything wobbled precariously, cups clanking, a pile of plates sliding to the edge.

"Shit. So sorry, Camille," Félix said. "I was heading to the washroom. Wasn't looking where I was going."

"Nothing broken." I was more interested in the car park.

I dashed the tray around to the washing-up kitchen, then darted back again, but Raphaël still hadn't appeared, and there was a long queue behind the till. I joined Guy, who was shuffling religieuses into boxes at the patisserie counter as he made up a large order. José came out and topped up the shelves with baguettes, pain de campagne and viennoiserie.

"How can I help you?" I asked Madame Ballon, who stood by the till in her flowing kaftan, her short grey hair brushed back, her pendant necklace glimmering. She always wore the most stunning chunky jewellery, and today was no exception. Against her chest lay a half-circle of what I guessed was black quartz, the crystal framed in gold that extended out in rays. The whole thing was like an upside-down black sunrise.

"A cappuccino and a madeleine, please, my dear. I'm a little tired. I was up with the ladies half the night. Dark mafia book club always keeps us chatting." Her eyes sparkled.

"And I have to make it through a meeting at the town hall." She faked a yawn. "You know how it is."

I plated up her madeleine. "I do indeed." René, the mayor and Gabe's father, could be seriously hard work. "I love your necklace."

"One of my favourites. Melville gave it to me on our honeymoon. I miss him every day."

"I bet." I turned to make up her drink.

Guy had transitioned to the espresso machine and was steaming milk. "Camille! Haven't had a chance to catch up with you all day." It was remarkable how all of him sort of bounced when he talked. "Man, that was a gnarly fight last night. I couldn't believe the doc. Didn't know he had it in him, the way he destroyed that guy. Eliot, wasn't it?"

Nope, not Eliot. "Yeah." I scooped coffee grounds into the filter, clicked it in place and switched the machine on.

"And then Eliot, well, he gave as good as he got. Lucas was pulverised." Guy swung his fists in a replay.

"Thanks for the rendition." Alice had been too much of a concern for me to think of that asshole Elivorn, but now cold trickled through me.

"But was Lucas alright?" Guy added. "He was wrecked. I felt for him there."

"Once we cleaned him up, he was good." I'd had a text from him during combat first thing saying that his locum was organised and he was heading into Fae. He'd be back in a week at the latest. I had to admit, it was strange knowing he wouldn't be sitting at his usual table gazing at me in his weird way, or that I wouldn't have to watch out for his annoying tricks for a while. I guessed it meant that I was on my own if anything kicked off, although there was always Roux, and things had been extremely quiet lately. Well, apart from the rat infestation in Super U. What the staff had seen as vermin were in reality the Men playing chase the badger rather enthusiastically through the supermarket aisles. The game hadn't actually involved a badger—the quarry was Snigger wearing a striped pelt—and the whole affair had been sorted in a flash when Lucas had roared at the Men for knocking over the display of local wine and getting plastered on the spoils. The troop had slunk back to their cave shamefaced.

The machine finished, I placed Madame Ballon's coffee on the counter.

"Thank you, my dear." She walked off to the nearest table and placed her things down.

Gabe and Nora passed by on their way out. "Madame Ballon, great to see you." Nora flung her arms around the portly lady. They embraced then fell into conversation. I didn't realise they knew each other.

Guy took the next customer. As the woman behind stepped forward, Félix darted in front. "Sorry to push in. But Camille, I found this on the floor. I think it's yours." The verity lay in his palm.

No. No. Nooooo. I stared at it for a second before snatching it back. It must have dropped out of my pocket while I was doing the tables. I couldn't believe I'd been so careless, especially as I'd been hyperaware of it all day. "Uh, thanks." I tucked the vial firmly into my pocket so there was no way it could fall out again.

"No trouble." Félix darted back to the nook.

I made to take the next order but noticed a shiny BMW arriving in the carpark. Raphaël. I had my chance. "Guy, I need a moment," I said as I walked away.

"No problem," he called.

I stepped into the car park as Raphaël climbed out of his car. He was dressed in his swanky but cheap estate agent's suit, a purple tie knotted neatly at his neck over a blue shirt. His glamour really was knockout gorgeous. What had he done? Studied *GQ* for some male model to imitate, then crafted a collude to fit the bill? Creep.

As I relaxed my gaze, his grey, wrinkled skin was all too clear, his limbs spindly, his suit hanging off him. He was playing dress-up.

He walked around to the back of the car, opened the boot and searched for something, his eyes googly, the small patch of hair on his head quivering. He paused, drew his hand to his mouth and bit his thumbnail with the sharp point of a tooth. How did he not skewer Alice when he kissed her? And when she slept with him... But no, I really didn't want to think about it.

I marched up to him, the sun hot on my skin. His eyes grew wide. Not only was I Alice's best friend, but I was a Keeper, and word had gotten out about the hantaumo queen, not to mention Anthras. I didn't have my blade, but with my recent combat training, I didn't doubt I could take him.

"What the hell do you think you're doing?" I growled.

"Uh, what, Camille?" He shut the boot and edged back against the car.

"You know exactly what I'm talking about, faker. Alice has no idea you're a goblin."

"Come on, Camille." His ears trembled. Yep, he knew I could take him, too. "Be reasonable. You know I love Alice."

I shook my head. "You're lying to her."

"What am I supposed to do? I can't tell her the truth."

"Then you're happy to lie to her for the rest of your lives together? That doesn't sound like the basis of a healthy relationship to me."

"I... I... There's nothing I can do about it. I want to be with her. She wants to be with me."

"Break it up," I said, though the thought of him shattering Alice's heart really wasn't much better. This was all so fucked up.

"No. No way." Raphaël's eyes flicked to something over my shoulder.

My stomach sank. Please, no.

"Break what up?" Alice said, scowling as she stepped to my side. She rammed her hands into the pockets of her ripped jeans, sunlight glinting on her studded belt and the layered charms that hung over her short-sleeved blouse.

Shit. Shit. Shit.

She twigged and her face closed in, her messy locks grazing her shoulders as she spun to face me. I could feel the anger radiating off her. "How could you, Camille? Why can't you be happy for us... for me?"

What on earth was I going to say? I attempted not to shrink from her gaze, my hands trembling. "Maybe you don't know everything about Raphaël," I tried weakly.

"Like what?" She glowered at me then turned to him. "What is there to know?"

He swallowed. "I have absolutely no idea."

I glared at him.

"Camille just doesn't like me," he added, "no matter what I do."

Bastard.

Alice glanced between us, utterly confounded. Then her brow narrowed. "You're jealous, Camille. That's what it is, isn't it? I never would've thought it from you, but as I can't see any other explanation—"

"No, of course that's not it," I spluttered. "It's Raphaël, he's a liar... You have to believe me."

"And even now," she growled, stepping closer, "you're still at it, dead set on breaking us apart. I don't know what your problem is. We have to work together, but apart from that, just keep away from me, keep away from Raphaël, and stop trying to destroy my life."

Chapter 6

Alice grabbed Raphaël's arm and pulled him into the café.

The ground swayed, my chest raw, as the best friend I'd ever known walked away. I couldn't believe this was happening. Years strobed before my eyes, years of Alice and me at school, sticking up for each other in front of teachers. Of us playing hooky and getting suspended. Of us facing the wrath of our parents, knowing we weren't alone.

That time Alice had been seriously ill with mono, I'd spent every hour at the hospital by her side. And when Grampi had his breakdown, only able to speak of goats from then until recently, she'd been there. She'd encouraged me to be patient with him and to try to communicate in another way. My relationship with my parents had been hellish back then, and she'd gotten me through. She was a part of my life. I just couldn't see a way forward without her.

Dazed, I walked back into the café and headed behind

the counter, pausing by the espresso machine with no idea which way to turn.

"You alright?" Guy asked. "You look terrible."

"Uh... I'm fine." I gazed at the entrance to the office corridor. Alice was along there, fuming, her heart possibly as broken as mine.

"You sure?" Guy said as he plated up a canelé.

"All good." A programmed response not minutely connected to reality.

Guy pressed his lips together in concern, but then a customer called.

"I don't want to rush you," she said, "but I've got an appointment in a moment."

"Crap." Guy raked his hand through his hair. "José has had to pop out for a minute. Alice and Raphaël want an espresso and a thé au citron. Would you mind making them up?"

I stared at him, the verity digging into my thigh. The solution to all my problems sat in my pocket, waiting for me. "Uh, yes... sure. No problem."

I had a chance to change this—to make Alice see. I had to do something. Lying to her for the rest of my life wasn't an option.

My heart beating with a low thud, I made up the tray with a teacup and lemon, then spooned tea into the pot and filled it with hot water. That done, I started Alice's espresso. She always had one at this time. As the machine dripped, I pulled out the verity and uncorked it. A faint aroma of cloves wafted up, mingling with freshly baked bread and burnt coffee beans.

This was my chance. If Alice was going to keep her distance, I might not have another, and it wasn't likely I'd have the nerve again. I drew my shaking hand to the cup. Just a drop, Lucas had said. She wouldn't even notice. If Raphaël really was the one for her, she'd accept him, goblin and all.

I tipped the vial, then stopped before the potion could escape.

My world had crumbled when Lucas had given me verity... I'd be putting Alice in the same position. She'd be able to share the truth with me and a few others, but not with her maman, her family or anyone else.

My fingers trembled, the vial shaking.

If she had verity, I'd be shifting my pain onto her, making her feel as bad as me, forcing her to experience this hellish divide, and she would have to live with it.

My hand sank. Nope, I couldn't do it.

"Gonna grab Alice's and Raph's drinks," Guy said. "I'll take them in while I have half a second."

I hid the verity in my fist. "Sure." My breath grew shallow as he lifted the espresso onto the tray, the room pressing in, despair welling up. I needed to be away from noise and people. As Guy walked off, I pressed the cork into the vial, a deep sob racking up. Not knowing where else to hide, I dove for the kitchen.

Thankfully, it was empty. The kitchens were always peaceful in the afternoons. I headed to the worktop in the far corner and leant over it, weeping, pain twisting through my body. This was it. This was the end of the closeness Alice and I had shared for so many years. And here I was standing in her café, in the kitchen her maman had made so cosy with its old-style charm. We couldn't continue working together. I'd have to lie to maintain the peace, but I couldn't. She meant more to me than that. I would have to find another job.

Feet shuffled behind me. I glanced over my shoulder.

Blanche paused in the doorway to the back kitchens, the swirl of hair on her head as white as the snows she commanded. "Oh, Camille, it's you, dear…" I thought she'd left ages ago. Her keen blue eyes took in my state. "Oh my dear." She strode over and wrapped her arms around me.

I wanted to shrug away. This was too painful to share. But Blanche's touch was warmth and comfort. She was an aspect of the mother goddess, the epitome of mothers every-where, and I melted into her soft form, unable to hold back my tears.

"There, there," she murmured against my head, her soapy scent soothing despite the pain that wracked through me.

"I… I don't know what to do," I stammered against her apron strap. "There's no way I can lose Alice, but there's this gulf between us. I can't tell her about the hidden world. We can't be open. She doesn't know what's going on with Lucas. It's a massive mess." It all came flooding out. "And I feel like I'm living a sham. I have a completely different existence to most people, and I have no idea how to deal with it. But Alice is the worst of all. I can't lose her."

Blanche squeezed me tightly. "Oh, Camille, I feel for you. Truly, I do. You're not the first to experience the chasm between realms. Some are given more knowledge than others, and it is indeed a burden of sorts, though it bestows a greater understanding of the world—"

"But Alice—"

"Have faith that things are as they are for a reason, hold that in your heart, and understand that it all tends to come out in the wash."

Scuffling came from the window at the other end of the kitchen.

I pulled back, the intelligence and depth in Blanche's eyes striking me afresh. Her words held weight. They always had. Even so, I had no idea how I was going to get through this.

The scuffling came again. Blanche cocked her head and rubbed my arms. "If I'm not mistaken, that's our dear little friend." She released me and walked over to the window, her long skirt swirling. She leant against the counter and unhooked the latch.

My chest smarting, I pulled off a load of kitchen roll, blew my nose and attempted to dry my eyes.

Mushum hopped onto the preparation counter, the tiny goblin no more than a couple of feet high. When there was a quiet moment, I often opened the window and let him in for some patisserie. He'd helped me so much with the whole hantaumo business, and it was him that had introduced me to Dame Blanche in the first place. I owed him big time, and it was lovely to have his company. But with my thoughts on

Alice, I'd neglected him lately. Today, he didn't look quite himself, his grey skin quivering and even more wrinkled than usual.

"Camille." His voice was high, his eyes bulging. "Mushum has heard something. Mushum knows information that is very important to Camille."

"Well, don't delay," Blanche said, tilting her chin. "Tell us what it is."

"It's Lucas. Mushum likes Lucas. Lucas is nice— Mushum knows it in his heart. But Lucas is in danger." He stretched his arms wide. "Very big danger."

The smarting in my chest sharpened. "What kind of danger?"

"Mushum doesn't know. The only thing Mushum knows for certain is that if Camille doesn't help, Lucas will die."

CHAPTER 7

I RACED ALONG THE COBBLED HIGH STREET IN FAE Tarascon, passing the Peppered Parsnip. Leafy boughs arched above, providing welcome shade from the sun, the canopy an extension of the trunks and branches that formed the structures of the brightly painted shops.

Thoughts whirred through my head. Lucas was in danger. He would die if I didn't do something. My chest ached for Alice and everything that had happened, but if Lucas's life was on the line, I had to put him first, and I couldn't deny that the distraction was helping me cope with the pain that threatened to swamp me.

I'd feigned sickness at the café, pulled on my Keeper gear in the washroom and left Guy and José right in it. Truth be told, I wasn't sure I could've stayed to face Alice anyway, and it wasn't long before closing time. But I had to help Lucas. Mushum's predictions had been accurate every time. As usual, he'd not been able to give me any more information.

His friend and informant, the wind, didn't bother with specifics, but Mushum had been certain that the threat was imminent, and it couldn't possibly wait even a moment.

But Lucas hadn't wanted me to accompany him to Grimmere. He'd said to trust him that it was no place for me, whatever that meant. Well, I wanted to trust him, and I certainly didn't want to tread on his toes, but I couldn't stand by knowing he was in danger.

I had to be sensible, though. In the past couple of weeks, I'd trained my butt off and learnt a fair bit about Fae, but I'd had very little direct experience. I would need to go to Grimmere to find Lucas, but I knew nothing about the place and hadn't a clue how to get there. On top of that, dracs were a mystery to me. All I knew from folklore was that they were incubi and succubi who changed form, and traditionally, they lured people to watery graves, which only went to highlight once again how little I knew about Lucas. I needed to speak to Roux, but he wasn't answering his phone.

Reaching the timber-framed building of the Keepers' post, the lattice windows glinting, I pushed inside. Gabe, Nora and Roux sat at the table in the meeting room, books open before them.

Roux's hands were raised in mid-instruction, his straggly hair and long beard as dishevelled as usual, although today his cloak was reasonably clean. "Good afternoon, Camille."

The other two called greetings.

I closed the door behind me. "Nora. I didn't expect to see you here."

She glanced up, her eyes narrowing, assessing me. "Lucas

thought it would be good if I had somewhere fae-related to hang out, and he said I could use the books to get myself acquainted with everything." There was more to Nora than met the eye. What actually lay beneath her pristine, alpha-girl surface, I wasn't quite sure.

"Yeah." Gabe grinned. "Means we can study together."

"We have a problem," I said, heading over to the library.

"Oh?" Roux asked.

I pushed the door open. The room was dark, the scent of old paper potent. "Lucas mentioned he was going into Fae, right?" I called through.

"Yes, we spoke first thing this morning."

"According to Mushum, Lucas will die unless I go help him."

"Hmm, that is a problem indeed," he muttered.

I placed my blade and bag on the central reading unit and pulled open the thick velvet curtains that kept the sun off the books. Daylight revealed shelf upon shelf of old tomes and rolls of parchment. "We need to find him. But I know nothing about Grimmere or dracs. What can you tell me?"

The books were grouped by subject, and there was a section on species. I scanned the spines. *The Devices of Elves*, *Nightly Habits of the Osencame*, *Twenty Types of Dwarf*. I hadn't realised there was more than one. *Creatures of Sickness and Blight*. *The Delights of Trolls*. Wasn't sure I wanted to read that.

"I'm really not an expert," Roux said, "but you won't find much in there. Lucas removed everything on dracs the other day. He said he didn't want you to find out about him via books. Wants to tell you himself."

"Huh." Strange. I wasn't going to judge him on what some musty old volume said. Honestly, denying me information that would help me learn about him seemed... well, kind of underhand.

I walked to the door. "You must be able to tell me something about them or Grimmere. I'd really like to be prepared."

Gabe and Nora were staring between us, their interest piqued.

Roux rubbed his chin, rucking his beard up some more. "I don't know very much myself. Only that Grimmere is approximately the size of France. Dracs are a lordly species, and there's not that many of them considering the number of lands they control. They have a close relationship with goblins. Particular families rule populations of them, much like the feudal system in this area in the Middle Ages. Grimmere is an awful place, by all reports. All kinds of terrors lurking in the forests."

Terrors, the Pyrenean term for things that went bump in the night. None of them pleasant. And I'd seen Lucas's drac form. I supposed because of it, I hadn't exactly expected a pleasant land. But that wasn't a lot to go on. "Really? There's nothing else?"

Gabe and Nora exchanged a glance. Nora's eyebrow lifted and Gabe's lip turned up at the corner. There was something going on there.

"Fae is huge," Roux said. "There are as many countries as

in the human realm, and although dracs are an extremely powerful race, they keep their affairs under wraps. It's like you asking me about Kiribati."

Gabe tapped at his phone. "Kiribati in the South Pacific. Population one hundred and twenty thousand."

I wished I could google Grimmere. "And Lucas, do you know where he's gone in Grimmere or the way marker he used?"

"He didn't say."

"Great. Then we have nothing to go on. If the place is the size of France, how are we supposed to find him?"

"As I said, there aren't actually that many drac families. It may be possible to ask around there—amidst the goblins, that is, if we can find someone friendly. Best not ask a drac." He scratched his nose. "I have to admit, the idea of going to Grimmere isn't filling me with joy. I believe the price for being there without permission is death."

"Delightful." I shook my head. "Well, we have to try. And how the hell do we get there?"

Roux got up stiffly and walked into the library. He retrieved a scroll from the rack and, pushing my sword and bag to the side, unravelled it in on the reading table. It was a map of a large city with points marked all over it. "Let me check... Yes. Here." He placed his finger on one of the points. Gabe and Nora joined us at the table, eyes poring over the parchment.

"Wow," Nora said. "Where is this?"

"Stinkhorn," Roux said. "The goblin city of doors. A very useful place indeed."

"Lucas mentioned it last week. Said it was one of the goblins' most strategic and important cities, and that one of the reasons Tarascon was a significant fae outpost was because the way marker here led straight to it."

"Indeed. There are doors to many places from Stinkhorn." He tapped the map. "This is the door that leads to Grimmere, not very far from the seat of power, Grimmere Castle. Which is probably a good place to start looking for Lucas, although I expect he took a more direct route to wherever he's gone."

"It's a start," I said. "And is there a map for Grimmere itself?"

Roux nodded. "Gabe, find me Grimmere, will you?"

"Sure." Gabe went to the rack and scoured the scrolls. He drew one out and handed it to Roux.

"Thank you," Roux said as he unrolled it. "I believe this is all we have. It's a list of the major ways into Grimmere."

The country was long and narrow, more like Italy than France, and it was covered in forest with countless lakes. There were only a few way markers scattered here and there. There was a note pinned to its edge in handwriting that looked suspiciously like Grampi's. *Information inconclusive.*

I chewed my lip. Even though Grampi had respected my decision to become a Keeper, there was barely a second when he didn't grumble about Lucas. "Do you think Grampi would know more?"

Roux shrugged. "It's possible, but the note implies perhaps not."

I could ask him. It would be the sensible thing to do, but

there was a chance he'd go off on one. If he didn't like Lucas being my partner, how was he going to react to me going into Grimmere? More than that, I didn't want to worry him. Nope. Under the circumstances, it was best I didn't mention it. After all, if there was something important, Grampi would've recorded it in the Keepers' post.

"Anyway," Roux added. "The path from the Stinkhorn way to Grimmere Castle is most likely well trodden, as are many of the main routes in Fae. It shouldn't be difficult to find."

I nodded. "Sorted, then. And what do we need to take? I guess a range of weapons." I headed out and strode through to the kitchen, looking for a pack. "We had better get going right away."

"Right away?" Roux followed. "I have poker with Shroom-Jean tonight. Plus, I'll need someone to secure the bounds every morning we're away."

A couple of leather backpacks hung on a peg out by the back door. I grabbed one and returned to the kitchen. "Mushum said I need to get to Lucas immediately. We can't risk a delay. I could go alone, but with my limited knowledge of Fae, that might not be the best idea."

Roux drew his shoulders back. "No, no, no, not at all. We can't have you going there by yourself."

Gabe and Nora peered in at the door.

"We could go with you," Gabe said. "I know some glamours that would be of help, and it's the school holidays, so we have the time."

Nora nodded keenly. "It's got to be better going into Fae

with you rather than wandering in on our own without guidance."

That was sweet. "I really appreciate that, but Grimmere sounds like a terrible place, and I'm not going to subject either of you to somewhere I know very little about." I waggled my finger at them. "And no wandering into Fae *ever* without one of us."

Then it hit me. Of course there was someone else who could come with me, quite a few of them, actually. "Slaughter," I called.

He appeared from the side of the range. "Yes, ma'am." He saluted, his chestnut beard sticking out a little as he raised his chin.

"Fancy an adventure, danger guaranteed?"

His eyes lit. "Just say the word, and me and the Men are with you."

I could always rely on Slaughter. "Great. We need to go find Lucas in Grimmere, and I'd like to leave, well, basically now."

Slaughter's face fell and his mouth opened and closed. "Grimmere," he squeaked. Very unlike him. "I'm sorry, Camille, the Men have been banned from Grimmere. We can't even take a step in. There's some kind of ward that stops us. It's damned inconvenient, what with Lucas being from there and all, but that's how it is."

"No, no," Roux huffed. "I'll rearrange bridge and get Stinking Stéphane to do the bounds. You'll definitely need me. Not to mention Lucas will probably tear me to shreds if I don't accompany you."

I was glad of his support, but... "Stinking Stéphane...?" The name didn't inspire confidence.

"Don't ask," he said. "But he'll get the job done... probably."

"Right then." I glanced around the kitchen. "What else do we need for the trip?"

"I have a load of food." I'd taken some viennoiserie from the café—croissants and pain au chocolat that wouldn't sell by the end of the day. "What herbs should we bring? Moonwort...?" It would be useful to make a lumière. Not that I could manage the collude if the glamours I'd attempted were anything to go by. Roux would be fine, though.

"Well, at least you have pastries," Roux muttered.

Chapter 8

"Honestly, Camille, would you give a mage a moment to get his breath back?" Roux wheezed as he struggled with the stone steps that wove up Coustarous, the foothill behind fae Tarascon.

At this rate we'd be lucky to get to Grimmere before tomorrow. I paused and waited for him to catch up, my muscles tight, tension spreading through my shoulders. I was having second thoughts about Roux accompanying me. His face was blotched, sweat beading all over him, and we'd only just started. It looked like the climb might actually kill him.

I pulled out my phone and tapped on the café for the fifth time, the hot evening breeze doing little to cool me as I gazed out over the town and river.

The café phone rang on and on. I'd already called Grampi to let him know that I'd be away on Keeper business for a week. I had no idea how long it would take, but I hoped that would do it. He'd asked me about the details, but I'd fobbed him off and said to cover me if anyone inquired from the café. My story was that I had Norovirus.

I'd been trying to call the café ever since we left the Keepers' post to give my excuse, my heart thrashing at the prospect of having to talk to Alice, the person most likely to answer the phone, but there had been no reply. It wasn't unusual if everyone was rushed off their feet, but I really needed to reach someone before we crossed the bounds into Fae and my phone stopped working.

The ringing continued as Roux lumbered up the steps below, his staff just about the only thing holding him up. "I wasn't made for climbing mountains," he said through wheezes.

The phone stopped ringing. "Pyrenee's," a cheerful voice on the other end of the line called. Guy. Thank heavens.

"Guy, it's Camille." I attempted to sound weak. "I'm still sick. It's Norovirus. I've got to keep away from the café until it's all cleared up." I was getting good at lying, and I hated it. "Most likely I'll be away for a week."

"Bummer. I'll let Alice know. You concentrate on healing up. Noro is a bitch. I had it last year, and I was on the loo for forty-eight hours straight. Got through so much loo roll."

More information than I needed. "Uh, thanks."

"Hey, before you go, did Alice say anything about what she was doing this afternoon?"

Roux joined me, his chest heaving.

I closed my eyes at the mention of her name, trying not to sink back into that well of pain. "Come on. Have you seen us speak for the last two weeks, arguments aside?"

"Well, no. Thought it would be worth a try, though. She's not picking up. I need to ask her about the opera gateau for Old Len."

"Uh, we had another argument. There's a chance she's a bit shaken up."

There was a wiping noise. Probably the sound of Guy dragging his hand over his face. "I wish you two would sort it out. Such a bad atmosphere."

"Yeah, sure is," I said. "Look, I'll let you know when I'll be back at work."

"Get better soon," he called.

Roux nodded that he was just about alive, and we set off again, picking our way over rocks as we climbed the steps.

I tucked my phone away and adjusted my pack. I'd opted to carry everything, knowing Roux would struggle. We'd packed various herbs at his instruction, and the food I'd taken from the café, plus some grapes, cheese and bread that had been in the pantry at the Keepers' post. We'd also packed waterskins and the map of Stinkhorn. The one of Grimmere was too large scale to be any use. In terms of weapons, Roux had secreted a fair amount of ironwork under his cloak, which might have been why he was struggling. I'd strapped a dagger to my thigh, but otherwise, I had my blade.

Roux was beginning to wheeze again, and he was almost purple.

I slowed down, my tension redoubling. Lucas really could look after himself, but Mushum's predictions had always been spot on. My worry was a curious thing, though. It made me realise that despite my doubts, Lucas and I had grown together since the midsummer's eve celebration. He was an excellent instructor, a reliable partner, and dare I say it, actually quite good company when he wasn't playing his latest caper on me. I supposed, if I admitted it, we were becoming friends. I hadn't really thought about it before.

And there was that attraction, that constant draw as he showed me a new move, his muscles playing. He repeatedly insisted on training with his shirt off. I got it. It was summer. It was hot. But it meant that I had to concentrate extra hard. Although it was quite possible he was doing it on purpose to distract me.

After a few more minutes of stepping onward at a snail's pace, we made it to the gentle slope of the rounded summit, the menhir a little way ahead. As we neared, deep crevices scored the dry earth here and there, along the usually invisible bounds between the fae and human realms. Light sank into the fissures as if it had decided to give up on existence, leaving only intense blackness. I shivered. I always did when I went near. It was as if the cracks drained all life from my soul.

Roux tutted. He was drenched in sweat, a little spit dangling from his beard. "Not good," he said between breaths. "When I secured the bounds this morning, I measured the growth of the cracks. Three inches since yesterday."

"That's a lot," I said. "Is it like that every day now?"

"It's erratic. Some days the increase is minute, but they're always expanding."

As we passed, the lifeless sensation increased, my

stomach lurching. The air shimmered, and we'd crossed into Fae. The summit levelled, and the small menhir stood before us amidst cleared ground.

"Andos," I said.

Through puffs, Roux did the same.

I'd not noticed another path from this way marker when Lucas had brought me here on midsummer's—I'd been so caught up in the magic of the evening—but studying the area carefully, several paths opened up other than the glimmer of the wildflower meadow in summer.

Roux headed toward a path that flickered with the verdigris stain of an old door. He pushed the handle and we stepped through.

Everything was a riot around us. There was so much busyness that I struggled to grasp any of it. We stood in a market square, goblins bustling about. A lot of them. Some were cloaked and hooded, some wore typical jerkins and breeches. Some were as small as Mushum, some taller than Raphaël. They were striding across the square or chatting to one another or bartering at the packed-in stalls. There were just so many, and there were other fae too—elves, dwarves and creatures that on first glance might have passed for human but could well have been dracs or dryads or any number of species I wasn't familiar with. Animals mingled with the crowd. Hens, goats, cows. And the smells were a riot. Spices, perfume, beer, cow dung and something that was possibly bolognaise. It was complete sensory overload.

Behind the market stalls stood hodgepodge stone buildings with countless doors that opened and closed as fae passed through. Some were standard wooden affairs, some were decorated and out of place, some were strangely shaped. A group of goblins emerged from a skewwhiff example to the side, a luscious forest beyond. A handsome elf pulled open a narrow door painted in red, and I caught sight of an ocean.

I may have accepted the role of Keeper, but I hadn't let go of the folklorist in me. I don't think I ever would, and this place was mind-blowing. Though I had no clue what to do with all the new information. Right now, I was acclimatising.

Something shoved us from behind and we stumbled forward.

"Watch what you're doing," a gruff voice said. A group of trolls had emerged from the door. Their glares clearly stated that it would make their day if it came to a fight.

We stepped gingerly back.

"What do you think you're doing blocking the doorway?" another of them growled.

I glanced at Roux and raised my eyebrows. "I'm guessing this is the moment when we get the hell out of here."

Roux nodded. We dashed away through the throng to the side of the square by the market stalls, then slowed to a walk.

"We need to find a quiet place to look at the map." Roux scanned the area. "Maps are precious, and I want to ensure we hang on to ours."

"Sounds like a plan." We skirted the square, passing stalls laden with cloth, cheeses and baskets. One sold mice. The little creatures were on their backs, lined up in rows, their eyes closed. They occasionally moved, so not dead. I paused to stroke the soft pelt of one. Its eyes opened and its mouth extended almost to its feet. Very spiky teeth flashing, it chomped toward me. I snatched my finger away just in time.

The stallholder, a squat goblin about half my height, laughed heartily, his jerkin straining. "Better watch out, little lady. Don't want to lose any body parts."

His voice caught the attention of a cluster of goblins nearby. They turned, their eyes narrowing as they took us in. A lanky one strode over. "Now, what have we here? Humans?"

"What do they want?" I whispered to Roux. "I'd really quite like to draw my blade."

Roux's gaze flitting around, taking them in. "I'd advise caution. Goblins love a fight, which would take up valuable time. It would be better to leave as quickly and quietly as we can."

One of them stepped behind me and pulled my ponytail. I swung around and glared at him. Another yanked Roux's cloak, then tweaked his beard. A third tugged at my elbow. Talk about invading our space. I tensed, desperate to feel the hard metal of my sword in my palm. Roux's grip tightened around his staff, but he managed not to react. The group roared with laughter and sauntered off, which went to show how little experience I had of fae. If I'd gone with my impulses, I would've probably caused an international incident.

I noticed an archway at the edge of the square. "Come on."

We wove through the commotion, skirting hens, a rather

irate-looking goat and a goblin who'd tipped a bucket of slosh over a now furious elf. Another goblin cut the strap of a fellow's bag, causing vegetables to spill everywhere. A small critter was teasing a stoat with a handful of food. Engrossed and not looking where I was going, I caught my foot on something and stumbled. A round goblin with long skirts had her foot extended where she'd tripped me.

"This is utter craziness," I muttered. "Is it always like this?"

"The place is known for it. Most goblins are nonsensical."

"You don't say."

There was an opening in the crowd, and we dashed for the archway. It led to another door-filled square, a quiet side street angling off. We headed into it, passing a few goblins who either laughed or leered. One rather large fellow crouched down into a doorway that was no bigger than a dog flap. He squeezed himself onto mud beyond.

"Here." Roux dove into a small passageway, his staff tapping against the cobbles. An empty barn stood to our right. We ducked in.

It was darker inside. That combined with the hint of dusk meant we didn't have much light. I pulled my pack off my shoulders and took out the map. "What a place."

"Indeed." Roux grasped the scroll, sank into the straw and laid his staff at his side. "By Abellion's braces, a sit-down is most welcome."

The map shook in his fingers as he unrolled it on the

ground. The climb up Coustarous really had taken it out of him.

I sat down, the scent of fresh straw tickling my nose as I fished in my bag and pulled out our waterskins and a pain au chocolat. I shoved the patisserie at Roux.

He almost tore it from my hand. "Just what I needed." The way to Roux's heart was paved with delicacies from Pyrenee's.

We leant over the map, peering at it in the half-light. Stinkhorn was made up of innumerable buildings that formed courtyards and squares, interconnected by a mish-mash of streets and passages. A large fortification stood in the centre. Everywhere, doors were marked by dots with names scrawled in tiny letters alongside.

"The city is huge," I said. A hen crooned, roosting on the rafters above us.

Roux munched his pain au chocolat and nodded, crumbs spilling onto the map. "It's an enormous confluence of ways. When the goblins built the city, they created a door for each one. How they managed to organise themselves to build anything is another matter entirely. Now they use the traffic that passes through for commerce."

"How curious."

"Although the city is overseen by a drac minister," Roux added, "which probably accounts for the organisation. If it was down to the goblins..." He shook his head.

The remains of his pain au chocolat gripped in his hand, he extended his little finger and pointed northwest of the centre. "I believe we're here."

Yep, there was the square where we'd arrived and the door labelled *Tarascon.*

"The door to Grimmere?" The scent of the viennoiserie getting the better of me, I pulled out a croissant and bit into it.

Roux scoured the map, his eyes darting here and there as he finished his pain au chocolat. "Here it is. Not too far." He pointed to an empty area a little further to the north. A dot was labelled *Grimmere.* "If we take the back streets, we shouldn't meet such a crowd."

"Perfect," I said through the last of my croissant. I could only hope we weren't too late to help Lucas.

We committed the route to memory as we drank, then we packed up and continued on. We passed the edge of a couple of squares, one where a brawl was in full swing, another where some kind of slapstick play was under way, goblins falling about laughing. But for the most part, we stuck to alleyways and didn't meet such a commotion.

Navigating a series of steps and then a lane, we rose upward to a quieter part of the city. Dusk drew in, a few lanterns here and there lighting our way until we stepped into an overgrown area too wild to call a park. Ivy and bryony fought for space over stone walls. Trees hung low over unkempt grassy mounds, each the size of a person or smaller.

A shiver of unease ran up my spine. Although there were no headstones, I was sure this was a graveyard. As we walked through, the vista of the city opened before us, revealing endless streets and a grand castle with conical towers.

Roux led the way to a high stone wall with a large weatherworn wooden door. "This is us."

As we approached, the unease I'd felt shifted to something deeper. The door, going by the nettles and cleavers growing up around it, hadn't been opened in a while.

"Not exactly a popular route," I said.

"Doesn't look like it." Roux frowned. "I think it might be advantageous if we have a little glamour going forward."

"Oh?"

"If you wouldn't mind passing my herb supplies. I have a little bogfoil. It was quite difficult to come by, let me tell you, but it will be perfect for doing a friend-or-foe glamour."

"And that is what exactly?" I pulled off my pack and rummaged through, my fingers brushing on the verity vial. I'd brought it with me not wanting to leave it lying around.

"The collude will render us unnoticeable to our enemies, although we'll be perfectly visible to anyone with friendly intent. It should have an action of a couple of hours or so, and during that time we'll simply shrink into the background. It masks smell and muffles sound too, but it won't cover our tracks, so we'll still have to be careful." He tucked his staff under his arm.

I passed Roux his herbs. "Sounds good." I needed to get the hang of colludes. Something like this, or even managing a simple clothes-hiding glamour, would be handy.

Roux poured some herbs into his hand. "That should do it." He glanced at me from under his bushy eyebrows. "Ready?"

"As I'll ever be." I thought back to the Collude of Exceptional Infiltration Roux and Gabe had attempted on Anthras's black ward. "Though there's no chance of my clothing catching fire, is there?"

He chuckled. "There's always the chance of that." He muttered an incantation under his breath. A glow grew around his hand then surrounded him. It extended outward to encompass me too, then it was gone, Roux's palm empty. "That should do it. I think I'll hold on to the herb bag for now, just in case we have need of another collude."

I shrugged my pack on over my scabbard. Together, we flattened the vegetation surrounding the door, then I grasped the ring handle and twisted. Nothing happened. Shaking it, I tried again. The latch raised, the hinges creaked open, and we stepped into Grimmere.

Chapter 9

We froze. Unease and emptiness seeped through my blood as though everything positive, everything good in my soul, had left me. And damn, it was cold.

We stood in a clearing, two guards stationed a stone's throw ahead, the goblins dressed in a soft-and-hard armour combo. The gibbous moon above reflected off their livery of tangled silver branches on black. They didn't notice us, so presumably our glamour was working.

It was still possible to make out something of our surroundings in the fading light. We stood on a high hill, a forest sprawling before us. Although there was little breeze, clouds scudded overhead, covering the moon then rushing off again.

Roux and I edged away from the guards, then curved toward the well-worn path and headed into the forest. Roux had said our glamour would dampen sound. Even so, my instincts told me to keep quiet, the back of my neck prickling.

Things shifted in the undergrowth. A flash of an eye to our side, a rustle of bushes before us. The pine trees were twisted and gnarled, gaping hollows forming yawning mouths, branches contorted into broken limbs. Something howled a little way off. And Lucas had grown up here. Perhaps it looked better in daylight.

Once well away from the guards, I said, "If there was ever a place that felt like hell, this would be it."

Roux was trembling again. This time not from exertion. "I have to agree with you there."

I spun around, sure something was watching, but with the glamour, we were safe. "It might have been better to come in daytime."

"We may be hidden," Roux said, "but we should stick to the trees in case anything comes up fast on the path. Although let's keep it in our sights so we don't lose our way."

We stepped off the track and continued through the forest, the going slower. I rubbed my arms. "I should've packed something warmer."

Roux paused, drew out the herb bag, tipped powder into his palm and muttered. A glow extended around us. "Clove and a little ginger should alleviate the worst of the chill." Warmth eased through me. "We can't risk a lumière, though, as it's impossible to glamour. Moonlight will have to suffice."

As we strode onward, a huge maloumbro floated by, cold tearing through me despite the collude. I supposed the dense cloud of sickness and death didn't know we were here, and it was just going about its business. A witchy thing passed us on the path, then a group of gnarly, unpleasant-looking goblins followed suit. Being invisible was strange. As we covered the miles, we were skimming over the surface of Grimmere, clearly not experiencing it to the full, although I wasn't complaining.

I spotted a hideous creature crouched on the ground. It looked rather like Lucas in his drac form, all desiccated skin and bone. It was eating something, possibly a severed hand, but it could've been a paw. I fought the urge to run.

After what had to be a few hours, my impatience building, the trees opened out, moonlight revealing craggy mountains and more forest. To the side, covering the entirety of a mountain, stood a massive castle with abundant spires, a moonlit lake shining below. Cold seeped through me again, this time worse than before.

Roux pulled his cloak tight. "I'm not sure why the collude isn't working."

A tendril of dark mist extended between us. We flung around to face another massive maloumbro.

"Run!" I yelled.

"You don't have to ask me twice," Roux called as we sprinted away. I'd never seen him move so fast.

"But how did it track us?" The maloumbro's intense cold was still freezing my back.

"No idea," Roux managed through gasps.

We needed a flame—maloumbros hated light and warmth—but there was no time for that. Glancing back to check how close it was, I slammed into something and tumbled down.

"What the hell?" a voice muttered. I could just make out

a man sprawled on the mulch. Roux was darting off into the distance. The man studied me then gathered himself. "Come on, that thing's almost upon us."

The maloumbro was yards away, its tendrils reaching out, but not for me, for the man. It had been chasing him, not us, and we'd gotten in the way. We sprang up and ran, catching up with a flagging Roux.

"Over the path," the man called. "Maloumbros don't cross tracks."

Interesting, but I wasn't going to ask for more details right now. Roux was slowing to a hobble. I grabbed his hand and dragged him across the path. The maloumbro seethed on the other side, sending out tendrils that recoiled as if stung.

Breathless, we came to a halt. The man drew a dagger and brandished it before us. "Forgive me if I'm a little cautious, but this land puts me on edge. Who are you and what is your business?"

We stood there panting, assessing one another. The guy appeared to be human, although I couldn't be certain. With his thick features and no-nonsense expression, he looked about fifty. He had a pack on his back over a large sheepskin coat. Sensible. He was better prepared for the climate than we were.

Roux and I raised our hands. The man had saved our lives. It was my best guess that we didn't have anything to worry about. Besides, he could see us. I met Roux's eye and mouthed, "Friend."

Roux nodded almost imperceptibly, and we lowered our hands.

"I'm Camille Amiel, and this is Quentin Roux. Thank you for helping us back there. We don't mean you any harm."

"Well, that's quite clear." The man's voice was gruff. "You're not like the dark creatures that dwell here, and I would be a lesser fellow if I didn't give you the benefit of the doubt." He touched his chest. "Pierre Roig, at your service. What brings you to such a wicked place?"

"We're seeking someone," I said.

The man sheathed his dagger. "You're not the first to come here searching for a missing person. There are plenty of folk who disappear in Grimmere."

Roux had said that friendly goblins might be able to help us. Surely a friendly human was just as good. "We're looking for someone by the name of Lucas Rouseau. You wouldn't happen to know of him, would you?"

Pierre spluttered. "Do you have a death wish? The likes of him are not for decent folk. Keep well away."

I didn't get it, and Roux appeared just as confounded, although Lucas *had* said his reputation wasn't great in Fae. "But you know where he is?"

"Grimmere Castle, of course." Pierre narrowed his eyes. "If there is a Rouseau to be found, it's there. The place is protected on every side, though. Nothing can get in."

"How curious," Roux murmured.

"If you're heading toward the castle," I said, "perhaps we could walk together. Only we need to be getting on."

"It's been a difficult journey from Sturkpike way. You're the first creatures I've met that haven't been pledged to the dark. I'd welcome the company."

We set off, the path as always in sight, pine forest morphing into deciduous woodland.

Curiosity got the better of me. "If you don't mind me asking, you're human, aren't you?"

"Indeed I am."

Fascinating. A human in Fae. "So, what are you doing in Grimmere?"

"I'm also seeking someone." Pierre's voice grew low. "My son. Disappeared a month ago. I don't think he's alive, not from the accounts I've heard, but I couldn't live with myself if I didn't find out. Lost my wife and daughter a year back. There's nothing left without my family. I'm ready to meet my maker if Narim has gone that way too."

Shit. The emptiness in my blood amplified tenfold.

"And how have you gotten through the forest with nothing more than that maloumbro accosting you?" Roux asked.

"No doubt the same way you have. By treading carefully, keeping my eyes open and running when necessary. I'm a tracker. I pride myself on my woodcraft, and I'm used to working at night."

"It sounds as though you live in Fae," I said. "How come?"

"Changeling," he replied.

Roux nodded. "It does happen now and again."

Huh. Changelings were the real deal.

"Grew up in Fae," Pierre said as he skirted a fallen branch. "Married an elf. I tried returning to the human realm, but it wasn't for me. I was living a quiet life until my son got involved with a group of goblins. Good fellows, they were. Had notions about dracs. They went on some kind of mission into Grimmere, and that was the last I heard of them." He glanced at me, hardness in his eyes. "And you're from...?"

"Tarascon," I said.

"I once passed through. I was born in Toulouse..." He trailed off and cocked his head. "There's something following us. Keep quiet and stay put."

Roux and I exchanged looks as Pierre crept forward silently and merged with the forest. Although nothing would see us due to our glamour, we instinctively positioned ourselves back to back, scanning our surroundings. A couple of minutes passed.

"We really have to get to Lucas," I whispered, "not wait around while Pierre goes off on a wild goose chase."

"The friend-or-foe won't last much longer—"

A cry came from deep in the forest. "Get your hands off me!"

I recognised the voice, but it was completely incongruous here. Pierre drew out of the shadows, pushing a guilty-looking Gabe before him. To our side, a figure stepped out from behind a large oak. Nora.

CHAPTER 10

"WHAT THE HELL ARE YOU TWO DOING HERE?" I seethed at Gabe and Nora. "What did you do, follow us? Of all the inconsiderate, dangerous, stupid things to do." I wasn't sure if my glamour would work if I shouted. Every part of me wanted to, but I wasn't going to risk it.

Roux spluttered as he glared at Gabe. "By Abellion's socks," he managed. "You could've been killed."

"Looks like you know each other," Pierre said, his watchful eyes scouting the forest. "It's an interesting day when I come across three humans and an elf in this dark land."

Gabe sank from our withering glares. "I... We just wanted to get into Fae, to see a bit of it."

"What's the problem?" Nora scowled. She was shivering badly. They both were. "You said that if we went to Fae to go with someone responsible, and that's what we're doing."

"My dear girl"—Roux drew himself up, bristling—"you

knew full well what Camille meant by that. And following us without our knowledge is beyond foolhardy."

I rubbed my face, taking in the implications. "Do you realise what you've done? The position you've put me in?" The time it would take to return them home might cost Lucas his life, but bringing them with us, deeper into this place... I shook my head, anger ripping through me. I was going to have to choose between them and Lucas.

Roux tutted. "And where do your families think you are right now?"

"We made up an excuse about a camping trip," Gabe stuttered.

"You're endangering all of us by being here," I said. "How did you even make it through the forest?"

Gabe couldn't meet my gaze. "Roux instructed me in the friend-or-foe collude..."

"You stole some bogfoil?" Even in the moonlight, I could tell that Roux's face had gone red. "It was extremely hard for me to procure. Quite rare. I trusted you as my student."

Gabe shot a glance at Nora, who did her best to look unimpressed, though she was twisting her fingers together. Whose idea had it been? It was so unlike Gabe to step out of line.

Pierre just glanced between us all, amusement dancing across his stoic features. "Seems to me that the young sir and lady have made their beds, and now they must lie in them. This land will be punishment enough."

"Agreed," Roux said.

I closed my eyes, thinking of René, Gabe's father. He was

an arrogant asshole, but he loved his son dearly. If anything happened to Gabe... I didn't know Nora's family, but I was sure the same applied.

"Roux," I muttered, "we have no idea where we're headed or where we're going to sleep. It's much too dangerous—"

Hollers rose from the brow of the hill, hooves thundering toward us.

"Scouting party," Pierre said, his voice urgent. "We must hide until it passes." He darted into a thicket of ivy and brambles.

I dove after him, Roux stumbling in beside me, Gabe and Nora not far behind. We crouched down amidst the undergrowth. Thankfully, we were well away from the path. From a gap in the ivy, I could make out maybe half a dozen night-dark horses on the path, the torches held by their goblin riders illuminating the party clearly. A mount shifted into view with two squirming creatures, possibly goblins, strung over its back.

"They're looking for those in Grimmere without permission," Pierre whispered. "Hell knows what happens when they capture folk, but prisoners are always taken alive, and they're never seen again."

"If they get close, they're not going to be able to see us," I murmured to Roux, "but they'll see Pierre."

"Hopefully they won't notice any of us..." Roux drew out the bogfoil bag and began the collude.

The scouting party paused. Had they found our tracks? One of the riders blew an agonisingly shrill horn. A light thunder of feet headed our way, and a team of boar nosed through the undergrowth before us.

My heart thrashed as a leathery nose pressed into the brambles to my side. Another snorted close to Roux's and Pierre's boots. One rooted between Gabe and Nora, whose eyes were wide. Roux continued the incantation, light encompassing his hand. But before the glow could extend outward, a boar burst through the bushes. Grunting and squealing, it pounced on Pierre.

No. Please, no. Roux was seconds from completing the collude.

The scouting party turned to the noise. "Looks like we've got something," one of them called. He cantered his mount over, halted by our cover and sprang off.

The boar grasped Pierre's trousers in its jaws and backed out of the ivy. It snorted and screeched as it attempted to haul him along. I grabbed hold of Pierre's arms, trying to pull him back so Roux could cast the collude, but the boar was unshakeable. Gabe and Nora helped, tugging at Pierre's coat. For a moment, Pierre fought against the creature, then he met my gaze and smiled—a smile of peace, of acceptance of his fate. It really wasn't what I wanted to see right now.

Two other boars joined the first, gripping Pierre's ankle and leg. Together, they were too strong. He slid from our grips and out of the bushes.

I sprang up and drew my blade as the goblin struck Pierre around the head with the hilt of his sword. His head lolled to one side, the boars pinning him down.

Lunging forward, I skewered the goblin. He fell as the

rest of the party charged over, torches illuminating the forest. The goblins stared at their comrade, slain by an invisible sword. One of them recovered quickly and dismounted. As I thrust to take her down, she blew her horn.

The noise was agonising, halting me mid-strike. I released my blade and grasped my head as pain pierced my ears. Roux, Gabe and Nora cried out. A terrible coldness slunk over me, and the world became black as a maloumbro wrapped us in its embrace. I dropped to my knees, so utterly frozen.

Torches glimmered through the chilling blanket of darkness. "Got no idea what took Rash down," the goblin said. "But whatever it was, the maloumbro will sort it." She waved her torch in our direction to hold the creature away.

Chill sank to my core, oblivion calling me, enticing me into an endless sleep. I could do nothing as the goblin tied Pierre up.

"Give me a hand, you lot," she said. "There's a fair bit of bulk on this human."

One of the goblins dismounted and helped her haul Pierre over the back of a horse. "That'll make four for the lord this evening," he said. "And he's going to love the man flesh. Might even give us extra rations."

They mounted and cantered off toward the castle, and with them, the maloumbro sank away, the relative warmth of the forest pouring over me. Gasping, Gabe and Nora wriggled and pushed themselves up, but Roux lay slumped in a heap. I hauled my defrosting body over to him.

He was unconscious. I grabbed his cloak and shook his

shoulders. "Roux, wake up. Wake the hell up." Shit, he wasn't responding. I shook him again. He opened his eyes and groaned.

"The maloumbro has gone," I said. "They've taken Pierre."

"So cold. So terribly cold," he murmured, his gaze unfocussed.

"We need to get you up and moving. Come on." I sheathed my blade. We hauled Roux up and guided him out of the undergrowth. He stumbled forward, teetering this way and that, Gabe and Nora supporting him.

I stared in the direction of the castle. I wanted to go after the goblins, to break their necks and rescue Pierre, but with a dazed mage and two underage, skill-less companions to protect, it wasn't going to happen. Right now we needed shelter so Roux could get his strength back. That had to be my priority. Maybe if I found cover for these three, I could attempt to find Lucas on my own.

The only sign of habitation was the castle. Pierre thought we might find Lucas there, but what with his warning about dracs, I wasn't going to knock at the door. But the place had to have servants who would be living nearby, though if they were as friendly as the scouting party, we'd have problems.

Despite Gabe and Nora's assistance, Roux was only managing to shuffle along, stumbling on ridged earth and roots. "So cold," he muttered again.

"He might find it easier to walk on the path," Gabe said, his face ashen. Nora didn't look any better. Pierre had been right. This place was punishment enough for their stupidity.

"Agreed." We guided him onto the path—we'd be hidden by our glamours, although how much longer they'd last was another matter. At least Roux appeared slightly more coherent, his eyes focussing.

As we headed onward toward the castle, something shifted to our side. A band of goblins emerged from the trees.

CHAPTER 11

BEFORE I'D HAD CHANCE TO DRAW MY BLADE, WE WERE grasped from behind, our hands bound.

These goblins were dressed differently to the scouting party. Some wore simple tunics and breeches, some patchy leather garments or soft armour.

"Either the friend-or-foe glamour has worn off," I whispered to Roux, who was now looking more alert, "or these are friends." What with the swords, the grimaces on their faces and the rough handling, I wasn't exactly getting loving vibes.

"It may have worn off," he muttered. At least he was speaking coherently.

"Gag them," said a tall goblin with a pointed face and a glower.

Nope, definitely not friends.

The goblins forced strips of cloth between our lips and tied them behind our heads, then they took our weapons. In my case, this constituted my blade and dagger. For Roux it was five daggers, a sword, a stun gun, a rabbit's foot on a keychain and his bag of herbs. I wasn't sure why they thought the rabbit's foot was a lethal weapon, unless their cunning plan was to take away our luck, though I was pretty sure that had deserted us long ago.

Panic creased Gabe's face as he too was stripped of herbs and a dagger. Nora's glare would've withered the toughest heavyweight wrestler as a rather mean-looking flick-knife was taken from her. Goblins gripped our arms, forcing us to walk onward. The tall one, possibly the leader, drew something from his pocket and cast it about, a glow suffusing the air.

We were guided away from the path and down the side of the mountain to lower ground. The goblins in front had to half carry Roux as he was forced onward. And with every step, I was further from helping Lucas.

I studied our captors, looking for a chance to escape. I might be able to pull free suddenly and catch them unawares. But I wouldn't be able to help the others or make it past the outer ring of goblins without my blade.

I caught a glimmer of the castle through the trees, the moonlight glistening on its spires. It looked like something from a horror film. But we *were* getting closer, albeit at an angle.

Down we went until the land sloped gently and the bare-branched trees thinned. The tall goblin led us to a bank and paused. He rummaged in the grass and pulled open a round wooden hatch. Light flooded out from a tunnel.

"Bring them in," he ordered. "The rest of you, dismissed."

He took our weapons from a fellow, then led the way. I was pushed in after him and forced down a flight of steps, the others grumbling through their gags as they were manhandled behind. I tried to ask what was happening, but it only came out as a grunt, and the goblins ignored me. But why hadn't we been taken to the castle? We were being led into a hole in the middle of nowhere.

As we stepped downward, the air grew warm. The tall goblin opened a rickety door at the bottom, revealing a small passageway with more doors, a sideboard and floor-to-ceiling shelving stacked with books, boxes, scrolls and vials. Confused, I glanced at Roux. He looked as clueless as I felt.

At the end of the passage, we were led into a blissfully warm kitchen. Our guards retreated, closing the door behind them, leaving us with the tall goblin and an old, rather squat female goblin who stood before a blazing range. This was too weird. I eyed the door, wondering if we should make a run for it.

"Come now, Blisterch," the old goblin said, taking us in with her bulging eyes. "Look at the dearies. You've gotten them all tied up." Her skirts rustled under her apron as she approached, the grey cloth a shade darker than her wrinkled skin, her tufty grey hair a contrast to both. She may have been old, but by the way she moved, she definitely wasn't decrepit. I had the sense she could quietly and determinedly move mountains.

"For their own safety," Blisterch said. "They were

making one hell of a noise in the forest. They barely escaped from a scouting party, though their comrade was taken." He propped up our weapons in the corner by a dresser.

"Well, they're perfectly safe here." She stepped behind me, reached up and released my gag. "I'm sure that's much better."

I just couldn't figure out what was going on. All I could say was, "Friends?"

"Yes, of course we're friends." She went over to help Roux. Blisterch untied my hands, then set about releasing Gabe and Nora, who were rather stunned.

I rubbed my wrists and glanced around. The ceiling was low and beamed, and ramshackle cupboards lined the walls stacked with crocks and jars. To my side stood a large table laid with bowls, mugs, a teapot and a loaf of rye bread, and behind it sat an old couch and several armchairs. A pot simmered on the range, the aroma rich and spicy. It was all so cosy.

"Where are we?" I asked.

"This is my hole," the wizened goblin said with a smile. "And you are most welcome here." A goblin's smile was a funny thing. It often looked creepy or evil, or at best mischievous, but this goblin's smile was something else—kind and thoughtful, strengthened by the glimmer in her eyes. Although it probably helped that I couldn't see her teeth.

"An actual goblin's hole." Gabe's voice dripped with awe.

Nora frowned. "Guess it beats being frozen to death or mauled by boar."

"Come now, my dears," she said, gesturing to the table.

"Have a seat. I've laid out a little food, and you must be hungry. It's a taxing journey through the forest."

"You don't have to ask me twice." Blisterch sat down, his glower softening slightly.

The others looked at me, eager brows raised, waiting for the nod. But we knew nothing about these goblins.

"And although Lucas has told me so much about you," the old goblin added, "I'm thinking I'd like to get to know you for myself."

Roux and I exchanged glances.

"You know Lucas?" I said.

She nodded, returning to the range. "Of course, he's told me all about you, Camille and Roux."

"Madame," Roux said, twisting his beard. "It appears you have us at a disadvantage. We have no idea who you are."

"I'm Wortle." She carried the pot to the table. "Sit yourselves down and tuck in."

"Pleased to meet you, Wortle." Roux eyed the food. "A friend of Lucas is a friend of ours." He shrugged, rushed to the table and sat down. Gabe and Nora followed without hesitation, practically salivating. That was clearly enough information for them, but I needed more. "What's going on? I don't understand."

"We watch the forest," Blisterch said, ladling stew into bowls. "You weren't difficult to recognise from everything Lucas said, though we had to wait for the scouting party to retreat before we could approach. I sent a message back to Wortle to get some food on."

I swallowed, thinking of Pierre. The look on his face as

he was pulled away. It was as if he'd known it was the end, and he was glad of it.

Seeing my inaction, Wortle stepped over, took one of my hands and rubbed it between her gnarly fingers. "My deary, one thing I'm sure of is that you need some food."

"Uh, yes, I guess." I should let my defences down. Wortle and Blisterch appeared to be good-natured, despite our capture. I stepped over and took a chair, attempting to relax my shoulders.

Blisterch passed the bowls around. Not waiting for pleasantries, Roux dove in, Gabe and Nora following suit.

"Though I don't understand for the life of me what you're doing here," Wortle added, pouring the tea. "Lucas didn't say anything about you coming."

"But Lucas," I said. "How do you know him?"

Wortle paused, teapot in hand, her gaze hazing over, as if her thoughts were years in the past. "Ah, little Lulu."

Nora snorted. "Lulu?"

I had to agree with the sentiment. Both *little* and *Lulu* weren't words I would've associated with Lucas.

"My sweet boy." Wortle smiled. "I was his nursemaid."

I stared at her. "Nursemaid?"

"Raised him myself. Did my best for him, I did." She passed mugs of steaming tea around. Blisterch pushed a butter dish and knife toward Roux, who happily obliged, spreading gold onto his crust.

"It wouldn't be like the Rouseaus," Blisterch said, "or any drac family, for that matter, to involve themselves in the upbringing of their children."

I ran my hands over my face, trying to make sense of it. "When you brought him up, it must have been quite a long time ago, then?" Fae were generally immortal, although vulnerable to injury and illness. They aged in mindset rather than years, which was reflected in their appearance.

"Oh yes. I don't follow human goings-on, but I believe there was a well-known professor called Pythagoras back then. Good man, he was, superb teacher. The Rouseaus sent Lulu to his academy, and he advanced quickly. He was only a child for a few centuries. His teenage years were another matter entirely."

Nora choked on her soup. "That's ridiculous—"

Gabe explained quietly to her how age worked in Fae. Wortle's words just added to my general Lucas brain-fry. But then it dawned. "You know where Lucas is."

"Of course." She sat down opposite. "Most likely he'll pop by tomorrow. You'll see him then."

I couldn't believe it. We'd found him. But there was a chance tomorrow was too late. "I can't wait. I have to see him as soon as possible. Now."

She shook her head. "Lulu wouldn't like that one bit. Not at all. He'll be along soon enough."

I leant toward her, my elbows on the table. "You don't understand. I've reason to believe his life is in danger. If I don't warn him immediately, he may die."

Wortle and Blisterch exchanged puzzled looks.

"Deary," Wortle said, "that's really nothing new. His life is always in danger in Grimmere."

I wasn't managing to make myself clear. "Take me to

him." I eyed my blade in the corner. If I couldn't convince them nicely, I could convince them nastily, though Blisterch might be trouble.

Blisterch wiped his mouth on his sleeve, his gaze fixed on mine. Yep, he knew what I was thinking. "She has to know sooner or later," he murmured to Wortle.

Wortle sat back, shaking her head. "He's not going to like it one little bit."

"Camille is Lucas's partner," Blisterch said, his voice tight, "and Lucas's handling of the whole affair has been atrocious. He had it coming."

Wortle nodded slowly at the goblin. "That, I agree with." She turned to me. "Alright, Camille. I'll take you to him."

CHAPTER 12

WORTLE EYED MY UNTOUCHED STEW. "THOUGH, I'M NOT taking you anywhere on an empty stomach."

What did she not understand about "life in danger" and "immediately"? "But—"

"Nope, I won't take an argument." Her voice was soft, but there was something unyielding there. Was this the tone she'd used with little Lulu?

"I'll have to gather my things anyway," she added, "and that will take a moment."

"A very quick bite, then." I pulled my bowl closer. "Just while you get sorted." The stew did smell tempting, and actually, I was ravenous. I tried a bit. It was utterly delicious, warming and satisfying, though I couldn't quite identify the herbs and spices. I wolfed it down, its nourishment seeping through my veins. Wortle had been right. I'd needed food.

She bustled about, refilling the teapot and banking up

the range. I couldn't see how any of those things were as important as Lucas's life. "Where are we going?" I asked.

"He's in the castle." Wortle placed another loaf of rye bread on the table.

It made sense. Pierre had said the Rouseaus were there, and Roux had mentioned something about drac families ruling over goblins. Why on earth the goblins put up with it, I had no idea. But Pierre...

"The man we lost to the scouting party," I said, "he was heading this way to find his son, Narim, who disappeared a month ago. Did you hear anything about it?"

Blisterch met my gaze. "We knew a Narim. He was killed shortly after he was captured. There's no chance for the man you lost, either. It's death to all who enter Grimmere uninvited."

My stew stuck in my throat.

"Fuck." Nora's mouth fell open.

Gabe appeared to shake a little at first, then indignation crossed his face. "Isn't there anything we can do?"

"I'm sorry," Blisterch said.

Roux shook his head. "It is, by all accounts, a terrible place."

I got up. I was done with the stew. "We need to get going. Roux, you're staying here." He was looking much better, but he didn't need any more adventures."

"You don't have to tell me twice," he said, sitting back.

I glared at Gabe and Nora. "You two, stay put as well. Don't get up to any mischief and do the dishes."

Their faces fell.

I forced my tea down, knowing I needed the fluid, then I headed to the corner, strapped on my weapons and pack, and threw Roux his herb sack. "I'm wondering if Wortle and I should have some friend-or-foe glamour?"

Roux took out a small pouch and looked inside, his brow narrowing. "We have much less bogfoil than I'd thought due to it being pilfered. Only enough for one person, and certainly not enough to get us all back through the forest to the way marker." He shot a glare at Gabe, who cringed, a splodge of soup landing on his cloak. Reddening, he scraped it off with his spoon.

"Warming colludes have a longer duration, though," Roux added. "Yours should still be working."

I definitely felt warm, but then the range was blasting heat.

"Glamour won't be necessary," Wortle said as she wrapped a steel-grey knitted shawl around her shoulders. "We'll be out of sight in the tunnels." She met my eye. "Well, Camille, it looks like I'm ready. Blisterch, sort out the sleeping arrangements for our friends, and we'll be back anon."

He nodded.

I followed Wortle into the corridor. She drew out some herbs and cast a silent collude. A door appeared where there had been a bookshelf. "You'll be able to see this entrance from now on, deary. Although the glamour remains for prying eyes." A couple of lanterns stood on the sideboard. She lit them and passed me one before opening the door. Light streamed into a dark passage. As we stepped in, the unease I'd felt in the forest curled around me once again.

Wortle secured the latch behind us, the light dimming to that of our lantern's modest glow, then she scurried down the tunnel at surprising speed. I had to stride out to keep up.

"It's a fair way along here," she said.

The tunnel was built from packed earth, the roof rounded, the floor solid, doorways leading off occasionally.

"So, we're going this way to keep me hidden as I don't have permission to be here?" I said. The soft pad of our footsteps and the rattling of our lanterns filled the passage.

"Exactly," she said without turning around. "When goblins built the castle, we ensured tunnels were secretly constructed throughout. They give us a degree of freedom under the drac rule and allow us to gather information. By gaining knowledge of drac affairs, we can subtly influence events in the land. Not all goblins know about them, though. And very few dracs have an inkling of their existence—we only share the information with those we trust."

And yet she was sharing it with me. I supposed because of my connection to Lulu. "I don't understand. Why are the goblins subservient to the dracs?"

"That's just the way it is here." Her ears twitched a little.

Nope, I didn't get it. Had they been forced into submission long ago and become comfortable with the status quo? "I just don't see why you should have to creep around like this."

Wortle was silent. Time for a new angle. "So Lucas is part of a drac aristocratic family?"

Wortle chuckled. "You could say that, deary. The house

of Rouseau rules Grimmere as well as the other drac territories. It also controls the goblin lands. It's one of the most powerful families in all of Fae."

"Okay..." This was news to me. "So what's it like up there in the castle? The place is massive. I'm guessing the Rouseau family is big."

She halted mid-stride and turned back. I stopped short, almost colliding with her. Frowning and shaking her head, she drew her hands to my cheeks and cupped them, her gaze almost pitiful. "My deary, sweet thing, he really hasn't told you anything, has he?"

I wouldn't have described myself as sweet, exactly, but I appreciated her kindness. "Understatement of the year." Not to mention Lucas had hidden away all information that might have helped me find out.

She squeezed my cheeks once more, then headed on. "There are only five Rouseaus, the others being Lucas's mother and father, Elivorn, whom Lucas mentioned you'd met, and Isarn, his younger brother. Lucas is second in line to the drac throne after Elivorn, not that they use that kind of terminology. Lucas's parents go by the title of Lord and Lady Rouseau, but you get my meaning."

I paused. "What?" I couldn't have heard her correctly. "Lucas, my partner, is some kind of fae prince?"

"That's right," she called over her shoulder.

"Are you kidding me?" I ran to catch up, not knowing what to make of it. Morion Auberon, the dwarf king, had said that Lucas was number four on the dwarves' most-wanted list. Was this why? Perhaps the dracs and dwarves had some kind of longstanding feud. "Was that what Blisterch meant when he said I needed to know sooner or later?"

"Well, partly, but not exactly. You'll see the rest." She lifted her skirts as she trod through a damp patch.

There was more? "But why didn't Lucas tell me?" The ceiling lowered for a few paces. I ducked under. Wortle didn't have to stoop.

"He'll have to explain for himself, deary."

And Roux... He must have known. Why had he kept quiet? I had to admit, though, I was curious, but the truth was, prince, lord, whatever, it didn't matter. Actions meant more than titles.

We reached an open gate, and from then on the tunnel was built of stone, huge slabs across the roof. Steps rose before us. Wortle hitched her skirts, and we headed upward, my sense of unease growing.

Small windows lay in the walls. I peered through one, but all I could see were metal bars lit by a shaft of moonlight. The smell was awful—mould mingling with excrement. The collude was keeping me warm, but even so, I could feel cold air leaching from the place.

"The dungeons," Wortle said. "Not used much."

An eerie cry rang out, the tone high and uncomfortably familiar. My skin prickled. The place was definitely inhabited today. Perhaps Pierre was inside, although it hadn't sounded like him, the tone too high. But whoever it was, to be trapped in there... The poor soul. If I got some intel on the place, I'd see what I could do about releasing them.

Set into the wall a little further along was a slab of stone with a metal lever at the top. Wortle noticed my interest. "It's a doorway. There are glamoured entrances into each part of the castle."

The stairs levelled, and we passed a series of windows revealing kitchens that bustled with goblins cleaning up after the day's work. Their bangs, clatters and shouts were crystal clear.

"And they can't see us?" I asked.

"The windows look like wall panels or stone from the other side, and they were specially designed to funnel noise into the tunnels."

I really wasn't comfortable observing folk without their knowledge. It only added to the unease pressing in on me. I attempted to shrug it off, to no avail.

As we continued up, we passed passages and stairs that branched off here and there, as well as window after window, many of them dark, but in some I caught brief glimpses of vast halls and sweeping staircases lit by glowing candelabra. I don't know how high we'd climbed, but I was feeling it. Wortle, on the other hand, was as quick as ever.

The tunnel levelled again, light blazing in from the occasional window. We were walking too quickly to see much, but I noticed a four-poster bed through one.

At an intersection of tunnels, Wortle paused. "This time of night, the family will be in the drawing room. We're almost there. To be on the safe side, with the dracs' exceptional hearing, we won't want to talk nearby."

"Noted."

She took my hand in hers and rubbed it. "When the

family leave, we'll follow Lucas and hopefully gain the opportunity for you to speak. But heed my warning, he knows his situation best. If he tells you to do something, do it."

I frowned. "Care to explain in a little more detail?"

"It's dangerous. The Rouseaus are dangerous. Just do what Lucas says."

"So, lots of danger, then." How lovely.

She led the way forward, then paused at the next window. It revealed a large drawing room panelled with intricately carved mahogany. To one end, a row of arched and leaded windows looked out over the moonlit lake. In the centre, a fire blazed, its glow blending with that of the many candelabra. Leather couches sat before the hearth, black again. The place was a goth's paradise.

And amidst it all, with one arm propped on the ornate mantel, stood Lucas. He was dressed in an open tailcoat, a waistcoat and a cravat, all of it black. A long breath streamed from my lungs. I'd found him and he was alive. But dressed up, much? And damn him, he looked good in that get-up, his tailored coat hugging the ripped torso I knew hid beneath.

He wasn't the only one dressed for the evening. Two figures sat on the couch to the right. A woman, her hair piled elegantly on her head above an evening gown, and a young, lean man. Opposite them, an older man reclined, a wine glass in his hand. Lord Rouseau, I presumed. It was as if power emanated from him, though I couldn't say why. Perhaps it was his bearing, but even from here, he unnerved me. He was casually observing a figure pacing back and forth at the side of the hearth. That utter creep, Elivorn. And from his scowl, he didn't look happy.

Lucas glanced at Lord Rouseau. "I honestly don't know why you bother, Father," he said, his voice strangely formal. "The entries to Grimmere are as secure as possible. The scouting parties and the terrors do a superb job at catching trespassers who slip through."

My breath caught. It sounded as though Lucas was condoning the scouting parties, but he couldn't be. He was many things, but he had an urge to preserve life, to help people—unless they were about to tear him limb from limb, of course.

"It's the damned woodland glamour the goblins use," Lord Rouseau said. "Yes, they like their privacy, but too many are using it. Who knows what they're up to."

"I suppose there's no harm in extra security," Lucas replied.

Elivorn turned to him. "And what would you know? You haven't been here." With a glower, he continued pacing.

"Well, *dear* brother." The sarcasm in Lucas's voice was notable. "It was brought to my attention what a remarkable job you're doing with the bounds. Your attempts to split them has thus far caused a rift larger than any other in history." He drew his glass from the mantel and downed the last of his wine. "How could I not return to support you on such a momentous occasion?"

The air congealed in my chest. I couldn't believe the words coming out of Lucas's mouth. He was emphatic that he didn't want the bounds to split. I wanted to ask Wortle about it, but I couldn't risk speaking. She caught my eye and shrugged, a gesture I couldn't interpret.

"Marvellous," Lady Rouseau said. She rose from the couch, the train of her artfully cut dress swirling as she glided over to Lucas. A myriad of dark jewels stitched to her skirt glinted in the candlelight. She laid a hand on his arm and planted a kiss delicately on his cheek. "We have missed you, out there in the world doing your own thing."

Lucas smiled softly. "I missed you too, Mother."

Lord Rouseau rubbed his chin. "I have to say, I really didn't understand all that gallivanting off with Charlemagne and then the Trencavels. Chivalry." He scoffed. "Not to mention those awful little Men."

Lucas's lips pursed. "Everyone has their rebellion."

Elivorn shook his head.

Lady Rouseau nodded. "But we understand that it's taken years to plan this ruse. Imagine that, a Rouseau managing to gain the confidence of the assembly and being granted a position as a Keeper." His mother laughed lightly. It should've sounded beautiful—it *was* melodious—but it was cold. She squeezed his arm. "Well done. And now you're perfectly placed to assist us."

I sank back against the wall, my ears humming, my breath too shallow. A ruse as a Keeper. No way. Despite my misgivings about Lucas, there was a warped sincerity in everything he did. Even his trickery had a purpose that was reasonably sound. But then, Grampi had never trusted him... and Morion... and the fae in Tarascon did their best to keep out of his way. Wortle scrutinised me, her wispy eyebrows narrowing.

"Your subterfuge is ingenious," the younger man, presumably Isarn, said. "I'm quite impressed."

A flicker of a smile crossed Lucas's face. "I appreciate the sentiment. It's taken time and perseverance."

"Undoubtably," Lord Rouseau said.

Lucas met his gaze. "Father, I would very much like to hear your plans for advancing the splitting of the bounds."

Elivorn leant on the back of the couch by Isarn. "I bet you would." He spat the words.

"And I look forward to revealing all," Lord Rouseau replied, "but tonight, I fear it is too late, and you have had a considerable journey. A change of lands always makes one tired—"

There was a knock at the door.

"Enter," Lord Rouseau called.

A goblin footman came in. He closed the double doors behind him and bowed. "My lord, the day's trespassers are ready."

"Wonderful," Lord Rouseau replied. "Bring them in."

The footman flung open the doors. A female goblin entered. She was a good match for the one I'd almost killed in the forest, although so much had happened back then, I couldn't be sure. She was followed by three goblins, their hands bound, guards at their sides. Last of all came the sturdy frame and heavy gaze of Pierre.

I drew up to the window, trying to work out why he was here. I wanted to call out to him, but Wortle raised her finger to her lips. Lucas and his father stepped back, and the captives were marched before the hearth.

"And there we go," Lord Rouseau said. "This is why we need to tighten security at our entryways."

"Indeed." Lucas raised an eyebrow, assessing the captives.

"And look at that. A human." Lord Rouseau inclined his head to the scouts. "Well done, goblins."

Their chests inflated.

Turning to his family, Lord Rouseau added, "I have to admit, if we do tighten security, it will be such a shame to lose our entertainment. However, if this ragtag bunch can get into Grimmere, anyone can." He met Lucas's eye. "My son, it is good to have you back. I shall convey this evening's honour to you."

Lucas set his jaw, his lips tight. "It would be my pleasure."

I couldn't figure out what was happening. Everything was so confusing—Lucas's opinions, Pierre being here, the goblins, the tunnels, all that had happened in Grimmere. In a flash, Lucas darted to the goblin at the end of the line, lowering himself to the creature's height. I couldn't see what he was doing, but when he stepped back, the goblin sank to the ground, his neck gouged out. Blood ran down Lucas's chin.

My throat constricted, I couldn't move, couldn't think, all I could do was gasp for air as Lucas dove at the second goblin and ripped into his neck, and then the third. I clutched my chest, unable to breathe.

Lucas turned his attention to Pierre, who stood level.

No, please not Pierre.

Their eyes met. Pierre's shoulders were back, his gaze fierce, defiant. He was ready to join his son. In one swift movement, Lucas shot forward and tore out his throat. Pierre fell to the ground, lifeless.

CHAPTER 13

I couldn't believe what I'd seen. I couldn't. That wasn't Lucas—he wouldn't do something like that. But it had been. I couldn't deny my own eyes. The walls, the window, the drawing room, all of it pressed in on me, the voices of the Rouseaus much too loud as they left the room, bidding one another goodnight.

"No, no, no, no…" The word repeated over and over, sticking on what little breath I could muster.

Wortle grabbed my wrist, bundled my lantern with hers and pulled me back down the corridor to the intersection of tunnels. "Not a sound by the windows," she said, her gaze stern.

I placed a hand on the wall to steady myself. "But Lucas… he… he just…" The pieces wouldn't come together.

"He's a drac," she said in a no-nonsense voice. "He does what he has to do, and you needed to know. He'll be in his chamber in a moment. We'll go there."

I shook my head. "No. I don't want to see him." He'd been lying to me all this time, about the assembly, about the bounds, about who he was.

"Now, now, my deary, don't make a fuss. You didn't come all this way for nothing."

She sounded as though she was berating me for leaving peas on my plate. "A fuss? Not make a fuss over what he just did? Didn't you just see..." My voice rose. The tunnel spun some more, nausea rising in my throat. But of course she'd seen. Of course she knew. She'd been a servant to the family for years. Her hole had been so warm and welcoming, but she'd lulled us into a false sense of security.

"Come." She placed her arm around the small of my back, as if to guide me along. "Let's find him."

"No." I couldn't be here anymore, in the castle, in Grimmere, anywhere near Lucas, and there was a chance Roux, Gabe and Nora were in danger. I snatched my lantern from her and fled back the way we'd come. I had to get away.

Wortle darted past and stopped before me, her hands and lantern raised. "Camille, look." She nodded to a window at my side.

Lucas paced about in a large room, a hearth to one side, a four-poster bed at the far end, an arched doorway behind him, all of it styled like the drawing room. His face was contorted in fury, the lines harsh in the candlelight. He wiped his mouth and chin with his fingers, blood dripping onto the rug. A low rumbling built from his chest. He paused by the door, placed his hands high on the wall and hung his head.

"No, Wortle. I don't want to see this." I turned to dive down the tunnel, but as I did so, something clicked, a breeze brushing my skin.

"Lucas," Wortle called.

I spun around. Wortle had opened the secret door into Lucas's chamber. I couldn't move.

"Wortle?" Lucas whispered. That voice, so familiar, the low tone instantly connecting me to feelings of support. We'd come so far since we'd met. But he was a killer. He'd killed Pierre.

Wortle stepped behind me once again, blocking my escape. Lucas ducked his head into the doorway, his eyes growing wide as they fixed on me.

"Camille..." His voice dripped with astonishment, his only movements the parting of his lips and the rising and falling of his chest.

My vision homed in on the rouge on his broad mouth and rough jaw, the way the stunning silver stitching on the collar of his tailcoat was blackened with blood.

He shook himself and glanced past me. "Wortle, what's going on?"

Something hot and fierce bubbled up in me then. Our partnership had been a sham from the start. He'd played me. I was a part of his plan to get close to the assembly, to be a Keeper for who knew what reason. One thing was for sure, there was no way his motives were pure. Fury roiled in my middle, stiffening my sinews. "You," I said, shaking my head. I stood my lantern on the ground, strode forward, and with everything I had, shoved him, sending him stumbling back into the chamber. I followed and pushed him again. "You killed innocent fae," I growled. "An innocent man. You killed them. You ripped their throats out."

Wortle, remaining in the tunnel, clicked the door shut behind us.

Lucas's breath caught. "You... you can't have seen."

"Oh, I saw alright, and I heard your plans. You're playing me just like you always played me. You don't care for the bounds. You're not here to find out what Elivorn is up to. You're here for your family."

He glanced down at his crimson hands and swallowed. "Camille, you don't believe that. You know I wouldn't—"

I laughed, a hard, dry laugh. "Wouldn't kill innocent creatures? I thought you wouldn't, but you just proved me wrong."

He shook his head slowly, as if not knowing what to do. Then hardness returned to his face. "We can't talk here. Not with my family's sensitive hearing. Don't say another word."

"What. How can you ask that of me—"

The door swung open and Elivorn stood on the threshold. "And what have we here?"

I could only stare at the evil gaze and sensuous lips of the snake who'd seduced me. Ice ran down my spine, my heart thumping.

"Camille, how lovely to see you once again," he drawled, "and dressed so nicely." He ran his eyes over my Keeper gear for longer than was comfortable. "It was such a shame we didn't make it back to my place the other night and—"

"What the hell do you want, Elivorn?" Lucas rumbled.

Elivorn stepped in, a devious smile drawing across his face. "I'm fully aware that you're up to something, brother. You may have Mother and Father duped, but you don't fool me. Imagine my lack of surprise when I was passing and I heard the voice of a trespasser. You know the price. There are no exceptions."

The thumping in my chest grew violent. I'd seen the price all too clearly. My own partner had carried out the penalty. Would he do the same to me?

"There is one exception," Lucas said, his gaze boring into me, loaded with significance. If we were fighting together, I would've said it meant, "Trust me, do exactly what I say. I can get us out of this," which brought back Wortle stating the same thing. The slightest shreds of trust we'd mustered over the past weeks had just disintegrated, yet the instinctual part of me that held self-preservation above all else screamed that it really would be sensible if I got out of this place right now, preferably not in a box or as a drac snack. In a castle full of killers, Lucas was my best bet.

"Not in Grimmere," Elivorn continued. "You know that. Or have you spent so long in the human realm that you've grown soft?" His eyes glinted. "Perhaps I could take her life. I would like to taste her."

Lucas shot forward and slammed Elivorn into the door, his hands around his neck. "You dare lay another finger on her," he growled.

"My, my. We aren't going to start this again, are we?" Elivorn looked anything but worried. "Fighting really didn't do us much good in Foix, did it? Although it was fun."

Lucas got right up in his face. "She's my mate," he said, malice lining each of his words. Then he stepped back with the meanest glare I'd ever seen.

I glanced from Elivorn to Lucas. Mate, huh? That was so far out of my comfort zone. I had to bite my tongue and force myself not to draw my dagger. I so wanted to make it impossible for him to consider such a thing again. But if it was a get-out clause, I could go along with it.

Lucas adjusted his cuffs, regaining his composure. "Why do you think I was so protective of Camille in Foix? If you hadn't used your powers on her, she never would've submitted to you. And I invited her to join me here as soon as she could. She's fully on board with the splitting of the bounds and my Keeper subterfuge. So... I suggest you get out of my chamber and go screw whatever goblin whore you have for the night."

Elivorn glanced slowly between us.

Lucas pulled me close—too close—my leathers against his bloody tailcoat. His loaded gaze urged me to play along. He laid gentle fingers on my chin, angling my mouth to his. No way did I want to oblige, but my desire to survive was stronger.

As Lucas drew toward me, all I could see was his mouth smeared with rouge. His lips met mine and a sharp tang of iron filled my senses. Pierre's blood. I restrained a gag, forcing myself not to pull away and run Lucas through with my blade.

The kiss was hard, deep and much too intense, lit with the passion that Lucas fought with, that I'd come to know from him. And all the time Elivorn was watching, assessing. It was an act, and I had to do my bit if I wanted to get out of here.

I took Lucas's head in my hands and pulled him closer still, forcing myself to respond, pressing against him. And even as I enacted the sham, a duplicitous part of me responded to him, to his lips fierce on mine, though he had the sense to keep his tongue to himself.

Then it was over. Lucas drew back and glared at his brother.

Elivorn snorted, a grim smile extending across his face. "Well then, it looks as though we have a guest for dinner tomorrow night." He left the room, closing the door behind him.

CHAPTER 14

As Elivorn's footsteps receded into the distance, I pulled myself from Lucas, all my fury channelled into a death glare. I opened my mouth to call him out so damned hard, but he drew his finger to his lips, then stepped over to the door, turned the key in the lock and pocketed it. I was trapped with a killer.

He strode to the back wall where I'd entered. There was only smooth mahogany, no sign of an exit. Lucas felt along the edge of a panel. Click. The door sprang open, revealing the tunnel and Wortle. Lucas grabbed a candle from the nearest candelabra and beckoned me in.

As far as I knew, the tunnel was the only safe way out of here. I joined them and picked up my lantern, the panel shutting behind us. "What the—"

They shook their heads, insisting on my silence. Not wanting Elivorn to return, I held my tongue. Wortle led the way down the tunnel. When we were clear of windows and doors, I let rip.

"You traitor," I yelled at Lucas, fury wild in my veins. "You rotten double-crosser. You were stringing me along from the beginning. You're here to help your family. I should've listened to Grampi—and everyone else." I spat out the metallic tang of fae and human life. Pierre's life. "And you had blood in your mouth."

Bewilderment covered Lucas's face. "Camille, I need to explain."

"I saw it with my own eyes. We're done, and I'm out of here. That's if you're not going to kill me, too." I pushed past Wortle, whose face was set with grim stoicism.

My route was clear. Only one way led downward. I took the stairs, needing to get away, needing space to figure out what was happening, needing Roux, Gabe and Nora so I could get us out of this goddamned place. Most of all, I needed to get as far as possible from Lucas.

He was behind me, his shoes clicking on stone. "What the hell did you bring her here for?" he shouted back at Wortle.

"Camille needed to know," she called.

The space between Lucas's footfall and mine closed. "Camille, I have to explain."

My skin crept as I saw Lucas tear out Pierre's throat once again. He was a lethal killer, and I had to get away. But with his drac speed, he could've caught me already. He was holding back. He wanted me alive to partner him in his Keeper pretence.

On I ran, my feet drumming as I passed window after window, Lucas repeating his pleas. I flew past the kitchens, then the dungeons. I was nearly at the earth tunnel when a cry rent the air, the same pitiful wail I'd heard earlier. I stopped in my tracks.

Lucas almost hurtled into me but managed to pull up short. "You have to listen," he said.

The cry came again.

"Camille." This time Lucas's tone was harder.

Incredulity flooded through me. "You do realise there's someone screaming in your dungeons, and all you care about is wanting to explain things. That pretty much highlights your level of compassion."

"I've no idea who they have in there. Trespassers are usually brought straight up." His voice was steady—too steady.

I gazed at the dungeon door. I'd not been able to help Pierre and the goblins. There was no way I could leave another soul to the Rouseaus. Anyway, there was something about the cry that tore at my heart.

"Go in there"—Lucas stepped down toward me—"and you'll risk blowing the cover we just made."

Shoving him aside, I darted up to the door, raised my lantern to make out the lever and pressed it. The slab swung open.

"Now, deary," Wortle said from the stairs above, "the dungeon isn't a nice place."

"That kind of sums up Grimmere. Not a nice place." I drew my dagger. "Anyone going to stop me?"

I eased backward through the door. Lucas's brow creased, annoyance flickering in his eyes. Wortle shook her head.

Inside, it wasn't as dark as I'd expected. Moonlight streamed in through high windows, a cold draught guttering my lantern. On either side of the central passage stood cells, the fronts barred with iron. The smell hit me anew—not just shit and rot, but death. The place was empty, though.

Lucas and Wortle whispered at the doorway, no doubt deciding what to do with me. I lowered the dagger to my side, turned around and stepped slowly along. There were dark patches on the stonework here and there. Blood or waste, I couldn't tell. Some of the cells had a layer of straw inside. Either an attempt to keep prisoners comfortable or a convenience to soak up bodily fluids. The stones beneath my feet sloped into a central gully that led into a drain. I hated to think what was washed down there. And rats—I couldn't see any, but there were bound to be rats in a place like this.

At the end, the passage continued around to the main dungeon door, a massive thing with studded ironwork, and beyond stood another row of cells similar to the first. The cry came again from the far end. I hurried toward it, Lucas's and Wortle's footsteps closing in. A beam of moonlight shone into the last cell. Lying amidst a thick layer of straw, shivering and muttering uncontrollably to herself, was Alice.

CHAPTER 15

WORDS LEFT ME. ALICE WAS PART OF THE SAFE, NORMAL human world. How could she be in Grimmere? But there she lay. I had to get in to help her. I placed my lantern on the ground and shook the bars. They didn't shift. There was a door in the metalwork to the side. I pulled at it to no avail.

Lucas drew up behind me, his breath hitching.

I swung around. "What were you going to do? Have her as your next tasty snack?"

His face was aghast, but all he said was, "Shhh, Camille. Careful what you say."

"Really? When my best friend is trapped in your psycho dungeon from hell. What the fuck?"

"I... I don't know anything about this."

Wortle drew near, her additional lantern casting more light on the scene.

Alice's hair was tangled, her cheek torn, one eye darkened with a bruise. What on earth had happened to her? I rattled the bars again. "I have to get in."

"Here you go, deary." Wortle jangled something, then pressed it into my hand. "I wouldn't be me if I didn't have the skeleton key." She tapped the side of her squat nose.

I studied her for a moment, confused that she was helping me once more. Shaking myself out of it, I fumbled with the key and tried the lock.

"Wortle," Lucas said. "Get four of our most trusted goblins. Secure the area so Camille and I can speak freely, then send for my pack and bring food and water."

"I'll be on it without delay." She scurried off.

The lock wasn't budging. I shook the key and tried again. The catch released and the door swung open.

I dove in and sank down by Alice's side, dropping my dagger in the straw. I took her hand in mine. She was cold, so cold. "Sweetie... honey... it's me, Camille," I whispered. "I'm here. Everything is going to be alright." My eyes pricked with tears. I couldn't believe she'd been drawn into this.

Lucas rammed his candle between a couple of rocks in the wall and crouched down on her far side. He drew off his tailcoat and laid it over her ripped blouse and filthy jeans.

"Camille," she murmured, turning her head one way then the other, her eyelids tightly closed, her face swollen. "What's happening?"

"I need to examine her," Lucas said quietly but firmly.

I bit my lip, wanting to tell him to go jump, but if he was going to kill Alice—or me—he would've done it already, and if he really did have nothing to do with her capture, he was the best chance she had. I nodded.

"Alice, can you hear me?" he said. "I'd like you to tell me your full name."

She garbled, then managed, "Inès Roger." Her mother. Not good.

As Lucas took Alice's pulse, I scanned the cell. It was empty but for a pail in the corner—the latest in Grimmere sanitation. At least the straw was fresh and dry.

Wortle returned. "The dungeon is secure, and the supplies will be with you shortly." She merged into the shadows, her soft footfall padding away.

"Camille." Lucas glanced up. "Listen, we may not have long to talk." He began his examination, checking Alice's skull.

"You don't need to talk at all. You need to help Alice, nothing else."

"I'm here working for the assembly." He moved down to Alice's collar bone, his fingers shifting in deft movements over her white rose tattoo. The charms she'd worn when we'd had the argument were missing. "I despise my family's way of doing things, and I don't... uh... usually kill innocent people." He studied Alice a little too intently, unable to meet my eye.

I glowered at him. "Spare me."

"I don't want the bounds split," he rumbled. It looked like I was going to hear it whether I liked it or not. "I've spent my life trying to be who I really am, not what my family are."

"Such pure motives." Sarcasm dripped from my voice.

Alice mumbled something about Raphaël. I rubbed her hand. "It's okay, sweetie. Everything is going to be just fine."

"I was honoured to be offered the role of Keeper," he continued, "and I support all it stands for. The assembly is well aware of my family, of the injustice in Grimmere and the other lands in their rule." His face was sincere. I had to give him that.

Lucas shifted his coat, examining Alice's arm, his eyes flicking from her to me. "We've been planning to take my family down for a long time. I'm key to that. But the goblins are split. There are those who support the drac rule and those who, whilst not exactly against it, denounce the killings and various other practices. They believe there are alternative ways forward."

"I think the brioche has been in the oven too long," Alice murmured. "Better check Guy has taken it out. Will you do that for me, Camille?"

"Sure, hon," I replied, packing straw around her body in an attempt to warm her.

"I've spent the past few years rebuilding my relationship with my family," Lucas added. "Wheedling my way back in. I'm the only one who can get close, but so many more are involved. Hundreds have died for this." He paused and shook his head. "And I haven't gotten close enough yet. My father has Elivorn whispering in his ear, and because of that, he hasn't shared his plans fully. But they're splitting the bounds, Camille, which will mean the end of the human realm, if not Fae too. I have to stop them."

My gaze flicked to his, and I was caught by the fervour in his eyes.

"You're everything to me, Camille," he said, his voice low. "Your trust means everything." He continued on with the examination.

I pulled my gaze away. I meant everything to him? That was a step too far. We'd known each other for weeks, and most of the time he'd been tormenting me one way or another. "You killed those goblins. You killed Pierre."

"The executions are part of Grimmere law." His lips grew thin. "You knew the human?"

"I met him on the way here. We encountered a scouting party. Roux and I were glamoured, but Pierre—"

"Shit," he growled.

"What does it matter if I knew him or not? They were lives, all of them. Pierre was looking for his son, who was taken a while ago."

Lucas slumped back, ran a hand over his face and released a sharp breath. There was still blood smeared on his chin. "I couldn't have saved them. Once they were brought into the castle, there was no escape. They would've died no matter what." He closed his eyes for a moment. "My father was testing me. I had to go along with it or my cover and that of countless others would've been blown. I had no choice." He drew in a breath then continued checking Alice.

"That makes it alright, does it?" I studied him as he palpated Alice's middle. I had no idea whether to believe him or not. "And if you have nothing to do with Alice being here, what's going on?"

"Alice isn't on my parents' radar. It has to be Elivorn. It wouldn't surprise me after Castle Rock. He knows me best of all and isn't fooled by my cover. I'm guessing he wants to hold something—someone—against me. He couldn't take you. He'd risk bringing too much attention on himself. As a Keeper, you have a degree of immunity, at least outside Grimmere. Perhaps Alice was the next best thing."

My blood boiled. "Do you think Elivorn intends to kill her?"

"It's unlikely, unless she becomes useless to him. I doubt she's in immediate danger." He flexed her leg.

I stared at Alice's battered face. "Other than being beaten up, that is."

"One of these days"—Lucas's voice was deadly—"I'll pay Elivorn back for this and so much else. But right now, I'm having to be nice. I almost went too far at Castle Rock. I might have been able to control myself if I hadn't been so pissed, but when he seduced you..." His teeth scraped. "My father knows we fight occasionally, but if there's too much conflict, he may become suspicious that I'm not aligned with his and Elivorn's plans."

Footsteps echoed through the dungeons. Wortle appeared holding Lucas's travelling pack, a bundle and a waterskin. She placed everything on the straw. "One of our guards reported in a moment ago," she said. "He had an inquiry from one of Lord Rouseau's personal servants as to his presence, but he fobbed it off. The longer the goblins are in position, the more likely they'll attract attention."

Lucas nodded. "We'll be as fast as possible."

As Wortle disappeared down the passage, Lucas dove into his pack and brought out a potion vial.

"So, what's wrong with Alice?" I asked. "Why isn't she fully conscious?"

"Some humans don't react well to being brought into Fae against their will. If they haven't had verity, it's complete mental overload." Tearing Elivorn limb from limb would be too kind.

Lucas uncorked the vial with his thumb. "Alice, I'm going to hold your head, and I need you to drink this. It will help you get a little better." He supported her and tipped the vial softly to her lips. She gulped down the contents. She had to be thirsty.

"We'll need to support her through the overwhelm. When she wakes, she'll be in a semi-conscious state. Everything will seem like a dream, and when she returns to the human realm, she'll remember it as such. Even so, it will help her to explain what's going on and tell her that we're here. She'll take it in on one level. We'll also have to impress on her that when Elivorn returns, she mustn't mention us." He set Alice's head down gently. "The potion should help with her injuries as well as the overwhelm, but not too quickly, which is useful. Elivorn would be suspicious if she was suddenly better."

I pulled the stopper off the waterskin. "But Elivorn isn't going to see her. I'm getting her out. Roux, Gabe and Nora too." Cradling Alice, I held the water to her lips. She drank a few gulps, a little running down her neck. I caught the drips with Lucas's coat.

Even in the pale light, I could see the flush returning to Alice's cheeks, but her cuts and bruises were just as evident. I ignored the desire to rinse my mouth out with the waterskin, the tang of blood still acrid on my tongue.

"I get why you brought Roux along," Lucas said, "but Gabe and Nora?"

"They followed us. It was too late to turn back."

He shook his head. "Camille, Alice can't go anywhere, not right away. Moving her would be too much, and the shock of returning her to the human realm immediately would be severe. We need to give her time to respond to the potion, which will strengthen and prepare her. Otherwise, those tales of people wandering into Fae and coming out insane..."

I stared at Lucas. How could I trust him? But I couldn't risk Alice.

"Not to mention," he added, "there's so much riding on my subterfuge, so many lives, and if Elivorn sees Alice gone, he'll think of us."

He drew a small bag from his pack and scattered herbs into his palm. A glow suffused his fingers and encompassed Alice. "Our scent will be all over the cell. This will disguise it. And"—he repeated the process with another herb—"this will keep Alice warm."

Alice's breathing grew deeper. A good sign, but even so... "This place is horrendous. Someone needs to watch over her. I'll stay."

Lucas sat back, the lantern light delineating his cheekbones. "No one can know we've found Alice. You can't remain here."

"No way. I won't leave her." My stomach clenched at the thought. I scoured Lucas's face. "You know, I have no idea what to think after today. Whether you're legit or supporting your family. You've had ample opportunity to mention Grimmere or your situation before now, but all you've done is hide things from me."

He fixed me in the eye. "I didn't want you to find out like this."

"How the hell was I going to find out, then?"

"I don't know." He released a breath and dragged a hand over his chin. "I hadn't figured out how to tell you. But now you're here, we have to maintain the ruse I told Elivorn. You must play the role of my loyal mate. If my family thinks you're anything other, they'll kill you. Besides, it will give us time to help Alice and find a way to get her out without raising Elivorn's suspicions. You have to stick by my side and act the part. There's no alternative."

CHAPTER 16

THE LAST THING I WANTED WAS TO PRETEND TO BE Lucas's mate, but I was well and truly cornered. I glared at him. "Doesn't look like I have a choice."

He straightened his waistcoat. "I may be able to arrange for us to visit Alice tomorrow, although we won't be able to use the tunnels from my chambers again without arousing suspicion. In the meantime, I'll have someone feed and care for her when possible, and watch her discretely twenty-four seven. I'll ensure they alert me if Elivorn returns to the dungeons. She'll have all she needs."

"All she needs," I snapped, "is to not be here."

"That's as may be, but it's the best I can do."

"Well, she can't stay here forever, and neither can we." The thought of it.

"I told you I'd be here for a week at most, hopefully less. My parents know that. I'm not sure how, but we'll have to get Alice home before then."

Alice's eyelids fluttered open. Her warm brown eyes struggled to focus as she glanced about the cell. "Camille, where are we?" Her voice was a little slurred.

"Good," he said. "The potion is helping."

"Hello, sweetie." I rubbed her hand, relief flooding through me. "It's great to see you back with us."

She cleared her throat. "This is such a strange dream. Lucas is here too, and you guys are in fancy dress again. Is there a party?"

I took in Alice's sweet face, then met Lucas's gaze. "I may have no choice but to go along with you, but I want to spend some time with her now... alone." I stroked Alice's head. "No, sweetie, there's no party this time."

She tried to focus on me, her full lips playing. "But you're wearing that leather combo again, and Lucas is giving me dark opera vibes. Love the addition of the fake blood. The way you've smeared it down your chin and neck creates the perfect vampire look. Very effective."

Lucas glared into the darkness, chewing his cheek, then he met my gaze. "You don't have long. The servants usually have free access to my chambers to tend the fire, amongst other things. The locked door will be raising suspicions." He got up and grabbed his pack.

Alice managed to prop herself up on her elbows and watch Lucas pull open the bars, retrieve his candle and walk away.

"Take it easy, hon," I said, supporting her.

"Camille, where am I? I... I don't know what's going on. I'm in a medieval dungeon, but it's all so surreal, so distant. I think I'm hallucinating. And"—she scowled—"I'm so damned mad at you for being awful to Raph."

We really didn't need that between us right now. "Look, I know we still have to sort everything out, but can we put that to one side for a little bit? At least until we figure out how to get you out of here."

She attempted to study me, but winced and closed her eyes, sinking back into the straw. "Damn, my head hurts. I feel like I've been pummelled by a baseball bat. But considering everything is a haze, and you're the only thing that makes sense at the moment, not to mention, I hate arguing with you, let's do that."

I squeezed her hand.

"But where's Raphaël?" she said. "I want him."

"I know you do. But we're stuck here."

"And I have to pee. Like, right now."

I should've thought. Nursing skills were not my forte. It took a couple of minutes to get Alice up, as dizzy and uncoordinated as she was. Once done, she lay back down, exhausted. I bundled the straw around her to make her comfortable, then gathered the supplies Wortle had brought.

"Water?" I held up the skin.

"I'm so thirsty," she said. "This reminds me of the time we dumped Gilles and Xavier a few days apart. Remember Barcelona and those Italians we partied with? This is like that hangover. One of the worst of my life."

I laughed. "That was bad. I mean, it was such a good night, but it took me two days to recover. We took the train back, but were too out of it to buy tickets, then we fell asleep only to be woken by an irate guard."

"I threw up on his shoes." She chuckled, then groaned. "You held my hair, looking after me just like now."

"Well, of course. You've done the same for me more times than I care to remember." Although none of them trapped in a dungeon in Fae. I cradled her and drew the waterskin to her lips. She took long gulps.

"But, Camille, I have all these bizarre images in my head. You know that cute guy you almost hooked up with at Castle Rock? He was out the back of the café. We were talking, then he showed me something that smelt strange. The next thing I remember, I was tied up and draped over a horse. Then, get this... I tried to escape, and the guy clobbered me in the head."

Freaking Elivorn. I unwrapped the paper around Wortle's bundle. Inside were hunks of thickly buttered bread.

"And," she continued, "the weirdest part was that there were all these goblins and strange creatures in the woods. Horrible things." She shuddered. "Hell, this is such a nightmare, or, no... I might be tripping."

Somehow, I had to give her an explanation on a level she would understand, and as Lucas had said, she needed to know the stakes. I passed her the bread. "This should help."

"Just what I wanted." She tucked in. "I have an urge to get up and rattle those prison bars," she said through a mouthful, "but I'm too tired. What does it matter anyway? I'll wake up in a minute."

I bit my lip. "Okay, Alice, just say we're having the biggest trip of our lives..."

"I'm with you on that."

"So, the creep from Castle Rock—Elivorn is his real name—he kidnapped you and took you into Fae... fairyland. You know all those old stories about elves and dwarves? Just like that." It was strange—I'd wanted to tell Alice about Fae for so long, and now it was happening, she wouldn't remember any of it.

She released a fragile laugh. "Oh, Camille. You and your folklore."

"Yeah, but remember, this is a trip. Go with it."

She studied my face, her brow furrowed. "Okay... disbelief suspended."

I passed her more bread, and she tucked in with bigger bites. "Then being in Fae explains all the weird creatures you saw, right?"

"I guess so."

"Well, Elivorn has you trapped in his dungeon, and it's highly likely you'll see more goblins, as they're everywhere. I can't stay, but I promise we'll sort this whole thing out, and there will be someone to keep an eye on you."

"I don't want you to go," she said. "This is all too crazy."

I swallowed. "I know, I want to stay too, but I can't." A lump filled my throat, my voice threatening to shake. "But Alice, this is important. Elivorn will be back. You can't tell him that Lucas or I were here, or he'll stop us helping you. Elivorn is bad news. Just do what he says and keep a low profile. When I'm gone, I'll be thinking of you every second, and we will get you out of here. Remember that."

She shuddered. "I won't say anything about you guys. But I need you here, Camille."

The lump in my throat grew.

"Just like when we had that sleepover," she said. "There were goblins there then, a lot of them."

I frowned. We'd had plenty of sleepovers when we were little, none of them involving fae, but we used to watch fantasy movies.

She closed her eyes. "And that sandwich on my canary..."

"What, hon?"

"Dancing like a dragonfly in a case." She snorted. "A thorny pain au chocolat." She mumbled on about patisserie, then something about Raphaël, none of it coherent.

My stomach sank. I didn't understand it—she should be getting better. I resisted the urge to shake her, to bring her back to me. Instead, I curled up close and wrapped her in my arms, listening to her murmuring.

I don't know how long it was before Lucas stepped up to the bars, but the candle in my lantern had burned a little way down. Alice was still muttering softly.

"You need to come," Lucas said. "The servants are wondering what's going on. We can't risk our absence any longer."

I sat up. "Alice is incoherent again. What happened?"

She shifted restlessly, her fingers twitching.

Lucas's brow knotted. "She's still struggling with being in Fae. We need to give the potion more time to work." He rubbed the back of his neck. "But it may be for the best that she's confused. She won't let anything slip, and if she does, Elivorn will think it's deluded ramblings."

The best for him, maybe.

"I have a trusted goblin in place, keeping an eye on Alice from a window that overlooks this part of the dungeons. She'll be in to check her at intervals when the coast is clear. Wortle will be around to help, too."

I glanced about and shuddered, wondering where this secret spy window was. "But rats..." There had to be rats.

"One thing I can say for this place, there's no vermin. The goblins are partial to a little snack. Rat heads go down very well."

My stomach lurched. No rats.

He drew his tailcoat from Alice and put it on. She'd be fine without it as she had the warming collude, and Lucas couldn't leave it here, but she looked so exposed. I tucked her up in the straw as best I could. She was drifting to sleep, her face relaxing, her limbs still.

I swallowed. Every part of me longed to stay, but the thought of the deaths that might result if Lucas or I were discovered was enough to force my hand. Lucas's truthfulness was in question, but at this moment in time, I had nothing to go on but his version of events. Homicidal tendencies aside, I had to give him an extremely wary benefit of the doubt. My survival and Alice's depended on it.

I forced myself up, and with an almost unbearable weight in my chest, I left the dungeon.

CHAPTER 17

LUCAS AND I STEPPED OUT OF THE TUNNEL AND INTO HIS chamber, the panel closing behind us. Weariness and the thought of leaving Alice alone in the dungeons was almost too much to bear. It had to be the early hours of the morning and I needed sleep. I could only hope that Roux, Gabe and Nora were alright. All I could do for the moment was play my part as Lucas's mate—whatever the hell that meant—in the hopes of getting us all out of here as soon as possible.

Lucas dropped his pack on the floor by an elaborate table and chairs. He strode to the chamber door and unlocked it, then headed to the massive hearth. The fire had burned low. He took a poker from the rack and nudged the glowing charcoal.

The chamber was vast. I'd not taken it in earlier, as distracted as I'd been. The decor was similar to the drawing room, the panelling and the furniture for the most part black and ornate. I ran my fingers along the back of the leather couch that stood with two armchairs before the hearth, my boots sinking into a massive rug patterned with dark grey and hints of violet.

Stepping through the room, my gaze was drawn to the ceiling, which rose in sweeping gables. Bare branches were carved into the stonework, the pattern much like the livery the goblins wore. Candelabras stood around, innumerable candles burning low, the light soft and intimate.

The walls in the centre of the room were lined with books, a couple of doors leading off. A large desk sat in a sweeping alcove to one side, and at the far end, a huge four-poster bed stood before arched windows framed by dark mullions.

"Were these always your rooms?" I asked, unable to restrain my curiosity. Lucas had warned me that we needed to speak cautiously in the castle, but this evening, he'd arranged for trusted servants to ensure we weren't overheard.

He nodded. "From my birth."

I passed the bed and peered through one of the windows. Moonlight bathed my face, rays glinting off the lake and glimmering in the distorted antique glass. Below, the shadows of the castle sprawled like a sleeping maloumbro. Beyond, forest extended all around, dark and impenetrable.

I shimmied off my pack and placed it on the floor, easing my shoulders. The bed looked extremely inviting, its canopy dressed in black silk with intricate silver stitching. I pressed the surface, my hand sinking into unbelievably soft covers. Such comfort amidst such hell. I glanced at Lucas through the pillars of the four-poster bed.

He rose from the hearth, having added a stack of wood to the flames. "The servants should've been in already to extinguish the candles, clean up and lay out our things for the morning. According to my sources, they're getting agitated, wondering why we locked the door. Though most are saying it's something to do with you being human and not knowing how the castle works."

"Sounds like a good excuse. Don't you dracs ever lock doors then? I get the whole servant thing"—well, in as much as I'd watched period dramas—"But surely you need *some* private moments."

Lucas took off his tailcoat and threw it over the couch. The contrast of his loose shirt tucked into the broad waistband of his breeches emphasised the straightness of his hips. Why was I noticing that, today of all days? I pulled my eyes away.

"Nope, not at all reserved when it comes to servants," he said.

As though they were pieces of furniture. "But don't you want some security? Surely Elivorn is close by."

"The caveats," he said.

"Ah yes. You're seriously injured if you beat each other up."

"There's more. There are certain unavoidable forfeits if one sibling kills another by their own hand. Titles are stripped, and the malefactor may be subject to a variety of horrific roles, carrying out atrocious deeds."

I stiffened my jaw. "I don't think I want to know the

details. So, back at Castle Rock, is that what Elivorn meant when he said you couldn't kill him?"

"Yes. In theory, I *could* kill him, but I wouldn't for those reasons." A thin smile ghosted his lips. "Having said that, it's possible for a third party to act on a family member's behalf, just as Elivorn attempted through Anthras. We each keep circles of loyal servants to safeguard against poisoned food, assaults while we're sleeping, that sort of thing. You've already met some of mine."

I was warming to the place, feelings of security abounding.

He walked over and leant on the bedpost, his face shadowed. "Camille, why are you here? I told you I didn't want you to come."

My lips parted. The reason I'd ventured into this hell pit had completely left me, what with everything else. But after Pierre's end, I'd be doing the world a favour if I didn't pass on the message. I could only hope with every fibre of my being that Lucas *was* helping the assembly. "I had a serious warning that you were in danger. That you would die soon if I didn't help."

"Mushum?" He raised an eyebrow, his lips quirking.

He needed to take this seriously. "Mushum has been one hundred percent accurate so far."

Lucas shrugged. "I suppose he has. No doubt he was being over general, though. Many fae find it difficult to interpret intuition into something actionable."

"Well, he mentioned me specifically, that I had to help. I couldn't let it drop."

He glanced out of the window for a moment, then met my eye. "Thank you. I'll be careful."

"I presume Elivorn is the most likely candidate."

"Got it in one." He loosened his cravat and pulled it off. "I'll keep my eyes peeled."

I buried my fingers into the luxuriously soft covers again. That aside, this place was unbelievable. "All this black. Were your family the first goths? Dark aesthetic wise, not the Germanic people."

"Quite possibly."

I followed the play of his fingers as he unbuttoned his poet cuffs. Then realisation slammed into me. "You're a fae lord. An actual bona fide storybook dark fae lord." I barked a laugh.

He grinned. "Now you know."

But there was still so much I didn't understand.

He strode to the side of the room and pulled open a door. "Wortle prepared a bath, if you want it."

"I wouldn't turn it down." The thought of getting clean was beyond appealing, but it felt treacherous with Alice in the dungeons below, though I supposed I had to act the part of Lucas's mate, and not look as if I'd been dragged through a forest.

As he returned, he scoured my face. "You look tired."

"Exhausted. Today has been something else." To put it mildly.

"Dracs keep late hours. You can sleep in."

My brow knitted. "I'd like to get back to Alice as soon as we can."

His gaze hadn't shifted, just like when he watched me at the café. There was intent in his eyes, but I had no idea what kind, and I wasn't about to indulge him by asking. He nodded and the intensity was broken. "Understood."

I stepped past him and headed through the door. The bathroom filled the entirety of a round tower. Similar to the roof of the main chamber, the walls were carved into branches like the bones of a forest in winter, the motif repeated in the leaded windows. Set into the floor in the centre was an enormous circular stone bath, although bath was an understatement. Swimming pool was more accurate. The steaming water was strewn with herbs and petals, the aroma spicy and organic. Innumerable candles had been set at the edge.

"Shit," was all I could think to say.

But I needed bed. I stripped off my scabbards and placed my dagger and sword on the flagstones, then pulled off my Keeper gear. To the side was a basin, water constantly trickling down then draining away in a whirl. I filled my mouth and swilled it before attempting to spit out every last hint of blood. No matter how many times I tried, I couldn't remove the metallic tang.

Giving up, I stepped into the bath. The heat soothed me immediately. The water had to be piped from the earth—I could feel the minerals. It was like when Alice and I bathed at Font-Romeu in the forest.

I lay back, floating. My thoughts grew light, images of forest and goblins and darkness flitting before me as I drifted away. But Alice. I jolted.

There was no way I could relax with her sick and in danger below. I grabbed a flannel and soap from the bath's edge and washed thoroughly. Once clean, I jumped out, towelled myself dry and pulled on my underwear. A shirt hung in the corner. I shrugged into the crisp, billowy cotton. It was massive on me, draping to mid-thigh, which suited me fine. Abandoning my Keeper gear and boots, I took a towel, tucked my scabbards under my arm and headed back out. I wasn't going to be parted from my weapons in this place.

The candelabras around the bed had been extinguished. Lucas sat at his desk, writing.

"What I don't get," I said as I padded over, towelling my hair with one hand, "is this whole mates business."

Lucas glanced up and paused, his gaze covering my shirt, then lowering to my legs before rising again. He looked dazed. I must have startled him, which was unusual. "What did you say?" His voice was tight. He rose and clutched at his throat as if reaching for his cravat, but it wasn't there, so he dropped his arm to his side.

"Mates," I said. "Why not girlfriend or partner? What does it mean, anyway?"

Shaking himself, he leant back on the desk. "It's a deep bond that is possible for dracs and other fae. Humans can share it too, but it's rare. Mates trust each other fully, which means my family will adopt that trust without question."

"Trust. After today." I shook my head.

He undid the top button of his shirt, then worked his way down, a smile playing at his lips. "In essence, as my mate, you become a Rouseau."

I gaped at him. "Nope. Not on my bucket list." But I got that it was the only thing he could've said to give me a free pass in Grimmere. "And your parents don't mind that I'm not a drac?"

He shrugged. "They might have had a problem if Elivorn bonded with a human. As I'm second in line to the rulership, it's not such an issue. It's rare for dracs to bond with another species, but not unheard of, and it's always respected. There's a degree of power generated by the partnership, and because of it, there's also prestige. I'm not sure if my parents would've maintained their rule without their bond."

"How peculiar."

"And if you have no more immediate questions"—he undid the last button, his shirt hanging loose, revealing furrows and ridges that I purposely ignored—"I need to freshen up." He strode into the bathroom.

Turning the concept over in my head, I made my way to the now-invisible window and tunnel entrance, the thick pile of the rugs underfoot squishing between my toes. The thought of being watched was too creepy. There was a folding screen nearby. I hooked my blades onto my shoulder, chucked my towel onto a chair and hauled the screen in front.

That was it. I was beyond shattered. I headed to the bed and clambered in on the window side, pushing my blades into the centre. I supposed I couldn't insist Lucas slept on the couch, what with our pretence and the servants having free access. Not that I cared. The bed was bigger than some rooms.

I sank into the unbelievably soft mattress, the pillows surrounding me like clouds, the covers warm against the chill radiating from the window. I hated that I was in a comfortable bed when Alice was in the dungeon, but I had to sleep.

My eyelids lowered then flicked open again in an attempt to avoid a vision of Lucas tearing out Pierre's throat. And I would be lying next to that monster. But damn it, I was so tired. I caught the soft tread of Lucas's bare feet. He stood at the end of the bed, the sculpted muscles of his back and butt contoured in the candlelight as he towelled himself dry. Would he please put some clothes on? I wasn't going to get any sleep like this.

He hung the towel over a chair and strode to the other side of the bed, offering me a full view.

"Clothes, Lucas," I murmured.

"I don't have anything. You have my shirt and—"

"And what? Dracs don't have underpants?"

"Exactly." He slipped into bed.

I turned to face him. The cover was drawn up to his waist, his pecs much too evident.

"Inappropriate," I said.

He smirked. "We've slept together. You've seen me naked when I change form."

"So not the point."

"What's inappropriate is taking your sword to bed with you."

"In this place? I don't think so." I pulled the covers up to my ear.

"You know, back in Foix when I was in Raymond Roger's

service in the early part of the thirteenth century, if two people slept in the same bed with a sword between them, it meant chastity."

"Well, perfect then." I turned onto my back and tried to get comfortable, the unease that laced my blood in this hellish land not helping.

The door clicked and there was a gentle scuffle. A goblin was tending the fire. I listened for a while as the creature pottered about the room, the sounds merging with the soft flow of Lucas's breathing, but try as I might, I couldn't sink into the vulnerability of sleep. I turned toward Lucas again, my scabbard digging into my leg, my shirt caught around me.

His eyes were open. "Still awake?"

I untwisted my shirt. "I don't get how you manage to sleep here with your life always in danger, or with what you did today on your conscience." If he had one.

Lucas placed his hand under his head, the hollows of his eyes black. "Everything you've seen here was normal for me. My family and I killed constantly, and my brothers and I learnt early to protect ourselves."

"To be brought up like that," I murmured. "How darkness must shape your soul."

"You've seen my true form. It's my nature."

I gazed at him, gazing at me. That intelligence, that shrewdness. "And yet you appear to fight it. When the hantaumo attacked, you gave everything for the town, for me. You give yourself daily to heal your patients. And today you killed to save countless others." That was presuming he really was helping the assembly. And if his motives *were* pure, did that indicate tremendous inner strength or show how easy it was for him to succumb to his true nature? I had no idea.

Doubt roiled in me. I'd struggled to trust Lucas from the beginning, but after today, what little we'd built had collapsed. Yet the remnants of our relationship burned deep within, the embers stoking something I hadn't realised was there. If I was completely honest with myself, I *wanted* to believe that Lucas was telling the truth.

We lay there gazing at each other for a long time, existing in the same space.

After a while, sleep still evading me, a question that had been playing on my mind pushed to the fore. "I don't understand the goblins. Why would they subjugate themselves to another creature's rule?"

Lucas turned onto his back and released a breathy laugh. "Goblins. The hideous creatures that make you cringe at the idea of anything intimate."

He was referring to my comments about Alice and Raphaël. Whenever I raised the topic, he winced or made some sharp retort. It was true. The thought of sleeping with a goblin turned my stomach—the wrinkles, the disproportionate limbs, the teeth. But it wasn't something I was going to do—ever—so what did it matter? I believed that love shouldn't be based on outer appearances, but I supposed I was drawn toward the human physique. And anyway, that wasn't why I objected to Alice and Raphaël's relationship. It was because Alice didn't know that her fiancé was a goblin. It had always been that.

"I don't understand what you're getting at," I said.

He angled his head, the moonlight glinting in his dark irises. His arm was draped over the cover, his fingers, strong yet elegant, playing with the cloth. "The answer lies in a little goblin history—history that dracs do their best to forget. Fancy a bedtime story?"

"Will it help me sleep?"

"If you don't mind nightmares."

I slid my fingers over my scabbard. "Couldn't be worse than today. Go for it."

"There are all kinds of goblins," he said. "Some are more helpful than others, like Mushum, and some actually manage to hold their shit together, like Raphaël, although it doesn't often last. Generally, their eccentric nature gets the better of them. They're scattered, irrational and harebrained."

"I noticed," I said.

"Long ago, before the world as we know it, goblins lived in complete chaos. As a race, they were struggling. All attempts at leadership fell apart, and they were prey to many dark fae purely because they didn't have the wherewithal to organise their defences."

I followed his lips as he spoke, the asymmetry of the creases drawing me.

"There came a moment," he continued, "when subject to the dark whims of other races, the goblins were on the brink of destruction. As one, they cried out for help, and the gods answered. Deep in the heart of the land that is now known as Grimmere, a goblin mother gave birth to an unusual child. The creature was beautiful, perfect. It was akin to an elf, though with human attributes, and so alluring was its charm that the power of seduction came naturally to it."

He turned to face me again, his dishevelled hair falling over his forehead. "Yet the child had another side which it had to embrace if it was to live. A dark side, so utterly hideous and more terrible than that of any goblin that had come before. The child was a goblin cleaved in two, embodying the brightest and best of the race on the one hand, and the most gruesome evil on the other."

The sinews of his arms striated as he tightened his fingers around the cover. "And so, the drac race was born. As they were able to live in their bright selves most of the time, they had the strength to rule goblins, to rein them in when they lost focus, to give them guidance and direction. The price the goblins have to pay for coherence and leadership is the dracs' dark nature. It's part of our culture to delight in killing. Most goblins are content to live this way, because otherwise everything would fall into disarray. Despite all this, dracs dissociated from goblins long ago, seeing themselves as superior and rejecting their heritage."

His lips stilled, his jaw relaxing as the shaky notions I'd pieced together about goblin oppression dissipated to nothing. "So what you're telling me," I said, my throat closing, my voice tight, "is that you're a goblin."

He smiled grimly. "I'm the thing that revolts you most of all."

Chapter 18

At some point during the early hours, I hadn't been able to fight my exhausted body any longer, and I'd fallen into a fitful sleep crowded with horrendous images.

I awoke once and found myself in the centre of the bed, facing the window, my weapons on the other side. Every part of Lucas was wrapped around me, his leg over mine, his arm braced protectively at my chest, his head tucked into the back of my neck, his soft breath against my skin. It seemed natural, his body guarding me from the horrors of this place, his warmth infusing me with strength. And in my uninhibited state, I sank into a deeper sleep.

I awoke to light seeping through the window, the wintery sun trapped behind a gauze of cloud.

Alice.

I turned over. The other side of the bed was empty.

Shit. How late was it?

I got up and peered out. The sun was already a good way

up. Damn it, I'd slept in with Alice in the dungeon. I hoped to hell she was alright. I supposed the guard Lucas had posted would've alerted us if anything had happened.

A movement below caught my eye. A figure swam in the chill waters of the lake, diving then breaking the surface again. From what I could see, it wasn't human. It was too skeletal for that. I don't know why I had the feeling it was Lucas. I barely knew the drac side of him, and I was too far away to see the creature properly, but it made me think of his words last night.

He was, for all intents and purposes, a goblin. A goblin split into perfect beauty and repellent horror. The hairs rose on my arms. The irony wasn't lost on me that I was in a similar situation to Alice, the difference being that Lucas hadn't hidden his true nature from me, though I'd been so much more revolted by it than I ever had by Raphaël. Even thinking of it now made me nauseous.

I shivered and attempted to bundle the covers around me, but they were too big. Abandoning them, I headed to the fire.

The servants had been in. The hearth blazed and new candles had been arranged in the candelabra. One of the doors leading off the main chamber was open. I stepped in. The room was furnished with cupboards, a dressing table, full-length oval swing mirrors and a chaise lounge in the middle. Clothing lay upon it. From what I could make out, it was a period-style side-saddle riding outfit of a jacket and skirt, with boots on the floor beneath.

I ran my fingers over the fine fabric. It felt exquisite. I

guessed I was the only one in the vicinity that it would fit. But no. Absolutely no way. I could pretend to be Lucas's mate, but I'd been born in jeans and a T-shirt. Yes, I'd adapted to my Keeper gear, but this was something else entirely. Talking of my gear, it hung from an ornate rail at the side of the room. That was more like it.

I pulled my trousers and top from the hanger. They were clean and fresh. Somehow, the servants had laundered them in the night. I couldn't complain about *that*.

There were a few other clothes hanging on the rail. Still feeling the cold, my warming collude having worn off, I grabbed a sheepskin jacket, then carried it all into the bathroom and got ready.

When I emerged, the aroma of chocolate and coffee filled the chamber. The table by the fire had been laid with breakfast while I dressed. What did the servants do, lie in wait for an opportune moment? I glanced around at the walls. Were they watching from somewhere right at this moment?

Steaming jugs sat on the table with a pile of croissants. I'd not eaten since yesterday, but the thought of Alice made my stomach churn, that and Lucas's mention of poison. Even so, I didn't know what the day had in store, and I needed to be prepared. I sat down, poured a coffee and a bowl of hot chocolate, then dunked in a croissant and forced myself to chew.

Lucas headed in, his hair wet, a robe hugging his frame. It had been him swimming. "Morning," he called. Good. perhaps now we could get to the dungeon, though if we couldn't go via the tunnels, I had no idea how we would get there without raising suspicion.

"Morning," I replied through a mouthful I'd chewed too many times.

He went into the dressing room and emerged a few minutes later, wearing something similar to yesterday but with knee-length boots.

He sat down opposite. "Did you sleep well?" He spoke with the formality he'd used with his family. He surreptitiously drew his finger to his mouth. He could've been scratching his lip, but the signal for silence was clear. We couldn't speak freely at the moment as his trusted servants weren't in place.

I studied Lucas's sculpted features as he poured coffee. The hope that had kindled last night, that he truly was faithful to the assembly, burned deeply. I supposed our partnership had begun to mean something. I couldn't trust him after what I'd seen, but I wanted to.

He angled an eyebrow, waiting for a reply.

Time to begin the charade. "I did indeed. What a comfortable bed, and how wonderful of the servants to lay out such a magnificent array of clothing." Putting it on, much?

He roared with laughter. "But you chose your Keeper gear."

Back to the real me. "I think it suits me better, if I'm not stepping out of line, that is?"

"Not at all. Although my parents will be offended if you don't dress for dinner."

"Sure, but I have nothing to wear."

"That will be taken care of." He took a sip of coffee. "I hope breakfast is satisfactory?"

I couldn't stop my lips quirking at his formal tone. "It's good. Though I guess I was expecting something different. Fae food or a raw animal carcass, perhaps."

He smiled. "Fae and the human realm reflect each other. Much of the food is similar." He bit into a croissant.

I leant my elbows on the table and steepled my fingers into an *A* for *Alice*. "So what have we got planned for the day?"

"I'm going to show you a little of Grimmere. The horses will be ready shortly." He inclined his head toward my hands. He'd gotten my meaning and had something arranged.

"Sounds perfect. But won't your family expect us to be sociable?" The image of Lucas's father as he called his evening's entertainment into the drawing room didn't exactly ignite my enthusiasm. I forced down another bite of croissant and a swig of coffee.

"They will be busy with state concerns. We'll have to entertain ourselves until dinner at sundown."

Plenty of time to help Alice.

A knock rapped at the door.

"Come," Lucas called.

A footman stepped in and bowed.

"My lord, your father requests a brief moment of your time. He'd like to see you in his study once you've breakfasted."

I smirked at the address the goblin had used.

Stifling his own smile, Lucas said, "Tell him I'll be right there."

The goblin backed out and closed the door.

Lucas gathered his napkin and dabbed the corners of his mouth. It really didn't reflect how he tore into baguettes in Tarascon, mayonnaise on his chin. "I shouldn't be long. Have a look around the place if you want. I'll find you when I'm finished, and we'll get under way."

"Sure." I hated the delay, but I had to do something whilst waiting.

He headed off. Having eaten as much as I could, I returned to the bed and fished out my blades, then slung my sword scabbard over my shoulder, ready to put on properly when we left. I'd manage without the dagger.

Despite everything that had happened in the castle, I couldn't deny my inquisitiveness as I stepped out of Lucas's chamber. I followed the corridor along, the place lit with candelabras and the dim light of windows, the decoration ornate and dark. Most of the doors were closed, but one had been left open. Inside was another massive suite.

I turned a corner into the next wing and found the morbid drawing room. Every sign of Pierre's and the goblins' blood had been removed. A little further on was a huge sweeping staircase. Windows to one side looked out over a courtyard. In the centre stood a menhir—a way marker, possibly.

On lower levels, I came across reception rooms, meeting rooms, a ginormous ballroom, a library that took up an entire wing and a spectacular entrance hall. The castle was utterly stunning. I guessed it paralleled the Palace of Versailles in its own dark way. Nonetheless, I couldn't shake off the feeling of unease.

Lucas had to be finished soon. I climbed the stairs and headed back along the passageway toward his chambers, thinking of Mushum's prediction. I had no idea if Lucas was in danger right at this moment, but he knew the place, and I was sure he would've communicated something if he was concerned.

I wasn't far from Lucas's chambers when a door opened to my side. Elivorn stepped out and leant against the frame. "Camille. How delightful to see you."

I glared at him. The monster had Alice below, and yet I had a role to play. "Elivorn." I nodded and continued on. He darted in front of me with drac speed. Pulling up short, my chin almost hit his chest. "What do you want?"

"Not so fast." His lips were close, his breath tickling my face as it had in Foix. "We missed out the other night, but now we can make up for it. Come with me."

"You have to be joking." But there was something about his gaze... and the way his dark waves brushed his cheekbone on one side... and his body in that tailcoat... He was goddamned intriguing, and I wanted to know more. Warmth kindling low in my centre, I turned and followed him.

But then, I didn't even like Elivorn, and there was no way I should be placing one foot after the other into his room. He was using his incubus manipulation. "What are you doing to me?" I growled. A small part of me screamed that I had to get

away, that I had to fight him, that I could draw my blade, but
most of me was beguiled. I wanted him now just as I'd
wanted him before. My breath grew shallow, the warmth
intensifying.

He laughed and closed the door, the thunk filling me
with dread as any chance of help was shut out.

The room was similar to Lucas's in decor, although
extremely cluttered. A desk stood against the far wall stacked
with books, and at the side of the seating area around the
hearth, numerous old parchments and scrolls lay scattered on
the floor.

I paused by the couch, attempting with all my might to
resist his sway. He walked toward me, undressing me with
his gaze. I wanted to shrink from him, and I wanted more.

"I do so love playing with my brother's toys." He drew
close.

Unwillingly, my body moulded to his. Shit. "Get the
fuck off me."

He ran his fingers from the collar of my Keeper gear
down to my breast. My skin burned at his touch. "We don't
have much time," he murmured. "My father will be finished
with Lucas any second."

He grabbed me and kissed me hard, too hard, dark desire
rushing through me despite his tongue invading, sickening. I
couldn't move, couldn't believe he was doing this.

He eased back, his teeth trailing painfully over my
bottom lip. "Camille, it will be so much fun to break you."

"Lucas is going to kill you." I tried to force myself away
from him.

He just laughed.

I didn't get it. Why was he doing this? No matter the caveats that prevented the brothers killing each other, Lucas was going to lose his rag and rip Elivorn apart anyway. But then, what had Lucas said back in the dungeon? He was having to be nice... He'd gone too far fighting at Castle Rock... Too much conflict and his father would be suspicious. "You're doing this on purpose. You want Lucas to react."

He shrugged a shoulder. "I look forward to you telling him. And if you don't, well then, as soon as we have a moment, I'll enjoy taking what's his, whether he knows about it or not." He stepped back and adjusted his coat.

Shit. What the hell was I going to do?

Every shred of desire dissolved as Elivorn released me from his sway. All that remained was a tight coil of fury. He'd said he wanted to break me, but I wanted to break him so damned hard, for this and for Alice, but if I raised a hand, I would ruin Lucas's plans and most likely get myself killed.

He gazed down the length of his nose, a smug smile pulling at his lips.

"You bastard," I said, and stormed out.

CHAPTER 19

WANTING TO PUT AS MUCH DISTANCE BETWEEN MYSELF and Elivorn as possible, I strode back to the chambers as fast as I could without raising suspicion.

That utterly vile creep beyond all creeps. For the second time in as many days, I had the urge to rinse my mouth out, Elivorn's taste nauseating. The memory of his touch oozed over my skin, but I wasn't buying into it. I wasn't going to feel used because I'd been subject to his influence.

Even so, fear trickled through me. I was Elivorn's prey, and he was waiting to strike. Lucas said he might have been able to restrain himself at Castle Rock if he hadn't been so pissed... Might. There was a chance he'd hold back, but that time in the cave when I'd taunted him about Pascale, he'd reacted badly, and Pascale and I hadn't even dated. I couldn't risk telling Lucas. If what he said was true about working against his family, there was too much at stake.

Shit. Shit. Shit.

I'd just have to be careful to avoid Elivorn when I was alone. I could do that. Or better, I'd find a way to deal with him—

Footsteps drummed behind me. I jumped inwardly, forcing myself to continue onward.

Lucas drew level. "Had a good look around?"

"Uh... yeah, sort of," I said nonchalantly.

He sniffed. "Elivorn?" His voice was guttural.

"Bumped into him."

"Literally, by the smell of it." He studied me intently. "What was he doing?" By the tension in his jaw and the fire in his eyes, he already looked as though he'd bite his brother's head off.

"He was just being Elivorn. Trying to wind me up— trying to wind you up if he knew you'd smell him. It was nothing." I met Lucas's gaze. I had to, or he'd know something was up, but I hated lying to him. Ha, I hated lying to the creature who'd torn out Pierre's throat. Damn, this was all so screwed up.

"You bit your lip."

I touched the sore spot with my finger, a dab of red staining the tip. At least this time it was my own blood, but fucking Elivorn. "Yeah, it's nothing." I licked my lip.

Lucas didn't look happy, but all he said was, "Let's get out of here, shall we?"

"Sounds perfect." All I wanted was to get to Alice.

We passed Lucas's chamber door. The corridor looped around and led back to the main staircase from the opposite direction. As we descended to the entrance, Lucas cast the occasional side-eye. He wasn't convinced of Elivorn's innocence.

Two footmen pulled open the massive doors at the front of the castle, and we headed out. The scenery was breathtaking. We were high above everything, a path winding down the mountain before us, the lake a silver expanse below. Forested terrain rose to peaks beyond, and wisps of mist trailed here and there. It was rugged, harsh, bitter and utterly awe-inspiring.

At the bottom of a short flight of stone steps, grooms held two night-black horses, their muscles defined beneath coats of rippled velvet, their manes sweeping to their shoulders. Lucas's pack and waterskins had been attached to the backs of their saddles.

"Your Keeper report from the assembly noted that you could ride," Lucas said as we approached.

A report on me. Now, that was something I wanted to read. "I messed around on the neighbours' horses for years as a teen."

He stepped over to one of the mounts and rubbed its forehead. The creature nudged into him. An old friend, perhaps.

I took the reins of the other. "What are their names?" I asked the groom.

He cringed as though being spoken to by one of Lucas's peers was extremely rare and very likely to result in death. "Uh... this is Crow, ma'am, and the other is Gloom."

"Thanks." I sent him a reassuring smile, then wondered

if I was supposed to. But to hell with it. No matter our charade, I wasn't going to treat the servants like trash. The "ma'am" reminded me of the Men, though. If only Slaughter and his comrades were here.

We set off at a walk. My body swayed as I shifted comfortably from side to side, rocked by Crow's gait. A small cove with black sand came into view under the castle. From what I could tell, it was where Lucas had swum.

I unbuckled the waterskin and swilled out my mouth, spitting Elivorn away and wondering if I could speak freely out here. Lucas placed his finger to his lips subtly, like before. I supposed it wasn't difficult to guess what was on my mind.

"So, I'll show you around, just as we planned." His gaze was loaded. We were heading to Alice, although as we were currently going in the opposite direction, I couldn't see how. And at this rate, we'd never get there.

"Wherever you're taking me, I'd like to get a move on."

"Let's get on with it, then." With a grin, he gathered his reins and broke into a gallop. I followed, Crow bunching and releasing under me, the wind whipping tears from my eyes as we thundered down the mountain and skirted the lake. I hadn't ridden for a while, and it felt so good, though the thought of Alice was enough to sober me, as were the maloumbros and other dark shapes that lurked in the pines to our side.

We charged up the adjacent mountain, not slowing until we'd rounded its summit. The horses' flanks were lathered with sweat, their nostrils blowing. In the distance, endless forest was broken only by a small town and the occasional cluster of rooks. Turning Gloom, Lucas inclined his head. Behind us rose Grimmere Castle in all its oppressive glory, mist wreathing its spires. It really was something.

"Come on," he called, spurring Gloom into a trot in the opposite direction. I followed, tension stiffening my arms at the thought of heading away from the dungeons once more. Crow, sensing it, jostled his head and pulled against me.

At the foot of the mountain, we followed a narrow path for a fair distance. Things lurked in the undergrowth—dark, indistinct, chilling things—though they were holding off, possibly deterred by Lucas's presence. I'd completely lost my bearings, my agitation at wanting to see Alice growing by the second.

A little further along, Lucas paused by a large pine, a scattering of mushrooms beneath. "Well?" he asked.

A goblin in a ragged jerkin stepped out. "The path is clear, my lord," he said in a low voice.

We wove in and out of the trees, the forest becoming deciduous, bare branches abounding. We passed another goblin and emerged into a gently sloping clearing.

"We can talk now," Lucas said, drawing Gloom to a halt. "The slopes are kept glamoured and secure by those loyal to me. If my family asks where we've been, we spent the day riding through the mountains, sightseeing. We avoided towns and villages, not wanting to deal with the folk there. The route we took shouldn't raise concern, and the goblins we passed will cover our tracks."

"That's all well and good," I said, Crow raking the ground with his hoof, "but where the hell are we?"

Lucas nodded to a hatch in the hillside, another guard standing nearby. I couldn't believe it. We'd doubled back on ourselves. "Wortle's hole," I said, my agitation easing away. "Which means we can take the tunnel to Alice."

CHAPTER 20

LUCAS DISMOUNTED WITH EASE AND HOOKED HIS PACK over his shoulder. I hauled my leg over the back of the saddle and slid to the ground, my muscles trembling from their unaccustomed use. Crow lowered his head and snatched at the grass. I scratched behind his ears.

We tied the horses to a tree, then headed into Wortle's hole and took the steps. As we entered the corridor, the aroma of coffee and toast mingled with the stink of rotten eggs.

A voice came from the kitchen. "When making glamours with sulphur, it's of utmost importance that you bind the mineral with the appropriate herb so the two can work in synergy." Roux was in full instructional mode. "Otherwise, you'll produce that awful stink."

"Yeah, I get that," Gabe said. "But what if you have two or more herbs—"

Lucas unlatched the door and we stepped in.

"Lulu," Wortle warbled, delight elevating her croaky voice. "Come, come. I don't see you often enough, and yesterday was too long ago."

With a broad grin, Lucas wrapped her in a bear hug, lifting her off her feet. "Dear Wortle." For a moment, I could see the boy in him. But that boy had been raised to kill, and the man might just be deceiving me. Seeing the delight on Lucas's face, it was hard to believe what he'd done last night.

Roux and Gabe, sitting at the table, watched with interest. A lump of yellow rock smoked in Gabe's hand. It was good to see them, even after this short time. They were a piece of home that felt like a million miles away.

The hole was a complete contrast to the cold opulence of the castle. The pans, jars, herbs and crockery stacked on shelves and sideboards were there because they were useful or treasured, and the place felt warm because of it.

"Lucas, good to see you alive and in one piece," Roux called. "And Camille, glad you survived the night in hell."

"You should see this, you two." Gabe pointed at the empty table.

"Uh, what?" I asked.

"Exactly," he said mysteriously.

"I'll be needing that back to make tea, deary," Wortle said to him as she straightened her apron and skirt.

Gabe's face fell. "We haven't gotten to the revealing collude yet. Can you manage with a glamoured kettle?"

Wortle tutted and shook her head.

"Now, now," Roux said, "the boy must experiment in the name of magical education. But I'll undo the glamour if I have the right herbs..." He rummaged in his bag.

Wortle bustled over, took my hands in hers and squeezed. I wasn't sure what to make of her after yesterday. She was helping us, but the way she'd revealed Lucas's true nature had been severe.

"Camille, deary, you slept well, I take it?" Her warm, goggly eyes sparkled, her wrinkles multiplying at the corners.

If you didn't count worrying about Alice in the dungeon, a castle full of killers and the chance my partner really might be the epitome of evil, it was sort of alright. "Yes, good, thanks, all things considered." Although the sensation of Lucas wrapped around me had been something else entirely.

Nora lay on the settee at the end, her knees bent. She turned her head as if she could barely find the energy to move, her make-up perfect as usual. I couldn't believe she'd brought her cosmetics with her. "Nice outfit, *Lulu*," she said.

Lucas lasered Gabe and Nora. "You two..." he rumbled. "You put everyone in danger, including yourselves. If I was Camille or Roux, I would've left you in the forest."

Gabe gulped. Nora put on her best defiant glare.

Wortle beamed at Lucas and me as she fished around randomly above the table. "Those two aside, I'm glad you're here. Blisterch and Digdeep will be back soon with some others. We have plenty to discuss. But in the meantime"—her hand closed on an invisible handle—"I'll make tea."

Roux looked up from his bag. "It appears we don't have

exactly the right herbs to undo the glamour. I may be able to give the kettle another appearance though." He scratched his chin, ruffling his beard.

"We have to see Alice first," I said.

"Yep, hold the tea. It's our priority." Lucas glanced about, looking for something.

"Very well," Wortle said, still beaming. "I've been down to check her already. Apparently there's been no sign of Elivorn."

"Alice?" Gabe asked, his brow knitting. "She's here?"

Roux and Nora looked as confused as he did.

"I wasn't sure what you wanted disclosed, dearies." Wortle tapped the side of her nose, then headed over to the sink. I appreciated her discretion.

"My brother has her in the dungeons." Lucas spotted a couple of lanterns amidst the general clutter and grabbed them.

Nora met my gaze, her eyes wide. "There's more than one man in the world with those genes?"

Gabe scowled.

Lucas smirked as he adjusted the lantern wicks. No matter the circumstances, he could always manage a good smirk.

"There sure is," I said. Did fae have genes? Not that it mattered. "There's a whole family of them in the castle and they're deadly."

"What time will you be back?" Wortle asked as she stoked the range.

"We'll meet here at noon," Lucas said, before darting out into the corridor.

"Uhhhh." Nora rolled her eyes. "Wonderful. Now we'll have to wait until then for something interesting to happen. This place is *so* dull."

"Serves you right for following us," I said. "And anyway, what do you expect, being somewhere dangerous like this?"

"I don't know." She twisted onto her side. "Maybe some danger? A little excitement?"

"Deary, you can go outside if you like," Wortle said. "Just make sure you stay in the slopes. The guard will warn you if you venture too far."

"At least we've got Roux here to go over the quantum mechanics of collude casting in variable dimensions." Gabe's brow rose. "Beats doing nothing."

Nora buried her head into the cushions and groaned. "What I wouldn't give for my phone to work."

Honestly, she'd been here five minutes.

Lucas came back in, lanterns alight. He passed one to me. "Ready?"

"Absolutely." The sooner the better.

We headed out and entered the tunnel, closing the door behind us.

Lucas strode swiftly over the packed earth. There was no doubt he was familiar with the route. I supposed he'd visited Wortle as a child. I had to admit I was curious about his goblin nursemaid. "You and Wortle are pretty close then," I called ahead.

"You could say that." He shot a glance back over his shoulder. "I don't know how I would've turned out without her. She told me stories of other lands. Made me see that there was more to the world—different ways of thinking. What you've seen of Grimmere is only the tip of a very dark iceberg. If it wasn't for her..." He sucked in a breath.

"I can't imagine growing up here," I said.

"I got out as quickly as I could." His voice was low, his gaze fixed on the passage. "I explored Fae and the human realm and saw how things were for myself. It soon became clear what I was. I studied healing and medicine because I... uh... wanted to make up for... various things."

There was so much beneath the surface of his words. We descended into silence, the scuffling of our boots filling the tunnel. The darkness yawning beyond the glow of our lanterns reminded me of the bounds cracks. "Did your father reveal anything about the splitting of the bounds earlier?"

"No. He wanted to discuss how I'm going to relay intel from the assembly."

We reached the gate and took the steps, then turned into a side tunnel near the dungeon door we'd used last night. A watchman sat on a stool before another window, a lantern at his feet. I hated to think how many of these passages and peep holes there were.

"Lord Rouseau." The goblin stood to attention, almost falling down the steps behind him. "Nothing to report, though Elivorn has asked for food and water to be given to the prisoner, and she's getting restless. She doesn't look too good." He itched his sides.

I didn't like the sound of that. Through the window, I caught a glimpse of Alice lying in the straw.

"Place the guards so we can speak freely," Lucas said. "We'll see that she's alright."

The goblin nodded, then grabbed his lantern and scooted off down the stairs into the darkness.

We followed him, descending a few steps and headed through a door. It opened in the wall nearest the cell.

Alice shifted restlessly, muttering to herself as Lucas unlocked the bars. The daylight oozing in from the small windows high above didn't improve the cold and filthy dungeon.

Lucas pushed open the door. I hurried in and sank to my knees. "Alice, sweetie, it's Camille. I'm back."

She rolled her head, her eyelids fluttering then closing. Her face was flushed, her skin clammy. "I don't know where Raphaël has gone. Where is everyone, Camille?"

Lucas knelt by her side and checked her pulse.

Alice murmured unintelligibly. The poor thing, and poor Inès, too. She would be going out of her mind with worry for her daughter, and if everyone was on high alert over Alice, would they have discovered Gabe and Nora missing?

"Shhh, sweetie, it's okay. I'm here now." I felt her forehead. She was much too hot. "She's burning up. What's happening?"

Lucas placed her hand down gently. "The potion should've worked." He scraped his teeth over his lip. "She's still struggling with being in Fae."

"What can we do?"

"We have two choices. I have another potion that should help her. If it doesn't, there's one last option."

"And that is...?"

His face was grave. "Verity."

"But you said she'd return home and think it was all a dream. If she has verity, then she'll remember... she'll know about Fae." I gaped at him. I'd wanted so much to share everything with Alice, before realising that I'd be putting her in the same position as me, never being able to speak of the hidden realm with those I loved.

He nodded. "And it's not reversible. But more importantly, when verity is administered to someone in a confused state, there are two possibilities. Either it helps, or it makes the patient worse. Much worse. It's our last resort."

I closed my eyes for a second. "I can't believe Elivorn has done this to her."

Lucas's jaw stiffened. "I can." He drew his pack from his shoulders and took out a vial. "Let's see how she responds to the other potion first and take it from there."

I supported Alice's head as Lucas tipped the vial to her lips. She swallowed the contents. As Lucas reinforced the warmth collude and glamoured our scent, I pulled a waterskin from his pack and offered Alice a drink. She took a couple of small sips.

A shadow slipped past. The watchman stood at the bars, his eyes wide. He gestured urgently for us to leave, then darted back to the door.

"We have to go. *Now*," Lucas said in the quietest whisper, his gaze darting to the dungeon entrance at the end of the row of cells.

I paused, the thought of leaving Alice tearing me up, but the look on Lucas's face was enough to pull me to my feet. We stepped out of the cell as quickly and quietly as we could. Lucas turned the key, wincing as the lock made the faintest of clicks, then we padded to the secret door and closed it behind us.

The goblin's jowls trembled as he stared out of the window. We joined him to see the dungeon door swing open.

Elivorn paused in the doorway, listening. He must have heard us. Even though I was sure from yesterday that the window afforded a degree of soundproofing, I held my breath. Lucas's lip curled.

In a flash, Elivorn disappeared around the corner, checking the place for intruders. He returned after a minute and stood before Alice's cell, massaging his chin. I willed him to stay out, to keep his slimy hands off her. He shook his head then strode out of the dungeon, slamming the door behind him.

The goblin raised his finger, indicating for us to wait. He disappeared down the tunnel, then returned a few moments later, itching his armpit. "The coast is clear."

I released a long breath. "I'm going to sit with Alice."

I turned to the door, but Lucas gripped my arm. "There's nothing you can do right now, although the potion will be helping."

I stiffened. "What I can do is be with her."

"It's too dangerous. Besides, we have to get back and sort out how we're going to get Alice and the others out of here."

I glared at him. I ached to be in the cell by Alice's side, but figuring out our next step was crucial.

His gaze softened. "We may be able to return later, before we leave with the horses."

"Alright." It was better than nothing.

CHAPTER 21

"How much information have you gathered?" Blisterch pointed at Lucas with his spoon, the handle gripped in his long, spindly fingers—every part of him was long and spindly. Apparently, he was the head of Lord Rouseau's security, which to my mind explained his constant glower. He was also Lucas's most trusted source in Grimmere.

Wortle fussed around, restocking the table as we devoured lunch. "Lulu has been back all of five minutes," she said. "It's going to take longer than that to get anything useful from his father."

Digdeep, another of Lucas's most trusted, shook his head, his tiny eyes glinting. "These things can't be rushed." He was a round goblin, made of muscle and a good layer of fat. His large cheeks along with his general solidity gave me the impression of a brawny mastiff. Very friendly, but could probably steamroll you, should he become over enthusiastic.

I dipped a wedge of bread into my vegetable soup, then took a bite. It was simple food, and a part of me registered that it was delicious, but I struggled with it, thinking of Alice. Roux, Gabe and Nora were tucking in, eyes on bowls, as were the other two goblins who'd joined us—the most committed of Lucas's advisers. Opposite was a small goblin with a serious overbite, his teeth digging into his chin, and the other chap, sitting next to Blisterch, was sort of pointy. Nose, ears, elbows—if any part of his body could have angles, it had them.

Lucas set his spoon in his bowl and sat back. "Despite Elivorn's suspicions, my father is beginning to trust me. He's confident in my desire to see the realms split. It's only a matter of time before he reveals more."

Gabe and Nora followed the conversation, their eyes darting back and forth. They'd been updated about our undercover positions, and Nora in particular was finding everything much more interesting now. Roux was completely absorbed in his lunch.

We'd already discussed the possibilities for them all returning through the forest to the Stinkhorn way marker, but Blisterch couldn't risk a goblin escort for a couple of days. We'd also explored ideas for getting Alice out, but we'd come up blank, especially as she was still too sick to be moved.

"It would be nice if you managed to hurry your father up," Blisterch said through a mouthful, shaking his head at Lucas. "This is just like that awful day we fought against the dark elves in Dimtrich. You're taking your time again."

The pointy goblin appeared to have lost interest in the

conversation. He positioned his knife on the edge of the table near Blisterch's arm and balanced a slice of buttered bread on the end. I couldn't see why. He saw me watching and sent me a sharp-toothed grin.

Lucas shot Blisterch a faux glare, a spark of humour in his eyes. "My horse went lame on the way to the battle. The five hours at the tavern with Digdeep couldn't be helped."

"Now, that was an afternoon to remember," Digdeep said, his eyes glinting some more.

Blisterch laughed, but there was a sharp edge to it.

It was interesting, hearing snippets about Lucas's life, although I couldn't figure out why goblins in Lord Rouseau's service would've been in another land fighting dark elves. Perhaps they'd had a feud with the dracs.

"It's taken years to regain my father's faith," Lucas added. "I can't rush it."

Blisterch shifted in his chair, his arm knocking the knife on the edge of the table. The bread catapulted up and stuck to his sleeve.

The pointy goblin and Monsieur Overbite cackled, Lucas roared with laughter and Wortle tittered. Gabe and Nora exchanged a look before creasing up with the rest. The whole commotion was enough to pull Roux from his soup. He glanced up for a second before clicking his tongue and returning to his bowl.

I gazed around at them as Blisterch peeled the bread from his arm, his sleeve coated in butter, his forehead marred by a rather pissed-off scowl. Digdeep didn't look too happy either. I got where they were coming from. It really hadn't been that funny.

Lucas caught my eye, still howling. "What?" he asked through his grin.

It was one of those ridiculous pranks that goblins seemed to delight in. But the pointy chap was one of Lucas's advisers. It did nothing for my confidence, and it was curious that Blisterch and Digdeep hadn't been amused.

And Lucas... what was he like? His words last night came back. He was a goblin. My partner was one of those crazed and oh-so-nutty creatures, albeit one with a degree of self-restraint when he chose to use it. I drew my hands over my face. And this was my life.

Blisterch's annoyance had set permanently on his brow, which only made his glower worse. "I think Lord Rouseau suspects me."

In an instant, Lucas's expression hardened. "What makes you say that?"

"Conversations I've overheard." Blisterch's ears folded a little at the tips. "The goblins are nervous, what with Lord Rouseau's plans. His trusted servants are bickering amongst themselves to gain his favour by providing him with even the most inconsequential information. Unfortunately, some of it involves us. He's beginning to put two and two together."

Wortle got up, lifted a large savoy cabbage from the centre of the table and poured Lucas a top-up, a stream of tea flowing from one of its leaves. Lucas wrapped his arm around her and pulled her close. She rubbed his hand and smiled—a wrinkled, sharp-toothed, pretty awful smile, but the love was clear.

"Those who support Lord Rouseau are always on the lookout for dissidents." Wortle reached across to top up Monsieur Overbite. "Blisterch ensures our activities are hidden, but it's difficult for him to cover our tracks all the time. Questions have been raised."

Blisterch nodded.

"Then you need to step back," Lucas said. "Have one of the others take on those tasks."

"Agreed," Digdeep said, his eyes narrowing. "It's what I've been saying for months now."

Monsieur Overbite nodded. "I'll third that."

"Then make sure it happens." Lucas pushed his chair back and crossed his ankle over his leg.

Blisterch tightened his jaw. "It's better if only one of us is under suspicion."

"We're all in this together," Digdeep said through a mouthful of bread.

Lucas nodded. "Absolutely."

"There's something I don't understand," I said.

"There's plenty *I* don't understand," Roux murmured, then ladled up more soup. He didn't look as though he was going to elaborate.

"Isn't that the truth?" I muttered to him. "You didn't even twig that Lucas was connected to one of the most powerful families in Fae, even though he had the same surname."

"The chance of an actual Rouseau becoming a Keeper," he hissed, "was so infinitesimally small, I presumed he was from a lesser house with the same name and that he was some kind of a rebel. Lucas wasn't exactly open about it."

All eyes homed in on me, waiting for my question.

I focussed on the subject matter, shooting a nervous side-eye at Lucas. "What with the stakes should the bounds be split, why don't we just... uh... dispose of Lord Rouseau and Elivorn." I was talking about killing Lucas's family. Harsh. It wasn't the sort of thing I generally went around recommending.

He shrugged. "I have no problem with that, but if there are other fae involved, by killing my family, we'll lose our information source. However, if it comes to it, that's what we'll do."

I tapped a finger on the table. "I just don't get it. The dracs have been pretty evil for centuries, right? Surely others have wanted to bring them down. With the tunnels, it wouldn't be difficult."

Wortle stepped over with the cabbage and poured amber into my mug. "The tunnels are our greatest asset. Through them, we've gained information year after year that has helped us in so many ways. If there were unexplained killings in the castle, there would be noses poked into all manner of things. What's more, deary, the rule would be seized by another of the drac houses, and they would root out the perpetrators."

Digdeep pushed his bowl away. "It's a case of better the devil we know."

"And what about you, Wortle?" Blisterch asked. "Has the mistress let anything slip whilst dressing?" Lucas had mentioned that Wortle, as head of housekeeping in the castle, had a host of goblin spies under her wing.

She slid me the milk jug. "Lady Rouseau is as tight-lipped as usual. The tunnels prove more reliable than maids' ears for gleaning information."

We continued our discussion well into the afternoon. As the conversation focussed on the minutiae of the castle, I grew restless, and I wasn't the only one. Gabe, Nora and I got up to help Wortle with the dishes, and Roux fell asleep in an armchair, still exhausted from yesterday.

The clearing-up done and the meeting finished, Gabe and Nora disappeared outside for some fresh air. I slumped down on the settee.

Lucas joined me, his arm against my shoulder. "Tonight," he said.

"What about tonight?"

"At dinner we need to gather as much information as we can about the splitting of the bounds. That aside, I'll have to put on a reasonable performance to convince my parents that our mates bond is the real deal."

"Sure," I said. That was given.

"You don't have to be anything other than yourself, though. You're human, and my family will be expecting foibles."

"Foibles? Like what?"

"Just certain mannerisms." He pressed his lips together, restraining a smile. "And we'll have to be of one mind. Whatever I say, agree with me. Our stance is that humans who refuse to believe in the existence of fae or lack the ability to see us are worthless—hence the splitting of the bounds to rid us of the burden they form. You'll have to be completely confident in your support for my family's plans."

He pulled a cushion out from between us and tucked it behind him. "And it will probably help if we gaze at each other with infatuation." His eyes sparkled. Yeah, he was going to love that. "But, Camille," he added, "the thing is... drac mates are... um... amorous. I'll have to be very attentive, or it will look strange. We need to set up some boundaries."

I couldn't help releasing a sharp laugh. "How far do you want to go? I guess I'd expected your arm around me and a bit of eye contact."

"All of that." There was mischief in his eyes.

"Alright. You can hold me close, and you can touch non-intimate parts of my body. Shoulders. Waist. Arms. Hands. Kissing on the cheek is acceptable. Will that do?"

"Perfect," he said.

"Anyway, considering we'll have to take the long route back to the castle, isn't it about time we saw Alice?"

A goblin burst into the kitchen—the fellow that had been guarding the hatch.

"Gabe and Nora," he said, tripping over his own feet. "Are they in here?"

"We've not seen them since they went out," Wortle called from the range.

The goblin swallowed nervously. "I've checked the slopes. They've gone."

CHAPTER 22

We sprang onto our horses.

"What the hell do Gabe and Nora think they're up to," Lucas growled. "It's bad enough they followed you here, and they're fully aware of the stakes. If they're captured and tortured—"

I raised my hand, my heart thrashing against my ribs at the possibilities in this hellish place. "Too much detail. Let's not go there yet."

He swung Gloom around. "We need a cover story for being in this area should anyone see us... We chased a boar on the way home, wanting some sport."

"Alright."

We dug our heels into our mounts and cantered through the forest. The guard had lost Gabe and Nora's tracks just after the pine with the mushrooms. We headed to the tree, then rode back and forth searching for any sign of them, the shadows of dark creatures flitting through distant thickets. Finding nothing, we reined the horses in.

"They can't have gotten much further," I said. "What were they doing, running?"

"I've no idea—" Lucas cocked his head. "I can hear something." He urged Gloom on through the trees. A minute later, we slowed, emerging into a clearing.

A mounted party stood on the far side dressed in clothes similar to Lucas's, all of them with imperious airs and the slightly sharp look that I was beginning to associate with dracs. One of the group had dismounted. He held a figure against a tree, her hair sleek and black, her eyes wild. Nora.

I caught sight of Gabe hiding behind an oak, herbs in his hand. He was desperately muttering a collude that didn't appear to be working.

"What a delicious specimen," the drac said as Nora twisted her face away. "It's not often we come across such mouth-watering game in the forest."

Lucas shot me an "I'll do the talking" look as we guided our mounts closer. "What do we have here?" he called, his voice clipped and confident.

The party studied us warily.

The drac, not bothering to glance our way, grasped Nora's chin and forced her head back. "First come, first served."

"I rather fancy her myself, Lord Dumoulin," Lucas said as we neared. "Give her to me."

The creep turned and flinched. "Lord Rouseau. An honour to have you back in Grimmere. Of course you may have the vixen. It is your right. But as I found her, perhaps I may take a little something first? Or maybe we could have one each. There is another in the trees over there." He nodded to Gabe.

Nora, still struggling, managed to push the distracted drac away just a fraction. Strange. Dracs were strong. I'd not been able to shift Lucas an inch when he'd been fighting Elivorn.

"I don't take seconds." Lucas guided Gloom closer.

Before he could reach Nora, she wriggled some more, then with a battle roar, she drove her knee firmly into the drac's family jewels.

"Argh. The little bitch." The drac crumpled to the ground.

Way to go, that girl. But I had no idea how she'd mustered the strength, never mind escaped the beast's incubus charms, which I presumed he was using. She sprinted over to Gabe, who dropped his failed collude herbs and wrapped his arm around her shoulder.

Lucas stilled Gloom by the groaning drac. "My dear Lord Dumoulin, you don't appear to be able to hold on to your prey. My father will be curious to hear that your powers are diminishing."

The other dracs laughed nervously, as though they had to agree with Lucas out of etiquette but hadn't a clue what was going on. I was with them on that.

Lucas's lips formed a chilling smile. "Let's see if I have a little more control." His gaze bored into Nora. "Girl, come here."

After everything Lucas had said, I was pretty sure he wouldn't use his powers on her, and by the hesitant glance she shot in my direction, she wasn't being compelled. It was a pretence. I nodded ever so slightly, encouraging her to play along. She got the message and stepped over to Lucas's mount.

"There we are," Lucas said. "I'll enjoy her and the other one too. Thank you, Lord Dumoulin, for this quarry. You have a long journey home. Best be on your way."

The drac fumed, his face scarlet. He stormed to his horse and leapt on. The party cantered away.

Gabe and Nora opened their mouths to speak. Lucas drew a finger to his lips and shook his head, rage burning in his eyes. The two of them cringed. His look summed up how I felt. They'd put themselves and everything in danger— again.

"Get on," Lucas said. He took his foot out of his stirrup and offered it to Nora. She managed to clamber up and swing her leg over Gloom's back with his assistance. Her perfect composure had slipped for once, her face tight with alarm, though it appeared to be due to her proximity to Lucas, rather than her ordeal. I managed to haul Gabe up behind me.

We returned to the slopes and halted the horses by Wortle's hole. The guard's face dropped with relief. Gabe and Nora slid to the ground and slunk toward the hatch, shamefaced. But they weren't getting out of it that easily.

"Where do you think you're going?" I said, my fists balled around my reins.

Gabe paused, looking anywhere but at me.

Nora pulled herself together, pursed her lips and drew back her shoulders. "Inside. Away from this stress." An impressive recovery. She was made of tough stuff. She grabbed Gabe's arm and dragged him toward the hole.

In a split-second, Lucas dismounted and shot in front of them, his glower impressive. I had to give it to him, he could do angry. "Camille. Is. Speaking. To. You."

Nora's fingers trembled at her sides. Gabe's bottom lip quaked.

I dismounted and strode over, the guard taking our mounts. "What on earth possessed you to leave the slopes?" There was a lethal edge to my voice. "Of all the stupid, moronic, unbelievable things to do."

"You put everything in danger," Lucas rumbled. "The charade Camille and I have established, not to mention the whole ruse I've been building for years. The lives of countless goblins are at stake. And you risked all that because of what? You fancied a walk?"

"I... I..." Gabe attempted, his skin grey. "We... uh... just wanted to explore... I thought I could glamour us—"

"You heard everything at lunch," I added. "You know what's going on. How could you..." I couldn't find the words, and there was no need to say more. Gabe and Nora were both about to pass out from fright.

Registering the sun low in the sky, its thin light seeping through the trees, I turned to Lucas. "Alice?"

"We don't have time."

"Fuck." I glared at Gabe and Nora some more. "And now I can't see Alice." The thought made me weak.

At that, their cringing grew to epic proportions.

"Get the hell inside," Lucas roared. "You're grounded." He caught the eye of the guard. "Ensure they don't leave again, and tell Roux and Wortle to make certain they don't enter the tunnels."

They slunk to the hatch.

Lucas met my gaze. "We need to get going, right now."

I nodded, made to mount Crow, then paused. "Just a second." There was something I needed to ask Nora. I supposed by Lucas's lack of concern about her ability to floor a drac, it was possible they lost their powers occasionally, but really... could she have been that lucky?

I jogged to the hole and descended the steps. Gabe and Nora were in the corridor at the bottom, muttering to each other. "Tell me one thing," I said to Nora, fury still swathing me. "How did you take out that creep?"

Her brow narrowed in confusion. "With my knee in his nuts."

"Dracs are incubi. They can force you to do what they want. You know that."

She shrugged. "Yeah, but I just presumed it meant they were super attractive and lured girls by looking hot."

"No, it means they influence your thoughts and feelings to manipulate you into acting." First-hand experience.

She shivered.

Gabe nodded. "I read about it in *Seduction of Our Times: The Last Three Millennia of Incubi, Succubi and Concubi.*"

I met Nora's gaze. "Are you saying you didn't feel any compulsion or desire?"

"Uh…" Her face softened as she considered the question. "I didn't feel anything at all. It was like he was really strong when he forced me back against the tree, but when I went for him, he just crumpled. I thought dracs were fit, but there was nothing to it."

It didn't seem right.

"Oh, I know what it is." Gabe's eyes lit, a little colour flushing his cheeks. "Your amulet. I knew it was special. That thing radiates power."

I cocked an eyebrow. "Let's see it."

Biting her lip, Nora drilled her gaze into Gabe as she tried to communicate something I wasn't party to.

Gabe shook his head slowly as he attempted to decipher her meaning. "What's the problem? Just show Camille the amulet. It's awesome. It was cool of your aunt to give it to you. I wonder if she's ever been to Fae."

Nora scowled back, her hand flat on her chest.

"I don't have time for this," I snapped. "You've already caused so much trouble. Don't make it worse."

Nora bit her lip as she pulled a necklace from her top. She let it hang against her T-shirt. It was a half-circle of black quartz encased in gold, rays emanating out like an upturned sunrise. Madame Ballon's pendant. I stared at Nora as it all fell into place, my anger morphing to Herculean proportions. By the way Nora jutted her jaw, she knew I had her sussed.

"Gabe," I said. "Go into the kitchen. Nora will be along shortly."

Nora just shrugged nonchalantly. With a puzzled backward glance, he pushed the door open and disappeared inside.

"I saw you," I hissed, attempting to be quiet but barely restraining the new layer of fury. "In the café yesterday. It was unlike you, hugging everyone, being so nice. That's when you took the pendant, wasn't it?"

She folded her arms across her chest. "What if it was?"

And she'd been so sweet when she'd picked up Shroom-Jean's wallet. "And Jean. What did you do, take his cash?"

She raised her chin. "It's so difficult to get any these days. Jean believes plastic is the route of all evil, which means he carries euros."

"Shit." I was thunderstruck. "Shroom-Jean has nothing. He's as broke as they come. And what did you spend the money on? Nail polish and a new outfit?" I seethed the words. Fuck. Shroom-Jean was barely managing at the best of times.

"Camille," Lucas called from the hatch. "We have to go."

I shot daggers at Nora. "I really don't know what to do with you, but you haven't heard the last of this."

I turned away to head out, but Nora caught my arm. For once, she looked so young, her skin soft, her features delicate, as if she hadn't yet grown into herself.

"Please," she said, her eyes beseeching. "Don't tell Gabe."

CHAPTER 23

"How long until we're required at dinner?" I asked as we strode up the sweeping staircase toward Lucas's chambers.

"About an hour," Lucas replied. "Just time to get dressed."

"An hour?" My tone rose. I was still riled at Gabe and Nora, which didn't help, but I could've seen Alice briefly then gotten back here to change in five minutes. Okay, maybe ten if I had to wear something nice. I was forced to communicate the sentiment with a look of outright incredulity. We couldn't speak freely for the rest of the day as Lucas hadn't been able to arrange cover.

"It will take all of that," he replied flatly, his expression dark. I wasn't the only one still worked up. We reached the top of the stairs and headed to Lucas's chambers, thankfully taking the route that avoided Elivorn's door.

I'd wanted to ask Lucas something since we'd left the

holes, but our fast pace had prevented me. I was pretty sure mentioning the matter wouldn't raise suspicions. Should anyone overhear, it would be interpreted as simple curiosity. "I was wondering, do dracs ever lose their powers?"

By the slight nod of his head, he acknowledged that I was talking about Nora. "Occasionally, and some people are immune to our charms. Both are extremely rare."

"Huh, curious." I supposed either could've been the case today, the necklace being powerless jewellery, but as Gabe had said, there was something about it. From Lucas's answer, though, it didn't sound as if he'd overheard my conversation with Nora. Perhaps he *didn't* listen in all the time.

"I certainly find your charms irresistible." My voice dripped with sarcasm.

He gazed at me from under his brow. "As my mate you're fully subject to my sway." We entered his door.

I laughed. "You wish." But damn, that look was smouldering.

He shot me a smile for the first time since we'd left the hole. "Wortle will be here to help you dress. As head of housekeeping, she wants to ensure everything is just so."

A maid emerged from the bathroom and curtsied. "I've prepared your bath, miss."

I wasn't going to get used to being lady of the manor. But what with the stress of hunting for Gabe and Nora, I was stinky, although it was the thought of washing away any remainder of Elivorn that was the greatest incentive. "Thanks."

I headed into the bathroom and undressed, inhaling the

warm, spicy air. The bath was scattered with herbs once again, innumerable candles glowing against the darkening sky outside.

I lowered myself into the steaming water and lay back. Now the adrenaline of Gabe and Nora's escapade had drained away, my worry for Alice pressed to the fore, my stomach aching with it. Perhaps there was some way I could see her later tonight.

But right now I had to brace myself to meet Lucas's parents. Fae royalty. Killers. I had no idea what to expect or how to handle the situation. Not to mention, Elivorn would be there. But if Madame Ballon's necklace really had protected Nora from that Dumoulin creep, there was a chance I could use it to protect myself against Elivorn.

I closed my eyes, the warmth and minerals transporting me far away, somewhere blissfully free of bizarre goblins and manipulative, murderous dracs. All until hands cupped my head, nails scrubbing into my scalp. I flew up and hugged my knees to my chest, my heart pounding, the water swishing.

The maid who'd run the bath was kneeling by the water, a bar of soap in her hand. She had an almost stoat-like face, the bristles on her grey chin quivering. Three more goblins entered, one carrying towels.

"Now, now, miss," the one with the soap said. "No need to be modest. Nothing we haven't seen before."

"You may have seen plenty of naked women, but goblins invading my bath is a first for me."

She chortled as she continued to work soap into my hair.

"Come now, Camille, deary." Wortle's croak filled the

bathroom as she scurried in. "You and Lulu returned late, and we have to clean you up pronto. Let the maids sort you out. Rest assured, they know exactly what they're doing. They've been under my tutelage for years."

"Uh, I can wash myself, thanks."

Wortle ignored me. "Chop chop. On with it, goblins."

The maid forced my head, and subsequently the rest of me, back into the water with surprising strength. For a moment I was entirely submerged. I surfaced, spluttering.

"I can't argue with Wortle," she whispered. "I'll lose my position."

Job on the line or not, this really was beyond belief. "How much choice do I actually have?" I asked Wortle as I sat up, placing my knees strategically before me once again. This wasn't my comfort zone.

Her innumerable wrinkles deepened in mirth. "Oh, deary, exactly no choice at all. You'll be having dinner with the family, and they have exceedingly high standards."

One of the goblins grabbed my arm and scrubbed it with a loofah, her eyes pivoting unnervingly before centring again. Another pulled my foot out of the water and pumiced it. I eyed my blade propped against the wall. I could force them off, but by the twinkle in Wortle's eye, I had the suspicion it wouldn't deter her. She grasped my other foot and did something to it. A pedicure, perhaps? But, really, the Rouseaus weren't going to see my feet.

"Many a time I bathed Lulu in here." She did something with my toenails. Was she actually cutting them? That was a rare occurrence.

"He loved his baths," she continued. "Used to splash around for hours playing mass genocide with his elven skiffs and eldritch monsters. Dracs do love water."

"Such a nice child," I replied.

My other arm was scrubbed by a wide-eyed goblin who clacked her teeth. Another bathed my neck and back. When the bristly one dove in to wash my nether regions, I'd had enough. I sprang up, pulling various appendages free. "Nope. Just no. I can do that myself, thank you very much."

They stared at me.

"Without you watching."

As one they spun around, and I finished up.

"Oh, my deary, you do make me laugh." Wortle smiled as she turned back, her wrinkles creasing, her eyes dancing with merriment. She held out a towel. "Come now, we don't have long to get you ready."

Heaven help me. "Is it too much to think that I might be dressing myself?" I said as a maid wrapped me in a luxurious towel.

"Indeed it is." Wortle drew over a chair built from branches. She clambered onto it and squeezed out my hair with a cloth.

My head felt lighter instantly. I twisted a lock around my fingers. It was almost dry. "Impressive."

"Aridroot, deary," she said. "Absorbs water like a treat."

Ignoring the maids attempting to buff me, I felt the cloth. A nail-and-chalkboard shiver ran through me. Weird. The bristly maid held up a robe. I shrugged into it and was herded out.

Lucas sat at his desk, writing with a long quill. He looked up as I passed. "Having fun?" There was a wicked glimmer in his eyes. He knew all too well what I was being subjected to.

I sent him a scathing glare. "I've been accosted by strangers whilst completely naked."

He laughed. "Sounds like fun to me."

The maids bustled me into the dressing room and shoved me into the chair at the dressing table. There wasn't a mirror, so I gazed helplessly into the carved mahogany panel before me, noticing the intricate detailing of bare branches, clawed hands and moons.

Under Wortle's direction, the goblin with the wild eyes rubbed cream into my face. Could she see straight? Then the one with the clacking teeth dabbed at my cheeks.

Clack. Clack. Clack.

I tried not to flinch. I had serious doubts as to how this was going to turn out.

"We do love dressing the ladies," Wortle said. "We help Lady Rouseau, of course, but what with her offspring being male, it's not often we get the chance with anyone else."

"Ouch," I yelled as the bristly maid pulled my hair tight. "This is torture. What the hell are you doing to me?"

Then it dawned on me. I had the full attention of Lucas's nursemaid. From what I'd gathered, she was the person who knew his young self best. I wanted to trust Lucas. If I found out more about him, it might help.

"So was Lucas a sweet child?" I asked. It was a stupid question, especially with his mass genocide bath play, but I had to start somewhere, and I had an idea that Lucas was everything in Wortle's eyes. No doubt he could hear me, but that made it better in a way—less underhand. If I crossed the line, Lucas could say something.

"He was the sweetest." Wortle beamed, her warmth a physical thing filling the chamber. Lucas had dealt with so much here, it was a grace that he'd had her. "The first thing he used to do when he killed was to rip into the jugular. It meant his prey didn't have to suffer. Though he really did get himself covered in blood and all kinds of things. The number of times I had to pick liver out of his ears."

My throat caught, and a volley of coughs racked through me. The maids paused in their dabbing of my face and looked on with impatience, one of them tapping her foot. "Sweet," I managed eventually, and the goblins returned to their onslaught.

"He got up to plenty of mischief, though," she added, her gaze distant. "He used to swim in the lake constantly, especially at night. Loved it, he did. And there was that time he came into the laundry afterward, looking for some clothes. He was fascinated with the washing back then. Helped out a fair bit. But that time, I'm not exactly sure what he was doing with the mangle, but before I knew what had happened, he'd caught his winkle—"

"I'm sure Camille doesn't need to know about that," came Lucas's shout from the main chamber. He was listening *now*.

"Winkle in the mangle," I called through, laughing. "I'm sure that wasn't your finest moment."

"Not my finest."

Wortle chortled. "Come now, deary, you look perfect." I had to take her word for it. "We need to get you dressed."

The maids ushered me to the centre of the chamber near the chaise lounge. Next to it stood a rail from which hung indistinguishable garments. A maid pulled the robe from my shoulders, leaving me naked once again.

"Could you just give me some warning?" Reflexively, I covered my chest with one arm and my nether regions with the other. I wasn't prudish, but the goblin assault was one step too far.

Wortle held out something large and black and gauzy. "Step into these and we'll get you sorted right away."

There were two leg holes—that was all I could identify. I climbed in. Wortle drew the cloth up and tightened a cord. Pantaloons. Hmm, draughty, but at least part of me was concealed. The bristly maid pulled something stiff around my waist and chest, jostling it into place before pulling it tight from behind. A corset. My insides squeezed together. "Ouch, really?"

"That's it. Tighter." Wortle nodded to one of the others. "Lend a hand. Camille has a good figure. We must make the most of it."

Another maid tugged the laces, the two of them pulling me backward.

"Hey, come on. What are you trying to do to me?" I glowered at them.

Wortle shook her head. "Now then, Camille, you're a Keeper. You can handle a couple of defenceless goblins."

"Defenceless?" I muttered. "I'm being crushed. Is it really necessary?"

"Of course."

They pulled again, my insides turning to pulp. "Aaaagh," I cried.

"Everything alright in there?" Lucas called. "No one dying?"

"Yes, I'm dying! They're freaking killing me!"

Wortle tutted as the goblins jostled me some more, presumably tying up the laces. Not that I could see.

The maid with the focus problem approached, swaying a little as one of her eyes gyrated. She carried a small bundle. Black stockings. I slid my legs into them, running my fingers over the dreamy silk. They were followed by matching garters, the lace knotted into a miniature woodland tangled with briar roses. Then black shoes with a small heel and side buttons were placed before me. I slipped them on and they fitted like gloves. It was all exquisite. I'd never experienced anything like it. The closest I'd come to haute couture was gazing at Margo Joly.

The maids unhooked more garments from the rail and carried them over.

"Pop these on," the clacking goblin said.

Clack. Clack. Clack.

I stepped into a skirt made of the lightest silk, then threaded my arms into a top that covered the corset. That done, the maids headed to a massive armoire in the corner and rummaged around.

I gazed down at myself. The skirt hung just above my

ankles, and the blousy thing was cut low with ruffles along my bust, my breasts barely concealed. It was all rather brothel-like. Not exactly the elegance I'd imagined. "I don't know. I thought I'd be wearing something more formal." But hey, I could rock the prostitute look. Not that I wanted to be anywhere near Elivorn dressed like this.

The maids cackled.

A broad smile extended from one side of Wortle's face to the other. "Camille, really? We're not going to send you to dinner in your underwear."

"Underwear? I've got about ten layers on."

The maids drew a shimmering mass from the armoire and placed it before me, opening it in the centre. The silk was thick and luxurious, the hue a deep, deep blue, almost black.

"There you go, deary," Wortle said. "Be careful now."

I stepped in. The maids lifted the dress, guiding my hands through the armholes. They pulled the bodice tight, fastening it at the back. Wortle fussed around, laying the fabric straight and fiddling with the lace that swept from the middle of my skirt up over my bust and shoulders.

Finally, she stepped back and nodded. "That will do nicely."

Two maids carried over one of the massive oval swing mirrors.

Clack. Clack. Clack.

They placed it before me, then tilted it so I could see the whole of myself.

My jaw dropped. That absolutely, one hundred percent wasn't me.

Silk draped from my hips and flowed to the ground, the fabric embroidered with a forest of dark branches, tiny jewels glimmering like stars between. The paler lace at the centre gave the impression that the dress was only just hiding what lay beneath. To top it off, my hair was piled perfectly upon my head, loose locks curling down my back, and my make-up was smoky and mysterious, my skin flawless. The only parts of me I recognised were my gaping mouth and the lines of my arms, the muscles just visible due to recent training.

The tallest maid, the one with the eyes, reached up and drew a necklace of inky stones and sweeping branches around my neck.

"What did you do to me?" I managed. I looked—I didn't know how to describe it—like a dark fae princess, perhaps. Not something I'd ever thought would cross my mind.

The maids stood back in a row, nodding in satisfaction. I turned to them. "Uh, you did a great job." Understatement of the year. I shouldn't have doubted them.

Clack. Clack. Clack.

"What do you think, my deary?" Wortle asked. "You do scrub up well. Although, my goodness, what a lot of fuss."

"But the dress... it fits perfectly. How did you—"

"We have the finest fae tailors, who've been working very hard."

"You don't say." There were a number of folktales about fae tailors who sewed exquisite garments overnight.

"Camille, you ready?" Lucas called.

"Uh... I guess so." I couldn't take my eyes off my reflection. It was so peculiar. But I didn't want to be late. We had information to gather. I shivered at the prospect of an evening with Lucas's family.

Pulling my eyes away, I turned and headed to the door, promptly catching my dress under foot and stumbling. The maids dove over and caught me.

Wortle chuckled. "You must be conscious of your dress at all times."

The bristly maid fluffed my skirts. "No damage."

I drew in a deep breath. "Right, conscious of the dress." I stepped carefully forward. One of the maids held the door, and I headed out.

Lucas sat at his desk, studying a letter. He'd cleaned up and dressed in his evening clothes, the fabric finer than his day wear, the cut more elegant.

"Ready," I said, flapping my hands against my sides and finding a lot of skirt where there was usually air.

"Just a mo—" He shot me a side glance and paused, those unfathomable, spellbinding, ruthless eyes absorbing me. Without shifting his gaze, he placed his letter down and stood up, his lips parted. The embroidery around his collar reflected the branches and stars on my skirt. He traced the contours of my dress, then met my gaze once again and held it.

Wortle came in. "Well, now, Lulu, it's not like you, forgetting your manners. Compliment the deary."

He released a sharp breath and shook himself. "Uh,

Camille, you look..." He bit his lip. "I... I don't have the words..."

I couldn't help the smile that tugged at my lips. "I'll take that. Haven't we got a dinner to attend?"

"Yes, of course." He straightened his jacket, stepped over and offered me his arm. I accepted, and he led me to the door.

"Camille," he whispered as we stepped out of the chamber. "You're utterly, devastatingly beautiful."

CHAPTER 24

"CAMILLE!" LADY ROUSEAU CRIED. SHE STOOD BEFORE the fire with her husband.

Silently, I gave thanks that we weren't meeting in yesterday's drawing room. This one was decorated similarly, though, the broad hearth positioned between two magnificent arched windows that looked out upon the lake.

We headed over, Lucas's arm supporting me as I attempted to look as natural as possible. I was pretty sure I wasn't carrying it off, but we were here to gather information about the splitting of the bounds, and that was all that mattered.

Lucas was playing his part superbly. During the walk here, he'd managed to project a combination of wonder and the desire to eat me. It wasn't something I was used to, although it reminded me of his heavy gazes in the café. I should've hated it after Pierre, but I didn't. Even though I knew it was an act, warmth blossomed deep within, the sense of Lucas's arm against mine doing nothing to lessen the heat. I had to admit, he was doing a good job of distracting me from the nerves that wrung out my stomach.

Elivorn and Isarn were in conversation by the window to the far side. Elivorn glanced over and tracked me. I tried to suppress the shiver that wove down my spine.

"Look at you, my dear. Absolutely stunning." Lady Rouseau stepped forward to meet us, her hair gathered expertly upon her head. Unsurprisingly, she was more competent in an evening gown than me, even though her dark skirts possessed additional layers, all of them embroidered with deep rouge. She gripped my arms, drew me close and kissed my cheek. I hadn't expected the intimacy, which was saying something from a French woman. I don't know what I'd thought would happen. Maybe mass carnage?

"Camille," she said, "we've been waiting centuries for one of these boys to take a mate." There was something in her wide jaw and broad mouth that she'd passed on to Lucas. "We're thrilled that we have the opportunity to get to know you."

Lord Rouseau joined us. "Utterly thrilled. It's wonderful to meet you, Camille." Goosebumps rose on my arms, a sense of lethal power radiating from his confident bearing. He was striking rather than classically handsome, the furrows between his brow and the permanent purse of his lips giving the impression that he held a lot within. "We have so many questions," he added.

"Of that, I have no doubt," Lucas said drolly.

"It's an honour to meet you, Lord and Lady Rouseau.

Lucas has told me so much about you." That wasn't true at all, but what else was I supposed to say? I made a mental note that Lord Rouseau hadn't kissed me. Perhaps *la bise* was a Grimmere custom solely between females.

"I have to admit," Lady Rouseau said, "we're so glad to have Lucas home. He's promised to return for so long."

Lucas placed his arm around my waist, his fingers gripping the bones of my corset under the fabric, his touch blazing through me. He swallowed me with his eyes. "And I was glad Camille decided to join me at the last minute. I couldn't wait to introduce her to you."

"Perfect," Lady Rouseau added.

Clothing and castle aside, their welcome and the small talk were so normal. It was ridiculous but they almost put me at ease. At least, they would've done if there hadn't been something intangible radiating from Lord Rouseau. I had to remind myself that they were killers. All of them—Lucas too.

A footman carried over a tray of delicate crystal filled with red wine. We each took a glass. Elivorn and Isarn finished their conversation and came over.

"Camille, how wonderful to see you again." Elivorn inclined his head. "It was an absolute delight to meet you in Foix the other day." He smirked at Lucas, then shot me a look, communicating that he would have me, one way or the other.

Lucas glowered.

"Lovely to see you, Elivorn," I said coolly.

Isarn's eyes darted between his brothers, curiosity crossing his sharp features, his cheekbones accentuated by the jaw-length hair tucked behind his ears. He hadn't missed the conflict. He dipped his chin. "Camille, it's a pleasure. I didn't think I'd live to see the day Lucas took a mate. All I can say is, you must be a strong woman indeed."

"Strong isn't the word for it," Lucas said. "She is working with me against the assembly."

"Absolutely," I said. "The splitting of the bounds makes complete sense. The ignorance of the human realm and the false reality maintained by the population are incomprehensible to me."

Lady Rouseau placed a manicured hand on Lucas's arm. "Your infiltration of the assembly and appointment as Keeper have already been of great value to us, but being partnered with someone of similar mind is beyond fortuitous."

I couldn't help wondering what use Lucas had been already, a thread of unease clamping my stomach tighter. I bit my lip, then released it quickly, hoping I hadn't given away my disquiet. Of course he'd fed his family information —he was working to gain their confidence. It was probably something prearranged by the assembly. Damn it. I really did want to believe him, so what was my problem? Pierre flashed before my eyes. Yeah, there was that. But this wasn't the time for doubt. I raised my chin. "Our partnership is perfect," I said. "I couldn't have asked for more."

My eyes locked with Lucas's, and his gaze sank into me. His attempt at communicating loved-up infatuation was remarkable.

"I'll say fortuitous," Elivorn muttered.

"Yet it makes complete sense," Lucas added, gripping me

tighter. "The assembly goes to great pains to partner Keepers. The pairing is only made between souls who have a certain attunement. It was likely that we'd have similar attitudes toward the assembly and the future of Fae."

It was news to me that the assembly thought we had some kind of rightness for each other. Mental note to ask Lucas about it.

Elivorn shook his head.

Surely a little acting wouldn't go amiss, especially if it would annoy the jerk. I drew my hand up and cupped Lucas's cheek. His pupils, just distinguishable from his irises, flared. His focus lowered to my lips—the perfect pretence that he wanted to kiss me. Damn, he was good at this. Something raw surged between us, my body shifting closer, responding to him—

"Well, I have no doubt about you two." Lord Rouseau clapped Lucas on the back. "Don't you think, Mireille?"

Lady Rouseau's cheeks filled as she smiled. "Indeed, the bond is radiating off you. Such a beautiful thing." She exchanged a knowing glance with her husband.

It appeared we were doing something right. But, really, that easily?

Elivorn was watching us intently. A muscle twitched in his jaw.

Lady Rouseau looped her arm around her husband's. "I have to say, we did wonder, what with your grandfather being Izac Amiel."

Grampi had divulged a few Keeper stories in the past couple of weeks. He'd fought tirelessly against dark fae like the Rouseaus. "My grandfather trained me, and for that I will always be grateful, but that's where my gratitude ends. He and I have completely different perspectives." If he could only see me now, the supposed mate of a drac, lying about him and plotting against everything he stood for. Although he would understand the ruse.

"How fascinating," she replied.

The door opened, and a footman appeared. "My lord, dinner is ready."

Lord Rouseau nodded. "Well, everyone, let's get to it, shall we? I don't know about you, but I'm ravenous." The image of Pierre flashed before me. Please let there not be trespassers tonight. I wouldn't be able to restrain myself if innocent people were killed. My stomach swam at the thought.

Lucas and I made to follow his parents out, but Elivorn stepped before us, a sadistic glimmer in his eye. "It would be my honour to escort Camille to the dining room."

More of Elivorn winding Lucas up. And from the amount of tooth-grinding coming from Lucas's direction, it was working. I didn't want Elivorn's hands on me ever again, but I had to make a show of politeness. As I took Elivorn's arm, a low growl escaped Lucas.

Elivorn pulled me a little too close. "My, my, Camille. You do scrub up well. It's nice to see you in something other than trousers, though I liked the jeans you were wearing at Castle Rock."

How could I answer that? "Fuck off, you asshole" came to mind, but we were a happy family. I gritted my teeth.

"Thank you, Elivorn, for such a lovely compliment." I hoped the sarcasm was clear in my voice.

We entered a bijou dining room with a floor of polished parquet, candelabras abounding as always. The room was smaller than I'd imagined, but no less ostentatious. I'd seen a massive dining room when I'd explored the castle, but presumably this was where the family ate on a daily basis.

Lady Rouseau directed everyone to the table. Elivorn pulled out my chair. I paused, uncertain how to sit down in the dress, but Elivorn was schooled in this sort of thing. He slid the chair forward, and I lowered myself in unison.

He leant in, just as he had in his chambers and at Castle Rock, his breath against my cheek. It was an intentional reminder of his powers. "There you go," he murmured. "If I can be of assistance in any way, do let me know." The absolute scumbag. He headed to his chair.

The table seated the six of us perfectly, with plenty of room for the mass of gleaming tableware. Lord Rouseau sat at the head, Lady Rouseau at the foot. Lucas was at my side, with Isarn and Elivorn opposite. The setting was stunning, the cutlery polished, the crystal sparkling. In the centre, the silver candelabras, shaped like barren branches, had been tangled with ivy.

Servants appeared and poured the wine. Red. Lucas always drank red. Was it a drac habit? When my own glass was being filled, I glanced at the footman. He flinched.

I noticed Isarn studying me as he unfolded his napkin. There was something distant in his eyes. "Camille has quite the reputation already, it seems," he said.

I winced. Had Elivorn told him about Castle Rock, or did he somehow know about the Italians in Barcelona, or that guy a while ago in Toulouse? But what was his problem? It was the twenty-first century, for heaven's sake. Although it felt like another century entirely here. Taking Isarn's lead, I laid my napkin over my lap.

Lucas noticed my bewilderment, his lips quirking. "The hantaumo queen. Many fae from both the dark and the bright lands attempted to kill her. None succeeded." He took a sip of wine.

My shoulders sank. *That* kind of reputation.

"Until now," Lucas's father pronounced. "Camille, consider us impressed." He raised his glass, and the family followed. "To Camille, slayer of the hantaumo queen."

"To Camille," they chorused.

I smiled graciously, although as Lucas's family were so dark, it would've seemed more appropriate for them to object to me slaying the queen.

Lucas ran his fingers down my arm, inflaming that heat once again. "I don't think there's a fae alive who isn't grateful for you ending that tyrant." The sense of him lingered. I hadn't realised my arm was an erogenous zone. Hell, this corset was tight.

The goblins served an amuse-bouche of goat's cheese on what looked like a tiny avocado macaron. Needing a distraction, I imitated the others and popped it into my mouth whole. Elivorn watched as I chewed. I ignored him and focussed on swallowing my hopefully poison-free macaron down.

"The hantaumo were set on victimising us all," Lady Rouseau said. "Their acts of horror had no discrimination. There were times, back in the distant past, when we tried to forge an alliance, but they were consumed by their own schemes."

That made sense. Just because the Rouseaus were darker than sin, it didn't mean they sided with the hantaumo. Just like in the human realm, there were many shades of grey. It only highlighted how much I wanted to understand the workings of Fae. "Well, glad to be of service." I fixed Elivorn in the eye. "I have no qualms about dealing with those who pursue me."

"My sentiments exactly," Lord Rouseau said. "I can see what you like about this woman, Lucas."

"Indeed," he replied.

"And with this talk of being pursued," Lord Rouseau added, "I have intelligence that our servants may have been infiltrated by those who disagree with our practices."

I froze, then tried to look as though I hadn't.

Lady Rouseau's jaw tightened.

"However," Lord Rouseau continued, "as always, I will ensure the traitors meet their end swiftly."

"Good." Elivorn said. "The servants take too many liberties."

"Undeniably," Lady Rouseau added.

Shit. I didn't dare look at Lucas. I could only hope that this didn't relate to his trusted goblins or our charade. Thankfully, the family was distracted by the arrival of the sole colbert.

"I have to say"—Lucas met his father's eye as he picked up his fish knife—"I'm keen to find out more about your plans. I'm intrigued that you've managed to cause so much disruption on the bounds already." *Finally, the reason we were here.*

Elivorn scowled at him.

Lord Rouseau swallowed a mouthful. "Of course. But I must explain a few details first."

"Oh please," Isarn said. "Don't bore them with the politics."

"We wouldn't want to take away your job." Elivorn lifted his glass to him.

Isarn rolled his eyes. "I'll have you know that Grimmere's home affairs are only in fine shape because of the meticulous balance held between the oldest houses. A balance *I* forged over centuries." A smile pulled at his lips as he gestured around with his fork. "The trade bonds are stronger than ever. Why, I had Lord Dumoulin here earlier to shore up the herb exchange in the western fells."

I exchanged the briefest of glances with Lucas before taking a mouthful of sole. We'd had first-hand experience of that creep, Dumoulin.

"How did it go?" Lord Rouseau asked.

"Very well. They are, as always, loyal to the rulership of Grimmere."

I listened politely as internal affairs were discussed, but names, places and policies went over my head. Lucas joined in, the perfect, patient son. As the topic petered out, Lord Rouseau narrowed his brow. "We really must get back to the subject du jour and our progress with the bounds. If Lucas is to assist us in gathering information, he should have a little background."

Lucas acknowledged Lord Rouseau with a dip of his chin.

"We have a particularly successful collaboration with the dark elves from the Webcap Mountains," Lord Rouseau continued, "and with the Brokenwater ogres, not to mention a small and rather new faction of dwarves from the eastern continent. Together, we've been able to raise considerable resources for the venture. But I think it would be best if we show you—"

"Father." A flush spread over Elivorn's face. "Be careful how much you divulge."

"Come now, Elivorn." Lady Rouseau's shoulders stiffened. "Lucas is your brother."

Fury lit Elivorn's eyes. "He's been siding with the enemy for centuries."

"I saw the error of my ways a very long time ago," Lucas growled. He placed his cutlery down, his fists tightening. "I've had to keep away from Grimmere to convince the assembly I'm on their side. And now, I'm the best weapon we have. With my infiltration I can relay information and sow mistrust. I'm in a position to do whatever we need." His voice rose. "And it never would have happened if I'd been friendly to you." Damn it, he was so convincing.

Every part of Lord Rouseau homed in on Elivorn. "Agreed." He said it with such intensity, I had to stop myself blanching.

Elivorn shuddered.

"It's taken a great deal of foresight for Lucas to get this far," Lord Rouseau added. "Don't let personal grievances come between you."

Elivorn dropped his fork with a clatter and sat back in his chair, shaking his head.

"I have to give it to you," Isarn said, studying Lucas. "You've got patience. I wouldn't have managed the isolation in the human realm. I'm happy keeping my nose in Grimmere while you lot go about reshaping the world." He gulped his wine.

Lord Rouseau shot Elivorn a glare then met Lucas's eye. "As I was going to say before we were interrupted, rather than spout dry details, it will be better to show you what we're doing with the bounds. However, it's not possible tonight. The mages are performing a series of critical colludes that can't be disturbed. I believe they will have finished this step by tomorrow." He inclined his head to Elivorn for confirmation.

"Tomorrow should be the calm before the storm," he said stiffly.

"Good," Lord Rouseau replied. "We're at an important stage. In a couple of days we will be ready to perform a ceremony that will aid the continuation of the bounds separation, and we have a delegation of dark elves joining us for the occasion. By that time, Elivorn may have obtained information enabling us to boost the colludes, which will allow us to accelerate the process considerably. And, well, one mustn't look a gift horse in the mouth."

CHAPTER 25

WE ENTERED WORTLE'S HATCH AND TOOK THE STEPS.

"What I don't get," I said, "is that, executions aside, your family is really quite... well, almost normal." It wasn't the burning question of how Elivorn was intending to speed up the process of splitting the bounds in a couple of days—we'd agreed that would wait until we were in the company of the goblins and the safety of the hole—but it had been on my mind.

The thud of Crow and Gloom pawing the ground reverberated from outside.

Lucas paused before the kitchen door and frowned. "What did you expect?"

What I'd expected was a bloodbath. To my utter relief, the evening had ended without incident. Only one trespasser had been caught that day, and he'd died on the way to the castle. Probably a better end than being drac entertainment.

"It just fries my brain that a family set on destroying the human realm loves and cares for each other, and that in their own warped way, they were being nice." Excluding Elivorn, of course.

Even more of a headmangle was that Lucas had the strength of character to bring down his own flesh and blood. I wasn't sure if it made me admire him or want to run away faster than Roux with a maloumbro on his tail.

"Anyway," I said as we entered the passage, "isn't someone going to get suspicious if we head into the forest every day?" We'd pulled the same trick as yesterday, doubling back.

"Agreed. I'm not sure what other excuse to use, but I'll think of something."

We reached the tunnel door. "Let's get to Alice." We hadn't been able to visit last night, and I was desperate to see her. My only consolation was that if anything had happened, we would've been notified. No news was good news.

"I'll let Wortle know we're here." He pushed open the door, then paused.

The kitchen was full of goblins. Tall ones, small ones, fat ones, bony ones. They were a mixture of strange ears, weirdly shaped noses, claws and slightly crazed expressions. Some wore the livery of Grimmere, some wore servants' clothes, others were in rags. Amidst the throng, I could just make out Gabe and Nora at the back, staring aghast at a goblin who appeared to be chewing on a large rat, the tail sticking out of his mouth. Roux was sitting at the table eating toast, surrounded by more goblins. He raised a hand mid-mouthful.

"What's going on?" Lucas said.

Blisterch rose from his seat on the other side of the table, glowering as usual. "That's what we want to know."

I didn't get it. And how early had they gathered? We'd risen at the crack of dawn, my concern for Alice preventing me from sleeping, even in Lucas's arms.

"First, we need to see Alice," Lucas said. "You'll have to wait."

Blisterch shook his head and pushed his way through the throng. "There's no time. Lord Rouseau wants everyone to report to duty in an hour. There won't be a single goblin to guard the slopes. We'll hide your mounts before we leave to give you some cover."

Lucas raised his brow. "What's this all about?"

Digdeep joined his side, his round head reaching Blisterch's chest, his small eyes narrowing. "The word is, Lord Rouseau is aware of informants, and he has plans to flush them out. Tensions are rising. The goblins are worried for their families."

The motley crowd bobbed their heads in wide-eyed agreement.

"He wants the goblins available for interrogation," Blisterch added, squeezing his flabby cheeks with his thumb and finger.

Shit. This was what Lord Rouseau had meant when he'd said he'd ensure the traitors met their ends swiftly.

Lucas's jaw stiffened as he looked around. "Can everyone here be trusted?"

"Every goblin in this room has helped us gather information," Blisterch said. "They've all risked their lives in one way or another, and they will be the first in question."

"Well, what can we do about it?" I asked. We couldn't let them end up like Pierre.

"Nothing from our end," Digdeep said. "We'll have to let it ride out. This isn't the first time there have been suspicions, and it won't be the last."

Wortle headed in through the door and patted Lucas's arm. "Alice isn't good, deary. I've seen to her, but she needs looking at soon."

My stomach flipped. We had to get there, or perhaps I could go to the dungeon whilst Lucas dealt with this, but if I was caught and our ruse discovered, these goblins would be the ones to suffer. And anyway, Lucas was the doctor.

Lucas nodded. "We'll be there in a moment."

Blisterch met Lucas's gaze. "Did you gather any intel on Lord Rouseau's suspicions last night, or anything else that might be useful?"

"Nothing about who he suspects." Lucas drew in a deep breath. "But he divulged that he has the Webcap Mountain elves, the Brokenwater ogres and a small faction of dwarves working with him. But more importantly, Elivorn is in the process of obtaining information that will enable them to accelerate the splitting of the bounds tomorrow."

There were mutters all round, the goblins appearing worried or afraid or just plain sad. One with spiky hair jerked nervously. Gabe and Nora glanced at each other. Roux continued on with his breakfast.

Blisterch drew a hand over his wrinkly scalp. "Never mind Lord Rouseau's suspicions. This takes priority. And if it's happening tomorrow, we're extremely short of time."

Lucas's jaw tightened. "We couldn't get anything else out of my family. My father wants to show us the rest tonight, so we should know more then. As for Elivorn, I have no idea what he's up to."

Seducing me, mainly. But that was him trying to wind Lucas up. I couldn't see that it was related.

"Somehow," Blisterch said, "we have to figure it out."

"What about Isarn?" Digdeep asked.

The goblins shrugged or shook their heads.

Lucas scowled. "There's no intel on him because he's completely wrapped up in the politics of Grimmere. He's not interested in anything else."

"My, my, he's a curious one," Wortle said. "Still no indication of how closely he supports your father?"

"No, but I like to think the best of him. What option does he have but to go along with my family's plans? Though he keeps out of the way as much as possible, and doesn't involve himself in the executions or Grimmere's more gruesome policies enforced by my father."

"He can't be trusted unless we know for sure," Blisterch said.

"Agreed," Lucas replied. "But I want him given the benefit of the doubt."

Blisterch and Digdeep nodded.

"Does anyone have intel on Elivorn?" Blisterch glanced around. "The smallest detail might be important."

Digdeep fidgeted with his livery. "He met with Dumoulin briefly, after Isarn had finished with him. I'll see if the staff have more information on it, but his personal servants are loyal. They don't reveal much.

Wortle's wrinkles deepened. "We've gleaned nothing from the window to Elivorn's chambers, and we haven't been able to enter as he's there most of the time. When he's not, his servants are carrying out their duties."

His chamber... I'd been in his chamber... and there had been all those parchments scattered about. The place had been cluttered, so maybe it was inconsequential, but it might be worth mentioning. I'd need to word it carefully, though. I couldn't risk sparking more of a feud between the brothers.

I shoved my hands in the pockets of my Keeper gear trousers, then pulled them out again. "Uh... I'm not sure if it's important, but I was exploring the castle yesterday and walked past Elivorn's room. I didn't know it was private quarters, and the door was open, so I poked my head inside. It was a mess, but I couldn't help noticing a load of parchments lying around in the far corner by the fireplace."

"That's the corner we can't see very well from the tunnel window," Wortle said.

Lucas frowned. "Are you sure it was Elivorn's room?"

Hell and damnation. More crappy lies needed. I could feel my pulse rate rising. "That was when I bumped into him. He was coming back in."

Lucas pressed his lips together. "It may be nothing, but

we need to check it out. With everyone reporting for duty shortly... who are we going to ask?"

Blisterch's glower deepened. "There's no one."

"Except us," I said, meeting Lucas's eye. "After we've seen to Alice, of course."

CHAPTER 26

WORTLE'S WORRIES ABOUT ALICE ECHOED THROUGH MY head as Lucas and I made our way along the earth tunnel, lanterns in hand. She'd said that Alice wasn't good, that she needed looking at. Later, she'd added that Alice hadn't eaten since yesterday, and that she'd only managed a few drops of water.

To make matters worse, we were heading to the castle at a snail's pace, waiting for the change of guard. Only once Lucas's goblins had taken position around the dungeon could we risk being there. It wasn't the full guard like before, and there would be no one in the tunnels keeping watch, but given the circumstances, it was the best we could do.

As Wortle and the others would be at the castle, and the slopes wouldn't be guarded, Roux had said he'd keep a firm eye on Gabe and Nora. The last thing anyone needed was those two making themselves conspicuous again. He'd also said he would keep a lookout for danger. If he was worried, the lot of them would hide in the tunnels. I could only hope that the goblins would be alright, and that Lord Rouseau's concerns would blow over as Blisterch had thought.

I tried to release my stress by shimmying my shoulders, but it only made them knot. "Can't we hurry up just a little bit?"

"We need to give the guards a couple more minutes," Lucas said without looking back.

My boot caught a loose stone and drove it into the wall. "We really need to get Alice out of Grimmere. And Roux, Gabe and Nora, for that matter." But if Alice was worse, how could we move her?

He shot me a frown over his shoulder, his hand clenched around the strap of his pack. "I still don't get what Elivorn wants with Alice. I presumed he'd use her as leverage to persuade me to keep away from his and my father's plans, but if that was the case, he would've done it by now." He ground his jaw. "And what the hell is he up to with the bounds? *Tomorrow*, Camille." He shot me a mean glare, every part of him tense. "Whatever he's doing, we only have until then to figure it out, and we have absolutely nothing to go on."

"You don't have to tell me," I said. "But Digdeep might come up with something, and let's at least see if we can get those parchments."

He shook his head.

Yep, it was doubtful they would be of any use, but we had nothing else to go on.

We walked on in silence, my concerns knotting my

shoulders a little more, although as we ascended the castle steps, something else came to the fore. "Your family was so convinced we were mates last night. It seemed too easy. A few gazes and intimate gestures, and they're like, 'Camille, welcome to the family.'" I don't get it."

He was quiet for a moment as we continued the climb, then said, "Dracs don't make that declaration easily or arbitrarily."

That didn't answer my question. The dungeon door loomed ahead. Lucas paused, his gaze meeting mine, drawing me as it always did. "You looked unbelievable, though. Absolutely stunning."

I hadn't expected the compliment now we weren't midcharade. Before I could react or say a word, he raised his finger to his lips and took the side tunnel to the other door. I supposed I could accept the compliment. I'd rocked that dress—all apart from tripping on it five times.

We paused at the window overlooking Alice. She lay on the straw, shifting from side to side.

"I'm going to check the guards are in place and the coast is clear." Lucas darted off along the tunnel, leaving me anxiously watching Alice, my worries building as she thrashed around. He returned a minute later with an affirmative nod. We stepped into the dungeon and unlocked the cell.

I dove down beside her and grasped her hand. Her skin was burning, sweat running down her forehead. "Hey, sweetie," I murmured, "it's Camille. Everything is going to be alright." She stilled at my voice, though her eyes remained closed.

Lucas, on her other side, took her pulse. "Alice, we're going to help you some more today."

Even now, I couldn't equate the gentle curves of Alice's face to Fae, to this hell hole. She should be back at the café doing the accounts or sorting out the customers who'd been spooked by Dame Blanche's knowing smile.

"So sorry I had to leave you," I said. "But we had people watching the whole time."

She murmured a little, her eyelids flickering. I grabbed Lucas's pack, pulled out the waterskin and held it to her lips. "Drink, honey."

Her mouth remained closed.

Lucas took her hand in his. "Her fingers are twitching on this side. What about the other?"

I squeezed her fingers, but they were still. "Nothing."

He fixed me with a steady gaze. "The potions haven't helped. The shock of being forced into Fae has been too much. She's developed focal clonic seizures, meaning her only chance is verity."

I studied Alice's bruised face. Then she would know, she would understand everything, she would see Raphaël for what he was, but she would also have to suffer the gulf I hadn't been able to bridge between the human realm and Fae. Right now, even though that rat of a fiancé had to be sorted, I couldn't believe I'd ever wanted her to have verity, or that I'd taken the bottle from Lucas.

"Camille," he said softly, "there's only a fifty percent

chance the verity will work, but now she's deteriorated to this point, the longer we wait, the slimmer her prospects."

"A fifty-fifty chance?" I swallowed, a lump sticking in my throat. But at least it was a chance. "Alright."

Lucas rummaged in his sack and took out the vial I'd brought with me. He'd asked for it in his chambers, just in case. Otherwise, he would've had Wortle brew a fresh batch, but it would've taken valuable time.

He uncorked it, then met my gaze. I nodded and supported Alice's sweaty head as he tipped the verity to her lips, but she didn't respond.

"If she won't drink water, how are we going to make her take this?" My voice was high and tight.

Alice's lips shifted then parted. Lucas allowed one drop to fall onto her tongue, the scent of cloves mingling with the awful dungeon stench. "Humans can't resist."

She stilled, her fingers relaxing, her breathing growing deeper. I hadn't realised how much tension she'd been holding.

"She'll sleep now," Lucas said, "most likely for a day or so. We can only hope that it will be healing."

I tucked the straw around her and dabbed her forehead with a cloth as Lucas renewed the warmth collude and glamoured our scent again. Despite her fever, the dungeon was freezing.

"Without the usual security in place, we have to go." Lucas rose, hooking his pack onto his shoulder. "She'll have water when Elivorn's guards come in. I won't be able to post anyone to watch, but I'll have goblins check the window as often as possible, and I'll do my best to arrange for someone to be here when she wakes." I appreciated that he hadn't said "if". "I'm sure my father will be finished with the servants by then."

We had to leave. I knew the stakes. I wrapped my arms around Alice and squeezed her gently, her heat burning into me. I couldn't allow myself to consider the possibility that I'd lose her. "I love you, honey," I whispered. "Remember that."

With my heart in a vice, my breath leaving me, I tore myself away and followed Lucas out of the cell. As we left the dungeon, I glanced back, sending Alice my love, as if that alone would keep her alive. As we took the steps ever upward to Elivorn's chambers, my chest felt as though it would tear apart.

CHAPTER 27

I PACED BACK AND FORTH ALONG THE LENGTH OF Lucas's chambers, pausing to stare into the roaring fire for a few moments before returning to the windows at the other end. It was late. Too late for me, but not too late, apparently, for dracs.

The day had been a failure. Lucas had stationed himself in the tunnels at Elivorn's chamber, waiting for an opportunity to enter, but Elivorn had been firmly ensconced there, reading parchments all day. The price for being caught was much too high for Lucas to risk entering during one of Elivorn's brief visits to the bathroom. We didn't even know if the parchments were important.

Whilst Lucas was on vigil, I'd gone back to the dungeon tunnel and sat on the guard's stool. I'd watched Alice until we'd had to leave for the castle via the slopes and the horses. The only relief today was a message that Lord Rouseau's suspicions about the staff had been revoked. They'd all returned to normal duties.

Lucas and I had dined here as, much to my relief, Lord and Lady Rouseau were occupied, then Lucas had been summoned by his father for something or other. It wasn't long until I was due to join them for Lord Rouseau's big reveal. I'd been advised to wear practical clothing, not evening wear. I still wore my Keeper gear, my hair tied into a plait. It would do.

All I could do now was wait for the word to join Lucas. I wanted to be back in the tunnels watching Alice. She'd slept deeply all day, but at some point she would come around... or... but no, I wasn't going to think about it.

Through the window, the ice-grey lake reflected the cold, fat moon. Beyond, the forest hid its horrors just like I hid horror within me. I would need to project a cool exterior as Lucas's mate once again, yet underneath lay the deep, unsettling fear I'd felt since I'd entered Grimmere. I couldn't pin it down to any one event I'd experienced here—it was as if the place exuded terror—and it wasn't really helping that Lord Rouseau was about to reveal his plans for untold misery to humanity through the splitting of the bounds.

A knock rapped on the door.

"Come in," I called.

A goblin bowed. "Ma'am, Lord Rouseau wishes you to join him. If you'll follow me."

Good. If we could find out what was going on with the bounds, at least there was a chance we could put a stop to it. Hating leaving my blade behind, I followed the footman toward the drawing room. As we drew near Elivorn's chambers, I breathed away the anxiety creeping through me.

The servant paused outside Elivorn's door and knocked. "What...? Wait." Shit. "What is this?"

The goblin narrowed his wrinkled brow and twitched his ears. "Lord Rouseau, ma'am. As I said."

Shit, of course. Double shit. All of them were Lord Rouseau. How stupid of me not to check. I made to vamoose back to the chamber, but the door opened.

Elivorn's eyes glinted darkly, his smile wicked. I tried to walk away, but I could already feel his influence. The blood drained from my face.

"Ah, Camille, so gracious of you to join me." He glanced at the servant. "You may go."

The goblin scurried off. I wanted to call for help before he disappeared, but if I did, Lucas would find out. Damn it. I should've asked Nora for the amulet, but I'd been too concerned about Alice and everything else, plus I'd been sure I could keep out of Elivorn's way.

"Come in," he said with a flicker of his lips.

"You have to be joking." I tried to back away, but part of me wanted to step closer.

"Speak louder and you'll have Lucas up here, which would be rather nice. I can't decide what I want more, to rile him or fuck you."

"Bastard." If looks could kill, he would've been mincemeat. Even so, there was a part of me that swooned, and that part felt damned real. But Elivorn was doing this to me—I had to hang on to that. And yet, the way he filled out his tailcoat... and the way his full lips gathered... I stepped in, my pulse rocketing.

Elivorn closed the door and leant on it. I was trapped, not just in Elivorn's room but within the part of me that wanted to do his bidding. But then it hit me—this was the chamber we'd been hoping to get into all day. Perhaps I could use this to my advantage. If the worse came to the worst, Elivorn was right. All I had to do was scream for Lucas. He'd hear, and if he didn't, surely one of the dracs or servants would. Lucas's reaction would cause all kinds of problems, but maybe we could smooth things over.

"It's a shame you're not wearing that dress," Elivorn drawled as he approached. "It only made me want to break you more. But those leathers are almost as enticing."

"Screw you," I growled.

He laughed. "Yes, please."

Unable to stop myself. I drew close to him. Too close. His scent was both alluring and nauseating. It wasn't churches he evoked, it was graveyards and corpses and rotting flesh.

Every inch of me pressed against his solid top-to-toe muscle. Part of me delighted in the sensation, and part of me balked at the reminder of his strength. I placed my hand under the high waist of his tailcoat, feeling his rigid abs. If I could only run my hands over... No, shit... no. I had to keep my wits about me, to do something about the parchments.

My hand was trembling. Elivorn placed his fingers over mine, his touch scalding like hellfire. "How you fight it. I'm impressed. It takes a lot of strength to resist an incubus, especially one with my power, but the fight makes it so much more fun." He grasped my hand and led me to the bed.

I tried to oppose him. I tried so damned hard. The only thing still under my control was my mouth. "You asswipe... you creep... you complete and utter prick."

He just laughed again.

If only I could slow him down. The parchments were in a pile by the couch. Perhaps I could get him over there. "The bed?" I said. "Really, Elivorn, so prosaic. Couldn't you be more imaginative?"

We paused by the bedside, his eyes glinting. "Oh, it's just for starters."

Against my will—but with every inch of my body craving it—I shimmied back on the bed, grasped Elivorn's cravat and pulled him toward me. Damn it, I wanted him. I wanted to get inside those breeches, and he knew it. A small voice screamed that I should call Lucas, but it was insignificant, not worth bothering about. All that mattered were the exquisite kisses Elivorn was trailing down my neck, skimming over my breasts, scattering on my midriff.

Desire coiled within me. There was nothing I wanted more. I dropped back onto the bed, my head hanging off the far side as I released myself fully to him.

"That wasn't so difficult, now, was it?" he crooned as he unbuckled my belt and pulled it off. "Hmm, could be useful." He threw it away and started unbuttoning my trousers, playing with the fastening, the sensation electric.

"Get on with it, you asshole," I growled. I couldn't

believe myself, but I was gone. Completely gone. All I wanted was Elivorn.

"It would be my delight." He smiled, his lips holding sin and pleasure and corruption. He lowered his head and kissed me over the leather of my trousers, one hand unbuttoning them much too slowly. I moaned, writhing in ecstasy, my eyelids draped with desire. And yet, I was sure I'd just seen something move in my periphery. There it was again, a small motion on the floor. A knee shifting as it stuck out from under the bed.

That snapped me back. What the hell was I doing? Elivorn almost had my trousers undone, and there was someone beneath us. Someone wearing skinny jeans.

That someone poked their head out just enough to glare at me and mouth, "What. The. Fuck. Are. You. Doing?" Nora.

I couldn't stop my body responding as Elivorn undid my last button. But what on earth was Nora doing here? She was in so much danger, and she was risking the whole ruse once again. But thank heavens Elivorn couldn't see her, as absorbed as he was with my nether regions. Then, as Elivorn kissed my thigh and tugged at my trousers, it dawned on me just how much danger I was in. "Help," I mouthed back.

A hand full of parchments emerged from under the bed, then the rest of Nora. I cringed, hoping Elivorn wouldn't hear, but he was too distracted. She propped herself up on her elbow and stuck out her other hand. The amulet lay in her grip. I had to reach it, and yet my body was still responding to Elivorn. I tried to fight myself yet again, only managing to tighten my muscles.

Taking my rigidity for pleasure, Elivorn grinned up at me. "All that resistance, and look how you're enjoying yourself now. When I'm finished with you, you'll never want to screw my arrogant ass of a brother again." Wonderful. I was being used for sibling-rivalry one-upmanship.

The amulet glinted in the corner of my eye just below the edge of the bed, and there was nothing I could do. But... maybe I could lean into the whole being-seduced thing. I couldn't push Elivorn off, but I could still move, as long as it involved reacting to his seduction. Perhaps I could work with that. At this point, anything was worth a try.

I linked with my desire to have Elivorn closer, to have him possess me. Groaning with pleasure, I arched my body into him, stretching my arms above my head. With a delectable grin, he tugged my trousers over my butt. As my arm arced back around, it lowered to the side of the bed, and Nora shoved the amulet, chain and all, into my palm.

In an instant, every shred of desire vanished, leaving me cold and so damned furious. My situation was all too clear. My trousers were around my hips, Elivorn's kisses lingered on my thighs like welts, and I had to get the blazes out of here. But first, I needed to give Nora a chance to escape. She must have come in through the tunnels for the parchments. Presumably her scent was glamoured, or Elivorn would've noticed. Well then, she needed to go back through the tunnel door by the hearth.

I sat up. From beneath me, Elivorn raised an eyebrow.

"Not the bed," I murmured as huskily as possible. "On the desk." It was opposite the tunnel door.

A frown marred his perfect features. Had anyone ever taken the lead under his power? Cold logic assessed the situation. Elivorn's chest was rising and falling, his breath ragged, his pupils dilated. Boy, was *he* still feeling it. I leant forward, pulled his mouth to mine and kissed him hard, forcing myself not to balk at his taste. Breaking away, I murmured, "The desk, Elivorn. I need you on the desk. Right now."

His jaw tightened, fire flaring in his eyes. Swiftly, he scooped me up, carried me over and placed me on top. Forcing desire into my expression, I grasped his belt and pulled him close.

For a second he acquiesced, then he pulled away, his predator eyes locked on mine. "How dare you?" he snarled.

Shit. I'd taken too much control. There was something furious in his face, something so hideous. His inner drac, maybe. But it was all too clear he'd snapped.

Growling, his features distorting, he tugged off his belt and ripped open his breeches. But most importantly, he was completely consumed with me. Nora poked her head out from under the bed. As he kissed my neck, I made a show of moaning loudly to cover any noise. She took the opportunity and darted out, padding to the wall near the seating area. The wooden panel shifted silently, allowing her access, and then she was gone.

Elivorn stepped back in all his glory. Oh, yeah, I'd forgotten. Dracs don't wear underpants. Yet I wasn't going to demean myself by looking... um... at least not properly.

"You're mine, Camille." At drac speed he drove his palm into my chest, thrusting me back against the wall, my head smacking into the wood. Pain split through my skull as he yanked my trousers further down.

Well, really? That had hurt, and I'd had enough.

With the amulet warm in my palm, I sat up, and as easily as brushing off a fly, I pushed him backward with my free hand. He tried to fight me for a moment, excited by my resistance, but he couldn't. I sprang off the desk and pulled my trousers up, fastening them whilst keeping the amulet concealed.

"What are you doing?" He gaped in astonishment.

This definitely hadn't happened to him before. And *now* I really was enjoying myself. But I had no idea how far I could go with the amulet, or how much danger I was still in.

He grabbed my forearms, his fingers digging in, his eyes blazing. I shrugged away, strode over to the rug and picked up my belt. I could've left it and gotten out, but that damn belt was from Wayland—a gift from a freaking pan-European god. Not to mention I loved it. The star patterning was exquisitely crafted, matching my scabbard.

As I threaded it, I kept my eyes on Elivorn. How much power did I have over him? How I wanted to kick him so damned hard that he'd never be able to perform again. Although, that would be much too merciful after Alice.

"Camille, come here, right now." Elivorn's voice was laced with fury. By the way his eyes bulged and his jaw strained, I'd take a guess he was giving me his full-blast incubus crap. Damn it. I so wanted to pay him back or at least rile him a teensy bit. But on top of everything else, I didn't want him to guess about the amulet. My safest bet was to act innocent and leave without making a ruckus.

"There we go," I said as I did up my buckle.

Sweat was beading on Elivorn's brow, his shoulders hunched, his glower boring into me. "Get here now," he rumbled.

"Not your best look, Elivorn." I couldn't help the comment, though I really needed to control my mouth. "I don't know what the time is," I said sweetly, "but your father will be wanting us at any moment. I'm going to freshen up." With that, I strode out.

CHAPTER 28

My head still hurt. Every step as I followed the footman to the courtyard sent shockwaves through my skull. Damned Elivorn. I'd wanted to take a healing potion from Lucas's pack, but if he noticed, it would raise too many questions.

I'd done my best to remove Elivorn's smell by washing, and I'd tried to wipe off my Keeper gear. I'd refrained from spraying on a spicy cologne I'd found in the bathroom as Lucas would realise right away that I was hiding something. If only I could manage the scent-disguising collude. But the main thing was, I had the amulet tucked safely inside my top. I had protection. Lucas didn't need to know what had happened, and we could focus on getting the information we needed to prevent the splitting of the bounds. Then we could all get out of here, Alice included.

The thought of the danger Nora had put herself in sent rivulets of fury through me. After her encounter with Lord

Dumoulin, she should've learnt. Once again, she could've blown everything. I tried to breathe away my anger. At least she'd gotten out alright.

Despite all that, I itched to see what was on the parchments she'd taken, though surely Elivorn would notice they were missing sooner or later. I hated to think what would happen then. A fresh round of interrogations for the goblins? Nora really had gone too far.

The footman led me into the drawing room where Lucas had torn out Pierre's throat. I took a deep breath and steeled myself against the memory. Isarn and Lady Rouseau were in conversation by the fire. Elivorn was nursing a whisky in the armchair opposite.

"Oh, Camille, wonderful," Lady Rouseau said. Her outfit, a sort of assassin-pirate get-up with tight trousers, long boots and an oversized shirt tucked into a wide belt, made me wonder how well she could fight... and kill. "We're waiting for my husband and Lucas. They should be here any moment."

I caught Elivorn's eye as I crossed the room. His head was lowered, malice coming off him in waves. My escape was only going to make him mistrust me—and subsequently Lucas—more. But perhaps he thought he was having an off day.

"Tell us about your rides over the countryside," Isarn said. "How do you like Grimmere? A little darker than the Pyrenees, perhaps?" There was a glint in his eye, maybe a tease.

I had no idea how to answer. I hadn't seen much more

than the inside of Wortle's hole. "There's an austere beauty about it—"

Lord Rouseau and Lucas strode in, talking. They broke off and Lucas headed to my side. I released a breath. Saved. Though as Lucas joined me, his nostrils flared and his gaze grew dark. He'd smelt Elivorn on my skin. Not saved. Just tipped from the frying pan into the fire.

Lucas glowered at his brother, his chest and biceps straining against his tailcoat. In return, Elivorn raised his glass, the corner of his mouth curving up. But I wasn't going to let Lucas blow everything on some jackass protective-male instinct. I grasped his hand and pulled him around to face me. After all, we were supposed to be making a show of being mates. I bored my gaze into his, communicating that he needed to snap out of it.

"Now everyone is here," Lady Rouseau said, "we can make a start, can't we?" She raised an eyebrow at her husband.

"In just a moment," he replied. "First, we have a small matter to deal with. I believe we've found our traitor."

Hell. I could only hope it wasn't one of Lucas's goblins. I'd thought they'd been let off the hook.

"Oh?" Lady Rouseau said. She fell into hushed conversation with her husband and Isarn.

Lucas was still bristling, although now he was glowering at me.

"How was your meeting with your father?" I said, returning the look.

His jaw shifted from side to side, then he forced his

shoulders back. "All good. It was excellent to spend a little time with him." His voice was calm, but his glare shot razor-sharp daggers. I had to defuse the situation.

"I visited Elivorn," I said softly. Yes, they'd all be able to hear if they were inclined to listen, but so what? We were in the same castle. Why wouldn't I visit him? But Lucas needed more than that.

The way we were positioned, with Lucas's back to the room, I was pretty much hidden. I raised a hand and balled it into a fist, then laid it flat for a moment before parting my fingers and snipping them together. The symbols for rock paper scissors. But would a drac know about that?

"We talked briefly. It was very pleasant," I added, emphasising my flat palm, representing paper—parchments. I'd been in Elivorn's room trying to get the parchments. It was sort of true.

He nodded, understanding, though he didn't relax.

"Lord Rouseau," a footman pronounced. "The traitor is ready."

My stomach flipped. Lucas's gaze, which hadn't shifted from mine, implored me to hold it together, come what may. His turn to support me. I swallowed as we turned to face the guards entering the room. A captive struggled between them, his hands tied behind his back.

He raised his bony head. Blisterch.

No. No. No. No.

"He's been interrogated," Lord Rouseau said. "And now he needs to be made an example of."

"Wonderful," Lady Rouseau trilled as though she was

complimenting the weather or my dress. She shot her husband a carnal smile. "I would so enjoy the honour, but it gives me even more pleasure to watch you kill." Lord Rouse-au's eyes shone with lust.

The world slowed and my ears hummed, a part of me noting that this was the real family, the family I hadn't seen last night because there hadn't been anything to tear apart. But most of me was reeling that strong, loyal Blis-terch, the goblin that had helped Lucas so much, was about to die.

Lucas wrapped his arm around my shoulders and pulled me to him. It was such a natural position for a couple, but the firmness of his grip imparted so much. That I mustn't react. That we would get through this. But I couldn't just stand there. There weren't any weapons, but I could grab the vase on the mantel and smash it into the nearest drac's head. Yet what good would that do? I was in a room full of the crea-tures, all strong and super-fast.

But Lucas... he had to do something. Blisterch was his friend. And yet if he did, the other goblins' lives would be at stake, and we'd be risking the whole human realm. Every-thing rode on us being quiet. Lucas's fingers squeezed tighter. They should've hurt, but it only grounded me in the knowledge that we had to get through this to save countless lives.

The guards dragged Blisterch to the hearth, where Pierre and the goblins had stood a couple of nights ago. Blisterch raised his head high, his gangly goblin frame resolute, his ears flat against his head. He glanced at us for the briefest of moments, conveying that at all costs, we had to be strong and finish what he'd worked so hard to achieve.

The guards retreated as Lord Rouseau strode over, smiling delightedly at Blisterch. "You thought you could pass drac intelligence back to the assembly. Not under my rule."

Faster than humanly possible, Lord Rouseau sprang at Blisterch and tore out his throat. I wanted to turn away, but I was rooted to the spot, the room spinning as Blisterch dropped to the ground. Lord Rouseau stepped back, blood covering his chin, his cravat, his tailcoat. He wiped his mouth with his hand.

Lady Rouseau joined him, gazing lovingly into his eyes. "Beautiful."

I barely managed to stifle the gag that heaved through me, Lucas's grip the only thing anchoring me to our ruse. Despite my nausea, I couldn't pull myself from Blisterch's lifeless form, his body motionless, his throat severed. For a moment, I thought I saw his skin shimmer. Or was it my vision swimming? But no, Blisterch really was glowing. The shimmer intensified, engulfing him. When it dulled, an elf lay in his place.

CHAPTER 29

"WHAT HAVE WE HERE?" LORD ROUSEAU'S EYES widened.

I gaped. Blisterch's body was stunningly beautiful, with golden skin, lithe limbs and long, lustrous hair. The Rouseaus flocked around him like crows on carrion, although Lucas stayed by my side.

"That's a turn-up for the books," Elivorn said. "He was glamoured extremely well."

Isarn shook his head and glanced at his father. "There's no doubt your intel was spot on."

Lady Rouseau shuddered. "He was the leader of the guard, privy to much that is confidential, and he has been here for years. There is a chance he has relayed a great deal of information. How many more do we have in our ranks?"

"I believe he was working alone." Lord Rouseau placed his hand on his wife's back. "The goblins have been interrogated. They have rock-hard alibis."

Interrogations... On top of this, the thought of the goblins who'd crowded into Wortle's hole this morning being tortured was more than I could bear.

It was only then that I noticed Lucas's hand trembling in mine. I glanced up. His face was red, his eyes fierce. Blisterch had been a close friend, but Lucas couldn't let on, especially not now Blisterch had given his life for us.

Lucas pulled away, his skin darkening, tightening, warping, his chest heaving as he paced back and forth at the side of the room. There was more drac in him than human, and he was beyond hideous. My pulse hitched. Blisterch's death had been one step too far. He was about to rip his family's throats out in recompense.

"I should've known," he snarled. "I spent enough time at the assembly. I wheedled so much out of them. But this... this they held close to their chests." He swung around to face his father, his coat-tails flying. "I swear, I will turn up everything when I return. I will root out every last traitor to Grimmere." This had to be an act. He was channelling his anger for Blisterch's death into the charade. He had to be, but he was so damned vehement. So convincing. What if he *was* pulling the wool over my eyes?

His father strode to him and gripped his shoulders. "This isn't the first plant, and it won't be the last. The assembly's methods grow cunning, their mages increasingly resourceful. But it shows that there is much more you can do. You are in the perfect position to infiltrate the assembly to its core."

Lucas's breathing levelled, the drac retreating, though the fierceness in his eyes remained. "And when I reach its heart, I'll ensure that every last one of them dies." I shuddered at the surety in his voice. Either he meant what he said or he was in line for an Oscar.

Elivorn, who was sitting in his chair once more, knocked back his whisky.

Lord Rouseau squeezed Lucas's shoulders. "Perfect. And that is only a matter of time."

Lucas nodded, drawing strength from his father's words.

"Now that's sorted, let us make a move." Lord Rouseau led us out.

As we followed, I was a picture of composure, though my face was too still. Inside, horror, grief and regret churned, my mouth dry, every part of me sick with what I'd seen. And all of it melded with threads of suspicion.

The corridor passed in a blur. Lucas's arm around my waist was solid and reassuring, but those doubts... Lucas had always been a trickster—he couldn't help himself—and I never knew what he was going to do next. But he couldn't be his father's man. I didn't want him to be, and yet it would be stupid not to consider the possibility.

It was this place, though. There was so much deception and betrayal. The atmosphere bred fear and doubt. All I could do was go along with our ruse and hope that whatever we were going to be shown would prove Lucas's loyalty to the assembly—to me—once and for all.

We descended the sweeping staircase, then entered the courtyard and paused before the menhir.

"Everyone set?" Lord Rouseau asked.

There were nods of agreement.

Around the way marker, a multitude of impressions flickered, a forest, a city, jagged mountains. Lord Rouseau turned toward a glimpse of darkness. Clasping his wife's hand, he led us forward.

We strode onto a mountainside near the summit of a barren peak, the wind whipping about. The sky was clear and the moon bright, but a swirling bank of cloud encircled us, extending down to engulf the mountains below.

The place felt... I didn't know how to describe it. Dark, evil, maybe? Wrong, definitely. I strove for steady breaths, but there was something about the air. As it seeped into my lungs, it kindled utter despair.

Lucas fixed on the rounded peak ahead, his eyes widening. "The omphalos."

"Indeed." Lord Rouseau smiled.

Lucas caught the incomprehension in my face. "This mountain is the heart of the dark lands, the focus of all that is horrific and wretched." Oh, joy. Although considering the Rouseaus, it fitted perfectly.

Figures moved on the peak. Lord and Lady Rouseau led the way toward them. Lucas released my waist, though he kept his hand firmly wrapped around mine as we took the rear along the rugged path. I caught chanting rising and falling on the gale.

As we neared the summit, the sense of despair intensified, cutting through me like knives. My instincts screamed for me to flee back to the way, but on we strode. We were here for a reason, and Blisterch's death wasn't going to be in vain.

The figures became clear. Mages stood amidst numerous menhirs, their hoods raised, their cloaks whipping about. The urge to run redoubled. I forced my legs to carry me forward. As we rounded the brow of the peak, the vista opened, and my heart froze.

Before us lay a vast crater, and within its centre, swirling right to the brim, was utter darkness. It wasn't dark in the sense of death—death was a part of life and had its own grim spirit. No, this was a lack, a complete nothing, oblivion. And from the crater, the nothingness flowed through channels to menhirs. Way markers.

"The malum," Lord Rouseau proclaimed, his features set in smug glee as he turned to his sons.

Elivorn wore a faint smile. Isarn looked disinterested. Lucas was agape. I wasn't sure I was doing a good job of keeping the horror off my face.

Lord Rouseau raised his arms. "Well, Lucas, what do you think?"

Lucas's lips were parted, his eyes lit with wonder. He stepped closer, pulling me with him. "So this is the source of the bounds cracks. Remarkable. But how did you manage it?"

Lord Rouseau's eyes sparkled. "By gathering the finest mages and scouring ancient sources of knowledge. The resulting colludes were able to call forth the malignant power of the dark lands from the omphalos. We concentrated the power, extracting every hint of light and life. Slowly, it fermented until it turned in on itself. It became more than darkness, more than a void. It became the malum. The only force capable of splitting creation."

Lady Rouseau smiled at her husband in adoration.

He turned to the swirling vat of darkness. "It is astounding, isn't it?"

Perhaps astounding in the sense of being so terrible that nothing compared to it.

"I wouldn't have believed it possible," Lucas said. "The old stories raise the idea, of course. But to have actually managed it..."

Elivorn stepped closer. "Now do you see what we've attained while you were playing nicely with the assembly?"

Lucas's brow creased. "I admit, what you've done here far outweighs anything I've achieved."

Elivorn stared at his brother for a little too long.

Isarn thumped Elivorn on the back. "And all the while this lot have been amusing themselves with the malum, I've had to keep Grimmere running."

"And you, Camille," Lady Rouseau said. "What do you make of it?" Her smile was cold but earnest.

I realised my mouth was open. I had no idea what was written on my face. Absolute revulsion, at a guess. My eyes were as wide as saucers and my jaw refused to move. I attempted to shape my revulsion into awe. "I have to say, I'm completely stunned." To put it mildly. "I don't know what I'd expected, but this is something else."

Her smile broadened. My turn for an Oscar.

"And the menhirs," Lucas said. "You created way markers to channel the malum to the bounds. That must have taken unprecedented power."

Lord Rouseau nodded. "That is where our allies have

been so useful. With their generosity we've had every herb and mineral needed to cast the colludes. Our mages have been working night and day to ensure the ways stay open, but it is a challenging endeavour, and the malum is restricted in its flow. However, if Elivorn manages to obtain the information he's seeking, the boost to tomorrow's ceremony will be unprecedented. The ways will be opened permanently, and the malum will stream forth unhindered. The bounds will be split."

CHAPTER 30

WE WERE GATHERED AROUND WORTLE'S TABLE, THE kitchen full of goblins, all of us silent in homage to Branhelm. Disguised as Blisterch, the elf had tirelessly infiltrated the drac guard to convey information to the assembly.

Digdeep had spoken of Branhelm's life, his family and his qualities as a leader. Lucas had spoken of the elf's passion for the freedom of fae and his respect for the human realm. Then, with a rough voice, he'd acknowledged their centuries-long camaraderie and deep friendship. Wortle had lit the candle in the centre of the table, and our silence had begun.

This morning, reeling from Lord Rouseau's disclosure, we'd informed the servants that Lucas was going out to hunt and that I wanted some air. It meant we couldn't stay out for long without raising suspicion. We'd already been to the dungeons to check on Alice, but she was still sleeping deeply.

When we'd returned to the hole to organise our counter-move, the kitchen had been full of Lucas's servants. They were distressed by Blisterch's death, their foibles more pronounced. Lucas had said they needed a mark of respect to help them through. We'd given an update about the Rouseaus' plans to split the bounds tonight, much to everyone's utter dismay, and then we'd commenced the ceremony.

Gabe and Nora sat on the other side of the table, their heads hung low. To my side, Roux frowned, stroking his beard. The crowd of goblins sitting and standing around us were lost in thought, one with a torn ear, one with twisted fingers, plenty with bruising. Signs of yesterday's interrogation.

The stillness in the room was tangible, burgeoning with grief. I sent Branhelm my thanks for all he'd done. Unbidden, those thoughts vied with images of his demise. The blood. The satisfaction on Lord Rouseau's face. Didn't the monster realise that with each execution, he was taking a life? A person with friends and family, a soul who'd been crafted by years of experience. And didn't he realise how many human lives would be lost if the bounds were split? I couldn't imagine why he believed he had the right to take away so much.

Yet Lucas had done the same to Pierre. I understood his argument that Pierre would've died one way or another, but so many twisted impressions rushed through my head. I couldn't shift Lucas swearing to take down the assembly, or the way he'd drawn succour from his father's support, or his wonder at the malum. But if I was so concerned, why had I slept once again with his arm protectively at my chest, his body sheltering mine? My gaze flicked to his face. He was staring at the wall, his otherworldly features set in stone, his cheeks lined with tears. Surely his grief for Branhelm wasn't an act.

Digdeep, sitting next to Lucas, shook his head. He seemed so solid and predictable compared to the goblins on either side of him, one with a long snout who was about to fall off his chair, and the other, the maid who'd helped me dress for dinner—Poky, she was called—who was doing her best not to clack her teeth. Was Digdeep also something other than he appeared to be?

With a glance at him, Wortle rose stiffly, her eyes damp, her wrinkles deeper than ever. She picked up the candle snuffer and held it reverently in both hands. "With all our goodwill and love," she croaked, "we send Branhelm onward along the path of the stars." After a moment, she extinguished the flame.

The whispering of sighs and the rustling of limbs filled the kitchen. I sat up, attempting to breathe away the tightness in my chest, my head aching from yesterday.

Lucas wiped his cheeks with his sleeve, his face darkening. He stood up and leant on the table. "I swear," he rumbled, "I will kill my father for Branhelm's death. But not before finding out what the lot of them are up to."

Wortle's expression broke. "Lulu, deary, you know the consequences." To my surprise, she burst into a hearty chuckle, the goblins joining in. Some kind of in joke, I guessed, but it dissipated the grief, the goblins appearing more themselves.

Lucas chewed his cheek, lost in thought, then he gathered himself and swept his gaze over us all. "Right. Time to get on with it. We know that Elivorn is in the process of obtaining information that will cause the bounds to split irrevocably this evening. We have to stop him. If we can't, we may have to use force against my family. In that event, our cover will be blown, and it's going to get messy."

Clack. Clack. Clack.

"Agreed." Digdeep placed his hands on his ample girth. "If it comes to it, we'll do what we have to do. But let's avoid that outcome if at all possible."

"My lord." The goblin with the long snout rose, inclining his head to Lucas. "We have to be going. Can't be missed for too long and all, but if we can be of any help, let us know."

"Of course," Lucas said. "Thank you for joining us."

I caught Nora's eye. I was so unbelievably pissed off with her for the risks she'd taken last night, but she needed to mention the parchments. I desperately hoped she wouldn't bring up my involvement. I'd not had the chance to warn her about it out of Lucas's earshot. She nodded at me, then glanced at Gabe. He gave a Vulcan salute and headed out the room behind a mass exodus of goblins. Of the castle staff, only Wortle, who was straightening the empty chairs, and Digdeep remained.

Lucas looked squarely at him. "Did you get anything on Elivorn's meeting with Dumoulin?"

"Nothing. Just a drink with an old friend."

"What I don't get is why my father believes Fae can exist without the human realm." Lucas began pacing back and forth between the range and the dresser. "It's not possible for one to survive without the other. Why would he even attempt such madness?"

"Could it be just that?" Roux's wild eyebrows drew together. "Madness? He wouldn't be the first tyrant to put everyone at risk because of his delusions."

"My father is many things," Lucas said, "but I'd be surprised if he let himself get carried away on a whim. Centuries of protecting his rule in Grimmere has kept him grounded."

Wortle fluffed a cushion. "I would agree with that, deary. Lord Rouseau is in possession of all his faculties."

Gabe returned and placed a huge bundle of old parchments on the table. Lucas studied him with curiosity.

"Uh," Nora said. "We have something that may be of help."

She shifted in her chair, looking anywhere but at Lucas. After the bollocking he'd given them, I wasn't surprised.

Gabe raised his brow. "Go on... or I can do it."

"No, I will." She swallowed, looking around nervously. "We... uh... I crept into Elivorn's room last night and stole his parchments. All of them."

"What?" Lucas bawled, this time leaning so far over the table he was almost in their faces. "After we told you to stay put? Are you continuously trying to put our lives in danger?"

The two of them shrank. "Uh... uh... we did our best not to be discovered," Gabe managed, trembling.

Wortle folded her arms and tsked.

"We found Elivorn's room and checked it out," Gabe continued. "I glamoured some of Wortle's papers to look like old parchments. We used them as replacements. And I glamoured Nora's scent too, so she wouldn't be detected. I wanted to go in and do the swap but, uh... she wouldn't let me."

Roux sat up, his eyes brightening. "Oh, well done, lad. You've come along so far with your glamours."

I glared at him. "Do you really think that's the point, Roux?"

His cheeks puffed. "Well... well... the boy clearly did a good job."

I tangled my fingers in my hair and rubbed my head, avoiding the sore spot. "Anyway, you said you'd keep an eye on them. How the hell did they get into the tunnels in the first place?"

"Wortle was at the castle," Nora said. "And I... we... I..."

"Passion flower." Wortle said. "Found a mug with it in this morning."

Nora blanched.

"You used a sleep potion on me?" Roux frowned, looking this way and that as he tried to piece everything together. "I did have the best rest I'd had in a long time. Very nice."

So not the point.

"Unbelievable," Lucas said. "And how did you get into the chamber without Elivorn noticing?"

"I snuck in when he was in the bathroom." The patch of table in front of Nora had become the most fascinating thing in the room.

Lucas shook his head, his teeth grinding. From our recce, we both knew how brief Elivorn's bathroom trips had been, which was probably why she'd gotten stuck in there. My fingers tightened, clamping into my palms. Was this where she revealed my part in it all? He was going to flip if he found out. The last thing he needed right now was to have to deal with his screwed-up territorial instincts.

"And what do you think is going to happen when Elivorn discovers the parchments are fakes?" he growled.

They glanced at one another.

"Anyway, the p... point is," Gabe added, "we've been studying them all night... they weren't easy to read. You know the thefts at the Musée Saint-Raymond and the Chateau de Foix recently? I think these might be the stolen parchments. Without having the internet, it's difficult to check but—"

"The important thing is," Nora said, "they all refer to colludes, ingredients and the like, dark stuff. A few of them mention harnessing a force to split the bounds, though it's written in airy-fairy language, and there aren't any details. It's more like stories."

Wortle sat back down, curiosity angling her wrinkles. The fire in Lucas's eyes had transformed to something a little more receptive, though most of him was strung much too tight.

Gabe nodded. "And a couple of parchments mention an incantation, a sort of super spell that could be used to make certain colludes so powerful that they are irreversible, but they don't say what it is."

"They claim that this knowledge was guarded by the Trencavels." Nora slid a parchment into the centre of the table. "And this one states that a scroll detailing the incantation can be found in a hidden room in the Chateau de Foix. More specifically in the grand chamber of the square tower."

I gaped. I knew the chamber. I'd guided tourists around there so many times.

Lucas drew his hand over his mouth. He'd served with Raymond Roger, so he must know it too, although it would've been a hell of a long time ago. "Go on," he said.

The enthusiasm returned to Gabe's face. "According to the parchment, only a Trencavel can access the room, and only when the moon is in Leo. And, well, that's it."

Lucas picked up the parchment and scanned it.

"The moon shifts through the zodiacal constellations every two to two and a half days," Roux said. "It would've entered Leo about two hours ago. The next occurrence will be in a month."

"Three hours ago, I think, deary," Wortle said. Roux frowned and counted on his fingers.

Lucas placed the parchment back down. "The Trencavels, Raymond Roger included, were rulers of vast tracts of land in the South of France, not to mention guardians of the mysteries. They were fully aware of the balance between realms. They were honourable to a tee, great leaders, and the most chivalrous people I've had the honour to know. They kept a number of secrets, holding them safely should man or fae have need."

That didn't surprise me, considering the family's reputation.

"But the Trencavel rule declined in the crusades," Digdeep said. "The King of France was edgy because of the power they wielded, and the Pope was nervous because of the so-called heretics they sheltered. The family disappeared in the fourteenth century, the lineage believed to have ended." His human history was good for a goblin.

Lucas drew a breath through his nose. "Some of the secrets they guarded were lost at that time."

"But it explains what Elivorn is planning," I said, gazing around at them all. "He wants this super incantation for the malum, which will make it all powerful. He'll attempt to retrieve the scroll today because the moon is in Leo, meaning he can access the hidden room."

A goblin poked his head through the kitchen door. "Sorry to disturb you, my lord, but the prisoner is awake and she's making a racket. If she carries on much longer, she'll attract unwelcome attention."

I jumped up, my heart thrashing. Alice had come around, which meant she'd pulled through. Relief swathed me. But if she was shouting, she wasn't happy. I glanced at Lucas. "Let's go."

"I'll find you some food for her," Wortle said, getting up.

"Digdeep," Lucas said as he grabbed his pack from the floor. "I'll be back shortly and we'll plan our next step."

"We'd better do something soon," Digdeep replied. "Or there's not going to be a human realm left to worry about."

Wortle passed Lucas a food bundle and a waterskin.

We headed to the door, but Lucas paused and turned back, his brow knitted. "There's one thing we haven't answered... Elivorn can't access this secret room without a Trencavel, but the line ended. Although part of the family went underground, so I guess he might have a descendent hidden away somewhere, but..." He met my gaze, realisation dawning in his face.

My heart missed a beat. "Hidden away in a dungeon?"

Lucas's lips parted. "Is Alice a Trencavel?"

"I have absolutely no idea."

CHAPTER 31

As we approached the dungeon, Alice's furious cries filled the tunnel. We'd been informed that the place was secure, so we could speak freely, but Alice's shouting was enough to wake the dead.

We left our lanterns in the tunnel and pushed open the door. Alice was shaking the bars, worry creasing her battered brow. She saw us and stilled, her jaw dropping.

I paused, my breath leaving me, as Lucas strode over to unlock the cell. I couldn't believe she was better. She looked terrible—her hair knotted around her face, and I had to fight not to wince at her bruises—but she was alive.

"Camille... Lucas... what the fuck is going on? I have all these memories... and you're still in fancy dress." She took a step back. "And I'm in a goddamned prison. Would you *please* get me the hell out?"

Lucas pushed the door open. I rushed forward and

wrapped Alice in my arms. "Sweetie, I'm so glad you're better."

She hugged me tightly. "I have the strangest feeling—no, I know—that I've been in here a while, days maybe. I think I was sick. And Camille, the things I've seen. Creatures, goblins... and you were here explaining everything, talking about fae and Elivorn." She shuddered. "I thought it was a dream, but now it all seems completely real."

I released her gently and her knees buckled. Lucas rushed forward and we caught her elbows.

"Sit down, Alice," he said. "You're right, you were sick. I'm going to check you over, but ..." He glanced at me. "Camille, you have to ask her."

I nodded. Once we'd checked Alice's lineage, we could figure out what to do next.

"Ask me what?" she said.

"Come on." Lucas guided Alice to the back of the cell and helped her sit on a pile of straw.

I joined her side and squeezed her hand, but this time it was my fingers that were shaking. I just couldn't help smiling, relief washing over me. She'd made it through.

"I'm going to check your pulse," Lucas said, kneeling down.

She nodded. Lucas held her wrist and looked pointedly at me.

I got the message. "Alice, I know you want an explanation, and I promise to give you one, but first, can you please answer a question for me?"

She took in the seriousness of my expression. "Sure.

Then I want to know everything. I mean, look at me." She gestured down at her filthy jeans and ripped top.

"Of course." Good. I drew a deep breath. "This is going to sound really strange, but do you know if you descend from the Trencavel family—maybe from the counts of Foix or Carcassonne?"

She glanced at me and then Lucas. "That is absolutely a strange question, although it fits with the dungeon. My aunt did our family tree a little while ago. She found a misplaced record. The archives noted that my great-great—I don't know how many times great—grandmother died of a fever, and yet she survived and had a child. And yes, she was a Trencavel."

Lucas's eyes widened as he lowered her hand. "I thought that Raymond Roger... that all of you had gone." There was a hint of a tremor in his voice. He cleared his throat.

She frowned. "You sound like you knew him."

He bit his lip and raised his hand. "Just follow my finger."

Alice obliged, her warm eyes shifting from side to side, her frown growing deeper.

"Then Elivorn will take her to the Chateau de Foix," Lucas added. "Probably tonight, under the cover of darkness, as he wouldn't glamour her in case it interfered with accessing the hidden room." That made sense. Elivorn couldn't force Alice into the chateau in the daytime with the staff and tourists around. But he'd let her get in such a state. What was he going to do, carry her there? Although that wouldn't have surprised me. And what if she'd died? I guess he would've kidnapped another of Alice's family.

"Elivorn," Alice murmured, her face falling. What had the ground slime done to her? She swallowed. "Camille, I've answered your question. Now, will you please tell me what the hell is going on?"

How was I going to explain? "Sure, only it's... bizarre. You're going to have to give me the benefit of the doubt."

"After the things I've seen, that's not going to be a problem."

For the first time, I could be completely straight with her, and she wouldn't forget. I drew in a breath. "It's all real, fae, goblins, everything that happened to you. Just like I said before, you're in Fae... fairyland."

Lucas sat back on the straw and took the waterskin and bread from his pack. He passed the water to Alice.

She pulled out the stopper and took a few gulps, staring at me. "Alright..." she said. "That explains a lot. But what are you and Lucas doing here?"

That wasn't a bad first reaction. Much better than mine. "I've known about Fae since Lucas moved into town. We've been asked to protect the boundaries between the fae and human realms." I tugged at my Keeper top. "Which is why you've seen the outfit... and it's why we got covered in glitter a few weeks ago... and why I've been off with Lucas all the time. We're not having a relationship."

"Apart from the drunken one-night stand," Lucas added with a grin.

I refrained from kicking him. "Apart from a drunken one-night mistake."

"Camille told me." She rubbed her temples. "Okay. It's

weird, but it fits with your strange behaviour lately, all apart from having it in for Raph." She raised an eyebrow.

"Do you remember we agreed to put that to one side until we get out of here?"

"Yeah, I did." She studied my face, trying to figure it all out.

I still couldn't believe we were having this conversation. "I hated that I couldn't tell you about Fae. I wanted to share everything, but I couldn't. I thought our friendship was over." My voice cracked. "If I couldn't be honest with you, it would've all been a sham. It's selfish of me, but I can't help being glad that you know."

She looked even more perplexed. "Selfish? I don't get it."

"Uh, I guess I'm struggling with some people knowing about Fae and some not. You seem to be coping with the transition a lot better than I did."

"I guess I believe my own eyes." I loved that she always had her feet planted firmly on the ground. She gazed around. "But where the hell are we?"

"You're in my family's castle in a Fae land called Grimmere," Lucas said. "Elivorn is my brother. Because of your Trencavel heritage, it appears he has a use for you."

"Your brother...?" She gaped at him. "Uh... what I saw... he, uh... he turned into something hideous. He wasn't human..." She edged away from Lucas.

He raised his hands. "I'm not going to hurt you. I'm a fae, a drac. I turn into that creature, too. But you know me, Alice. I'm not like him."

"But you had blood all over your mouth the other night. I remember that. It wasn't fake, was it?" Her eyes were huge.

Lucas grimaced.

"Long story," I said. "I'll explain later."

"Alright." She bit her lip. "But why am I in the cell? And you were here. Why didn't you get me out?"

"Lucas's family are..." Oh hell. May as well call a spade a spade. "They're sort of evil tyrants who want to take over the world. They kill people, and they're generally really nasty."

Alice stared at Lucas, her brow peaked, her mouth forming a circle.

"But we're working against them, undercover," I said. "They have plans to hurt a lot of people. And we couldn't get you out of here because you were too sick to move, but also because we couldn't raise Elivorn's suspicions, or our cover would be blown. We've had people... uh... goblins caring for you, watching constantly and providing food and water."

A draft from the high windows chilled my skin. "I hated leaving you here, hated every moment of it, and I wasn't going to let anything happen to you, but there are so many lives at stake if Elivorn discovers our ruse."

Alice sat back against the wall. "Shit, my head hurts."

"You've been through a lot," Lucas said. "Drink a little more. It will help."

Alice peered at the waterskin, remembering it was in her hands. "I wish Raph was here. He must be so worried, and Maman."

There had to be a lot of anxious people back home, although there was a good chance Alice wouldn't be excited to see Raphaël once she realised what he really was. I hated to think what it would do to her.

I grabbed the bread and unwrapped it. "Here, we have food."

"I'm ravenous." She took a chunk and tucked in.

"We need to plan our next move," Lucas said. "We don't have much time before we're expected back."

"We can't let Elivorn get the scroll," I said. "But what can we do? Trap him? Kill him?"

Alice spluttered through her mouthful. "For goodness' sake, Camille. What are you, a waitress or an assassin?" She wiped her mouth, then sipped some water.

"If we do either," Lucas said, "we'll ruin our cover. And I'm sure there's more my father isn't telling us. There are too many unanswered questions. But it's there as a last resort."

Alice looked perplexed. "I'm not following. What is this scroll?"

I met her gaze. "We believe Elivorn has you here because he needs you as a Trencavel to access a hidden room at the Chateau de Foix. There's a scroll inside containing an incantation that will give him the ability to..." More drama. "To destroy the human realm."

Alice blinked hard. "This just gets better and better."

"We have to get to the scroll before Elivorn does," Lucas said.

My thoughts exactly. "If the scroll is missing, he'll think someone got there before him, possibly centuries before, and he won't be able to boost the malum." I folded a knee up in front of me and leant on it. "So we take Alice out via the tunnels—I'm guessing she's well enough to be moved—and we set up some sort of excuse for her escape, so Elivorn doesn't think we're involved."

"It's too risky. We're the first people Elivorn will think of," Lucas said. "But what if the information in the chateau wasn't missing? What if we glamoured a replacement scroll with an incantation that instead of aiding the malum destroyed it?"

"Can we do that?" I asked.

"I believe Roux can."

"It sounds promising. But it will only work if Alice is willing to get us inside in the first place."

She crossed her legs. "I don't mind helping you get a scroll. Least of all, it means getting out of here."

Lucas shifted, the straw rustling as he met Alice's eyes. "Uh, if we plant a false scroll, we'd have to bring you back to the dungeon, so Elivorn can take you to the chateau later to retrieve it."

Shit. Of course, Alice would have to return.

She glanced nervously between us. I couldn't imagine how she was feeling.

"And once Elivorn has used Alice to get into the room...?" I didn't want to spell it out, but dracs killed freely, and she was a witness to her own kidnapping. She wasn't going to get out of there alive.

Alice swallowed. It wasn't difficult to guess what I'd meant.

"I don't want to put you in danger, Alice." Lucas raked a hand through his hair then thrust it down into the straw. I could see him weighing it all up. Risk Alice or risk the whole damned world. He'd had to make some terrible choices, and this was one more.

"Fuck," he said. "There's so much at stake, but I can't send you to your..." A sensible choice not to say the word, considering how Alice was shaking.

Her gaze narrowed, her breath tremulous. "When Elivorn took me, I... uh... I saw something... We were in a forest on the way here, I think, and there were these goblins. I didn't know what was happening. I was completely out of it after he..." She gulped.

Lucas clenched his fists.

"Alice," I said softly. "You told me before that Elivorn hit you. Did he do anything else?" If he'd used even a hint of his incubus influence on her, I would pulverise him.

She shook her head. "No..."

I released a long breath.

"But those goblins..." she continued, her lip shaking. "Three of them... a family. One was very small... a child. I don't know what they were doing, but he found them in the forest and he... he killed them." Tears beaded in her eyes.

I gritted my teeth. "I'm so sorry you had to see that." It was horrendous, but after everything I'd experienced here, I wasn't surprised.

Alice wiped her eyes, a fierce glimmer in her gaze. "That man is evil. If there's anything I can do to stop him hurting others, you can count me in."

This was what I loved about her. She was stalwart through and through. But the danger was too great.

"The only way we can go ahead," Lucas said, "is if we can somehow ensure your safety when Elivorn takes you to the chateau."

I studied him, realisation unfurling. There was a way to keep Alice safe. That way hung around my neck, the gold warm and comforting against my skin.

"Are you sure you want to take the risk?" I asked her.

Alice's jaw was set, her lips clamped together. When she looked like that, she never changed her mind. "Completely sure."

"Then I know how to protect you." I pulled the amulet from my top, the quartz and gold glimmering even in the dull light of the dungeon.

Lucas's face was blank. "Not getting it, Camille."

I grinned, thinking of Elivorn's impotence. Not that I was going to mention it. "Nora was wearing this when Dumoulin attacked her. It's why she managed to knee him. It gives the victim the strength to defend themselves."

Lucas studied the amulet with disbelief.

Alice appeared extremely confused again. "That's Madame Ballon's pendant. I'd know it anywhere."

I nodded. "Dracs are incubi and succubi. They use the power of seduction to manipulate people. This necklace stops them."

Alice was back to gazing at Lucas as though he was the creature from the abyss, which wasn't completely incorrect. I let her go with it.

"A sospes," Lucas said softly. "It can't be. They're mythical treasures."

His turn to be shocked by stories being real. "Try it. Seduce me. I give you permission to do your worst."

"No," he said flatly. "It's something my family do, not me. Besides, I gave you my word at Les Profondeurs that I'd never seduce you again."

"I understand that," I said. "And I appreciate it. But in the interest of confirming that this really is a sospes, and that it will protect Alice, you have to try."

He chewed his gum. "I don't like it, but agreed. We need to be sure. Although the second you yield, I'm done."

"Let's do it," I said.

Alice sat up. "This is getting interesting."

I had to agree.

Lucas squared his shoulders and fixed me with his gaze. The intensity was difficult to ignore, but that was about it.

My lips quirked. "Have you started?"

The muscles in his face tightened. "Camille, come here," he said in his best bedroom voice.

I laughed. "I don't think so."

"Impossible." His jaw dropped.

Alice tittered. "Way to be a charmer, Lucas."

I rose to my feet. "Try a little harder. See if you can grab me or something."

In a flash, he pounced at me. I caught his shoulder and pushed him aside as though he was nothing more than a breeze. He tumbled onto the straw and lay there clutching his arm. I stepped over and placed my boot on his chest. "Gotcha."

"Jeepers, Camille," Alice said. "I knew you could fight, what with Grampi and all, but this..."

"It's not me. It's the necklace."

Lucas's body shook as he tried to move. "I like it." A broad grin expanded across his face. "Do it again."

I couldn't help chuckling as I released him. "In your dreams."

He sat up, still grinning. "But then it is a sospes. I can barely believe it."

"It means we have a solution," I said. "Alice, you'll have to pretend to be subservient to Elivorn until you get to the hidden room. Once Elivorn has the scroll, if he does anything other than leave you in the chateau, you'll have to defend yourself. The amulet will only work if you strike out."

"Alright," she said.

"As long as we can create a replacement incantation," Lucas said. "It looks like we have a plan."

CHAPTER 32

I WAS CLOAKED AND HOODED DESPITE THE WARMTH, THE graveyard wall digging into my back. The Grimmere door stood to my side, and Stinkhorn sprawled below. The city extended so far that I couldn't see its end, the buildings jumbled next to one another. The dull hubbub of the goblins' daily lives drifted over, although in this small oasis, it was peaceful, dandelions inclining happily toward the sun, wrens and tits chittering in the trees.

I could hardly believe I was out of Grimmere. The place had consumed me, the rest of my life drifting away like the mists in the forest. And now, much to my relief, everything was easing back. Our plan was in motion. Alice and I would find the hidden room in the Chateau de Foix, and we'd replace the scroll with a fake containing the false incantation that would, fingers crossed, destroy the malum.

I tapped my foot, attempting to vent the tension knotting my stomach. I'd had to leave Alice again, although this time she'd accompanied us through the tunnels and we'd left her with Wortle. Lucas and I had returned to the castle. I'd gathered my things and taken the way marker in the courtyard to Stinkhorn. The menhir was surrounded by a potent ward, meaning that only a Rouseau or those accompanying them could access it. As Lucas's mate, that included me. Much to my joy, it appeared that I was part of the family, which was actually worse than that time Extreme Sports Alex's uncle, a slightly deranged swineherd, had declared that I was one of his best sows.

Lucas was staying behind to ensure that, at all costs, Elivorn or his servants didn't descend to the dungeons and see that Alice was missing. He'd be returning the parchments to Elivorn's chambers, just in case, and he'd make my excuses, saying I had business in the human realm for a few hours. He thought that would be justifiable, as long as I was back for the ceremony at midnight. Lord Rouseau was adamant that we should all be there. And why wouldn't I wish to attend such a wonderful occasion? What a super family outing.

The way had brought me to the other side of Stinkhorn, and I'd navigated across the city using Roux's map. Digdeep, Roux, Gabe, Nora and a few guards were heading here with Alice via the forest way marker, a woodland glamour protecting the whole entourage. Alice would be riding one of the goblins' ponies. When we'd left, she was doing well, but she was bound to be weak.

My foot gained tempo. They should've been here by now. The sun was descending, and we needed to get to the

Chateau de Foix before closing time, or the plan would become a whole lot more difficult. Not to mention, we were relying on the likelihood that Elivorn would break into the chateau under the cover of night. The assumption was bolstered by him having meetings all day, but what if he made his move early?

The door creaked, then opened.

I sprang up.

Digdeep stepped through, escorting Alice, Roux, Gabe and Nora, all of them swathed in hooded cloaks. I caught a glimpse of a pony, guards and that monstrous forest, then the door swung closed, and Roux latched it firmly.

I flung my arms around Alice. "You made it. I was so worried."

"Sure did, hon." She squeezed me tight.

"Everything went according to plan," Digdeep said.

"All apart from me getting seasick riding that pony," Alice added, peering about. "So this is Stinkhorn?" It was so good to see her anywhere but in that dark cell, even though she still looked as rough as hell. She couldn't clean up or have the full healing potion until Elivorn had taken her to the chateau.

Gabe blinked into the sun. "Can't say I'm sad to leave Grimmere."

"Complete agreement." Nora tried her phone.

Roux leant on his staff, catching his breath. "Camille, if you don't mind, the map."

"Of course." I pulled it out of my pack and handed it to him.

With shaky hands, Roux tucked his staff under his arm and studied the parchment. "The door we need is a little way south, so we'd better get started."

"Hoods up, everyone," Digdeep said, his small eyes darting about, his sizeable cheeks quivering. "Our glamour was limited to the forest, and this land is under drac rule. There will be informants about. Roux, take us by back streets, if you can."

Everyone pulled their hoods over their faces, and we set off down a narrow alley, Roux in the lead. We passed doors of all shapes and sizes, some elaborate like entrances to mansions, some glossy with oil, some plain and nondescript. A few of them were high above the street with no access. Really useful.

Alice was taking it all in her stride.

"Are you alright after the ride through Grimmere?" I asked.

She frowned. "Camille, I've been lying in a dungeon for days, then swaying about on that blasted pony. There's nothing I want to do more in the world right now than walk somewhere—anywhere."

I could accept that.

A wooden door opened to our side, and a group of foot-high figures, cloaked and hooded in leather, bustled through, weapons on their shoulders. One of them, bearing an axe, sprinted over and drew back his hood surreptitiously before covering himself again. "Glad to see you back from Grimmere, ma'am," he said. "Terrible place. Not to mention, we've been missing all the fun stuck outside."

I grinned. "Slaughter, great to see you."

Alice goggled at him.

Time for an introduction. "Uh, Alice, this is Slaughter. He's a Man of Bédeilhac, from, you know, the cave of Bédeilhac. He's a very good friend of mine."

She nodded slowly. "And I was just about getting used to the goblins."

"Nice to meet you, ma'am." Slaughter shot her his best black-toothed grin. "Though we've seen you around the café a fair bit."

Her brow wrinkled. "You've been in the café?"

"We come in occasionally, delivering cheese and the like."

"Huh," was all she could say.

We turned into a narrow street. The bustling square at the end was filled with goblins going about their business. Alice watched them, wide-eyed, before Roux led us into another alley at a fast-for-him walk.

I stepped back and joined Digdeep, leaving Alice with Roux at the front. "Let's go through the next part of the plan," I said. "Everything has to run smoothly."

"Absolutely." His beady eyes darted about, on the watch for Grimmere informants. "Two hire cars and changes of clothes will be waiting for us a short walk from the Ménac way marker."

"Right," I said. Lucas had sent a messenger to Stinkhorn, enlisting a trusted goblin to enter the human realm and arrange the cars. We'd decided on the Ménac way as we wanted to avoid Coustarous and fae Tarascon. Alice's abduction would likely be widely known, and we had to keep her out of sight.

"At the chateau, Alice and I find the room." The parchment had been specific about its location within the tower. "We take the original scroll and leave the replacement, then get out." Roux and Gabe had constructed a false incantation and written it on a counterfeit scroll that had been meticulously glamoured to look ancient and authentic. It was now carefully wrapped inside my backpack.

Digdeep nodded. "Then I take one of the cars and escort Alice back to Grimmere, where she'll wait for Elivorn in the dungeon."

"One thing I can't figure out is how Elivorn will get into the Chateau de Foix. It will be locked up for the night." Though when I'd worked there, the security had been terrible, the locks old, Herbert the security guard even older. They might have improved things, I supposed.

"No doubt Elivorn will use goblin locksmithing equipment. Magnets can be used for door sensors, and certain kinds of glamour can mess with surveillance cameras. With the resources at his disposal, he shouldn't have a problem."

I glanced back to check on Gabe and Nora at the rear, but Gabe was alone. He cringed.

"Where's Nora?" I growled. I couldn't take more of her antics.

"Uh... she said she'll just be a moment—"

She sprang out of a side alley with an armful of packages wrapped in brown paper. Angry shouts came from the square. She grinned. "Lunch, anyone? I could only get three..." She peered into one as we continued on. "Uh... I'm not sure what they are, some kind of filled baguettes, I think."

I fell back level with her and Gabe. "And you happened to have the local currency on you, did you?"

Gabe's eyes narrowed.

"What?" she said. "I was hungry. We didn't have time for lunch before we came. Who wants one?"

Boy, did I want to kick her butt. "Slaughter, make sure Nora sticks with us."

"Yes, ma'am." A group of Men circled her.

"What? Why?" From the scorn in her perfectly made-up eyes, anyone would think I was the most unreasonable person on the planet.

"Because," I hissed, "there is so much more at stake than you getting your lunch."

"I wouldn't have gotten caught."

Gabe's lips shifted as he tried to piece everything together. "You stole them...?" he managed finally. The two of them fell into quiet conversation, Gabe's tone tight. I heard, "I can't believe you actually shoplifted," then, "I can't believe you drew a load of hantaumo to the town to kill everyone." Yep. Nora was on the defensive.

"Oh, baguettes!" Roux cried from ahead, not having heard any of it. "Wonderful! My tummy is growling."

Nora handed him one, looking rather smug. "Anyone else?"

"Decent food?" Alice said. "Yes, please."

"Happy to help." Nora bumped her brow.

She offered one to Gabe, who shot her an evil glare. She,

Alice and Roux tucked in as we walked. Roux, juggling his staff, the map and the baguette, led us under an arch and through a particularly narrow street.

I joined Digdeep again. "Alright, when you head back to Grimmere, Roux, Gabe, Nora and I will wait in Foix in the other car for Elivorn to return with Alice. When he does, I'll be there to ensure she's okay."

"Perfect," he said.

"This is the part I don't like. I trust the amulet, but Alice has no idea about self-defence."

He locked his eyes on mine. "Is there a way you can cause a distraction? Get Elivorn out of there quickly?"

I shrugged against my cloak. I was too damned hot wearing it in this weather. "I'll have to think of something."

Roux led us through a series of passages, then an area with stables and livestock, the dung pungent.

"Are you sure we're going the right way?" I called. It was taking a little too long.

"Completely sure," he replied. "It's because we're having to keep to the back streets, but it's not much further."

I hoped everything was going alright back in Grimmere. Our plan depended on Lucas keeping Elivorn away from the dungeons. Once again, I thought of Lucas standing in the drawing room swearing to destroy the assembly, his face contorted with his drac form. My hot skin prickled. Damn it, my doubt was poisonous, lying in wait deep within to hook on to the slightest uncertainty.

I glanced at Digdeep, who strode with a steady footstep. In fact, every part of him was steady and dependable.

"Digdeep," I said. "All of Lucas's goblins... you trust them. But how can you trust anyone in a place like Grimmere, where there's suspicion and secrets and so much darkness?"

He sucked in a breath, his chops wobbling, his brow narrowed. "It's a question I've asked myself plenty of times throughout my life. I find it's necessary to weigh up each situation, and place trust where it's warranted. But without it in some form or another, life becomes hellishly impossible. Then one is always second-guessing, never able to commit fully to a cause." He shook his head. "Mistrust is a worm that will eat you alive."

I had to agree.

We ascended a flight of steps. At the top, a vista of the city opened before us.

"If it's worth anything," Digdeep said as we surveyed the view, "I know Lucas trusts you."

I scoured his wrinkly, flubbery face and his beady eyes that were a little too steady for a goblin's. Had it been so obvious that my question was about Lucas?

Anyway, I wasn't so sure Lucas did trust me. He'd not been open about his drac origins. But was that lack of trust or a delayed attempt to introduce the horrific reality gently? He'd trusted me with everything else. And Elivorn... I hadn't thought about it before, but I'd been covered in his scent both times he'd seduced me. Lucas must have known something was going on, but he'd trusted that I was dealing with it.

"Oh, look," Roux called from ahead. "The door is just along there. I... um... well, a small dollop of mayonnaise may have dropped onto the map, making me think we were in a completely different place, and we may have taken a slight detour, but... um... well, it's all sorted now."

I shook my head as Roux led the way to a blue door surrounded by a cloud of periwinkles. Digdeep paused and placed his hand on my arm, his gaze steady. "I've known Lucas for centuries," he said. "I know what lies in his heart. From what I've heard, you've known him for a couple of months, plus he's a drac from one of the most notorious and dangerous houses in Fae, to say nothing of him being one hell of a trickster. You're sensible to be wary. But be sure to listen to your instincts, and then after that, the best way to trust someone is to, well, actually trust them."

CHAPTER 33

Two black Audi SUVs had been waiting for us near the Ménac menhir. They'd been stocked with clothes, trainers, make-up, rucksacks and spare mobiles. The tinted windows were perfect, but considering Lucas had done a great job providing us with everything we needed, didn't it occur to him that most of the population didn't drive around in cars worth more than my loft? They were massive too, and not ideal for the narrow streets of central Foix. Digdeep, who now sported an average-Joe glamour, had obviously spent some time in the human realm if his driving was anything to go by. Despite his height, he was doing a fine job chauffeuring Alice and me through the town. Roux, on the other hand, who usually drove a C1, was struggling. He was following with Gabe and Nora on board, and there had been more than a few horn blasts from oncoming traffic as he veered into the centre of the road. So much for being inconspicuous.

Alice and I were in the back as we'd changed our clothes on the way, pulling on T-shirts, jeans and extra-large but thankfully lightweight hoodies. Perfect for hiding ourselves. Roux had glamoured my scent earlier as a precaution, although in such a busy place he thought smells would be muddied and impossible to distinguish. Alice couldn't be glamoured, but Elivorn would be overwhelmed with her scent when he returned with her and shouldn't notice traces from before. I transferred the fake scroll to one of the rucksacks, then cracked my window, the deliciously familiar fresh mountain air streaming through. Boy, was I glad to be home.

Alice stared out at the townhouses.

"You ready?" I asked.

She twisted her lips. "It seems strange to be back here when everything inside me has changed."

I knew the feeling. "That's been my default setting for a while now."

"But, yeah," she added, "I'm ready. After all, we're going for a nice walk around a tourist attraction—I can't see any problem."

"There's a bit of concealer out of place," I said, dabbing her cheek to cover one of her bruises. The rest were well hidden.

Digdeep drove us right up under the chateau, the three massive towers looming above. In the words of a troubadour, "the castle was so strong it could defend itself". What secrets lay within that I'd missed when I'd worked here?

We drew up by the museum. Digdeep turned in his seat. "Good luck. I'll be waiting here unless I get moved on. If so,

I'll be nearby. Just call." Parking was a problem this time of day. It was a problem at night, too, not that Lucas had taken any notice when he'd left his car here the other evening.

I nodded. "We'll be back as soon as possible."

We pulled up our massive hoods, climbed out and strode toward the museum. Not only was there a chance that Alice might be spotted, but there was a possibility that the place was being watched. The chateau grounds entrance lay inside the museum these days, the old gate no longer used. I met Alice's gaze as we entered the refurbished building. Her eyes communicated exactly what I was thinking. Please, let us not meet anyone we knew. Fortunately, I didn't recognise the woman taking entrance fees. We paid and headed up the steep path that crisscrossed the outcrop of rock on which the chateau stood.

"Kind of weird to think that this is my ancestral home." Alice was flagging a little, which wasn't surprising after the trek through Stinkhorn.

"It really is pretty amazing. Such a great family." I adjusted my pace to hers, then unzipped my hoody and brushed my hair forward over my face in an attempt to make myself look more natural whilst still maintaining my anonymity. Alice would have to manage with her huge hood hanging down before her eyes.

We passed under the gatehouse arch and continued on upward, meeting a few tourists. The view was stunning, the red roofs of Foix scattered below, the foothills beyond encircling the town.

"All we need to do is get in and out," I said as we approached the keep. "It should take minutes."

"Sounds good," she replied.

We took the steps up to the parapets and the twelfth-century central tower that housed the hidden room. Its open doorway led into a chamber that was full of tourists gazing at an exhibition of medieval weaponry, shields, spears and swords hanging on the walls. A spiral staircase stood by the entrance. I led the way up, almost bumping into a tour guide trotting down.

"Oh, sorry," he said, stepping to the side.

Shit, that broken nose and the ever so slightly dazed eyes were much too familiar. Alice turned her head away. Neither of us paused to reply, our hoods doing a great job of concealing us. The guy continued on his way.

"Wasn't that Extreme Sports Alex?" Alice whispered through gritted teeth. "I thought he didn't work here anymore."

I glanced back at her. "Me too. He finished years ago. I don't think he recognised us."

We stepped into the grand chamber. A few tourists milled about, peering out the windows and taking in the arched gables.

"It's here," I said softly, walking over to one of the windows. I'd fully acquainted myself with the directions in the parchment before I'd left Wortle's hole. The hidden room lay somewhere behind the nine-foot-deep alcove wall. Stone ledges on both sides extended along to the window. We sat down facing the wall in question, waiting for the tourists to vamoose.

"I don't see how there's a door in there," Alice whispered. "It looks solid to me."

I didn't either. "The parchment said you'd have to touch it. There's probably some kind of magic." Had I ever sounded more flaky? And I wished to hell that we weren't riding on "probably".

We gazed through the leaded glass until the tourists left. Alice got up and passed her hands over the wall. After a couple of minutes and plenty of doubtful glances, she paused on a low block near the window. "There's something here. I don't know what, but my hand is tingling."

Footsteps sounded on the stairs. We sat down and gazed outside again, as nonchalantly as any two burglars in hoodies could. We had to wait a full five minutes before the place cleared.

When we were alone again, Alice placed her hand on the stone. Part of the wall swung inward to reveal a small room. We'd actually found it. I turned on my phone torch and shone it in, curiosity burning. Alice did the same.

I'd expected the room to be dusty, but it was pristine—perhaps more magic at work. It was empty but for a beautifully carved oak plinth, a scroll in pride of place on top.

"You better do the honours." I pulled the fake scroll out of my rucksack and passed it to her.

"Sure." She stepped inside, swapped the scrolls and passed the original to me.

I wrapped it up and stashed it as she came out and

tugged at the stone door. It swung slowly and grated shut just as a family entered.

"Let's go," I said.

We headed down the spiral staircase and passed the exhibition.

"Oh, Camille, I thought it was you," Extreme Sports Alex called.

We drew up short, Alice turning away from Alex, my stomach leaping into my throat. We could make a run for it or walk out without saying a word, but Alex might come after us. There was nothing for it. I'd have to talk to him.

"Alex. I didn't expect to see you here," I said as calmly as possible. I could only hope he wasn't going to do his usual and hint that we should get back together again.

"I'm between jobs and the chateau was short-staffed." He eyed me up and down, looking confused, which was pretty typical for him. A hoody and trainers weren't my usual style. "Some fight at Castle Rock the other night. Looked like you knew the guys."

I hadn't realised he'd been there. "Yeah, fun night. Look, it's great to see you, but I'm... tight for time. I'll catch up with you again." I caught Alice's arm and pulled her past.

"Cool," he called. "And my uncle said to send his regards if I caught you. He says you were the best sow since Madame Truffle." He stepped out after us as we descended the steps. "Terrible news about Alice disappearing, though. I was thinking of you guys."

"Thanks," I called back.

"And, uh... we really should go out again sometime..."

I wasn't going to reply to that.

We strode down the chateau path as quickly as we could without drawing attention to ourselves.

"That was much too close," Alice whispered. "And Madame Truffle…" She sniggered.

"Most definitely best forgotten," I muttered. "I don't know about you, but I'd like to get out of here."

We headed through the museum. Digdeep was outside. As we approached, he started the engine and rolled down the window. Alice climbed into the back.

"Everything is sorted," I said.

Digdeep nodded. "Good. Time for the next step."

Over his shoulder, Alice was buckling up. She looked exhausted. "Honey, you don't have to do this," I said.

She smiled softly, her warm brown eyes glinting. "I know, but I want to. Just make sure you're here when I return."

"I will be. And just *you* make sure you keep safe." I wanted to hug her. I wanted to pull her out of the SUV, hail a taxi and take her home, but instead, I stepped back, and Digdeep pulled away.

CHAPTER 34

I SAT ON THE STEPS THAT LED FROM THE SQUARE outside the museum to the Rue du Palais de Justice. Traffic murmured in the distance, the town settled for the evening. The heat of the day remained, even though the vestiges of dusk were blending into the black of night, the sky inky behind the three illuminated chateau towers.

I'd been here for hours in case Elivorn made an early appearance. It would've been ideal to do the stakeout in the SUV, but there hadn't been anywhere inconspicuous to park. I felt exposed, despite being disguised with the scent glamour and the last of the friend-or-foe. The dagger fastened to my pouch and hidden by my hoody was a small comfort.

I hoped to hell that this was the best place to keep lookout. Elivorn was strong, but surely he couldn't climb up to the chateau via one of the rock faces with Alice in tow. Just in case, I had the Men watching from all sides, although I'd given them strict instructions to remain concealed. If Elivorn saw them, he'd know something was up.

My aim was to follow Elivorn and Alice to the tower. She had the amulet, but it was still possible for Elivorn to hurt her if she didn't defend herself. On Digdeep's advice, I was planning to cause a distraction once Elivorn had the scroll, to ensure he left immediately.

My stomach churned, doing bad things to the few bites of pizza I'd managed once Alice had left. There was so much that could've gone wrong in Grimmere. I could only hope that Digdeep had returned Alice to the dungeon without incident, and that Elivorn wouldn't harm her on the way here. At least Roux had the original scroll safely in the SUV a few streets away. He was planning to take it to the Keepers' post later and store it securely. Gabe and Nora were still with him. I'd offered to pay for them to take a taxi home, but they were concerned about Alice and wanted to stay.

A small but extremely wild chestnut head appeared from the corner of Rue du Palais de Justice. "Elivorn is here, ma'am. Just turned into Rue du Rocher."

The churning in my gut escalated. "Thanks, Slaughter." Their arrival meant that Alice was alright, and that everything had gone according to plan, but now Alice would be in the greatest danger of all.

Headlights flooded the square. I hid in the shadows, not wanting to catch Alice's attention. The Range Rover parked, and Elivorn jumped out dressed in a shirt and linen trousers. He held the passenger door, and Alice, wearing her ripped clothes and a large hooded coat, stepped onto the cobbles.

They headed over to the old entrance, and Elivorn fiddled with the massive padlock on the gate for a moment before it swung open, giving them immediate access to the chateau path.

I followed, glad that the friend-or-foe glamour covered sound, as in the still evening air, my footfall echoed about. I pulled my hoody down over my face. There were surveillance cameras here and there. Elivorn might be glamoured against them, but I wasn't. Slaughter had said that Herbert the security guard was inside the office in the gatehouse watching *Lord of the Rings*. Possibly one reason why the chateau was vulnerable to break-ins, but it worked for me.

Alice walked stiffly. She was doing amazingly. Today would've been too much for anyone. I sent her be-strong vibes as she and Elivorn passed under the gatehouse arch, then I followed as quietly as possible. My glamour wouldn't be effective against Herbert. As I slipped past the office window, I glimpsed a row of security-camera screens displaying the chateau grounds. Elivorn and Alice weren't showing up on the one of the path, so it looked like Elivorn had done something to the system.

We continued on up to the chateau. Elivorn and Alice took the stairs to the tower door. At the top, Elivorn paused, his body still. Shit, he was listening. I held my breath, my heart thrashing. But there was no way he could hear me. He surveyed the darkness, his gaze sliding over my skin, then turned to the tower door and worked on the lock.

I released a breath. He must have heard something else.

The door opened, and they headed inside. As a precaution, I waited for a moment, then climbed the stairs and pushed the door. It wouldn't budge. I tried again, harder this time. Nope, it didn't shift, and there wasn't a handle on this side. My heart rate hitched. Elivorn and Alice would be up in the grand chamber by now. There was nothing for it. I shouldered the wood. It refused to move.

What the hell was I going to do? Without tourists around, Elivorn would have the hidden room open already, and as soon as he had the scroll, I hated to think what would happen. There was no other way into the tower, but perhaps I didn't need to enter if someone else could...

"Slaughter," I whispered.

The Man appeared from behind a parapet.

I drew my finger to my lips. Elivorn would hear if he spoke.

He nodded.

"Can you get into the tower?" The Men seemed to pop up anywhere.

He gave me the thumbs up.

"Go inside. Make a noise... something unsuspicious. Maybe pull one of the weapons off the wall so it looks like it fell down, then get out of there. Don't let Elivorn see you."

He vanished. A second later, there was an almighty crash. Job done.

I strained to hear what was going on. I could only hope with every fibre of my being that Alice was alright. Catching footsteps, I slunk back. Elivorn burst out and headed down the steps. Before the door could swing shut, I darted inside and propped it open with the shield the Men had thrown off the wall. My heart in my throat, I sprinted up the stairs and into the chamber.

A heap lay in the alcove.

Chapter 35

My breath stuck in my throat as I ran over and crouched down.

Alice groaned. "Camille, you're here," she managed.

"We have to whisper until we're certain Elivorn is gone," I said softly. "But what the hell has he done?"

I helped her sit up. She drew her hand to her forehead and touched it gingerly. "He struck me. I was going to defend myself, but he lashed out before I realised what was happening. There was a crash and he ran off."

My blood boiled. I had no idea what I could do to Elivorn with our ruse in play, but I would damned as hell think of something. "I wanted to get here earlier but..." But she didn't need to hear about that right now.

I opened my pouch and pulled out a vial of healing potion. "This will help. Drink it all."

She tasted it cautiously then tipped it back. "Not bad." Narrowing her eyes, she touched her head again. "It was killing a moment ago, but now I can hardly feel it." Her bruises had faded a bit.

"Good. We need to get you home." And I had to get back to Grimmere for the ceremony. "Can you stand?"

Slaughter appeared in the doorway. "There's a problem down at the square. I think you better see." He rushed out.

Alice clambered up, wobbling.

I grasped her arm. "Alright?"

"Yeah. Actually, I feel better than I have in days." She steadied herself, then took a couple of steps, but she was fine. We headed down, Alice in the lead so I could keep an eye on her.

Slaughter was waiting at the door. He gestured to the parapets. We followed him over and gazed out. Elivorn stood in the square far below, facing five large goblins, their aggressive stances visible even from here.

The goblin in the centre stepped forward. "What do you mean you've no idea what I'm talking about? What have you done with her?" His voice was distant but clear in the still night air. Holy crap. Raphaël.

Alice frowned, attempting to pair the voice of her fiancée with the goblin standing below.

"We had everyone out looking for Alice," he continued, "and someone saw her heading through Stinkhorn with you. You're the one who kidnapped her. Where is she?"

Elivorn shook his head and made to stride along the street, but Raphaël stepped in front of him. Not good. He didn't stand a chance against a drac. None of them did.

Alice opened her mouth to speak. I raised a finger to my

lips, my wide eyes communicating the urgency that if we could hear Elivorn, he could definitely hear us. I grabbed her hand, pulled her back into the tower and closed the door gently.

"That goblin sounded like Raph," she whispered. "Really like him. And he was talking about me."

I fiddled with the old metal handle. "Right at this moment, I'm more concerned that whoever they are, if they threaten Elivorn, they're going to be toast. I have to stop them somehow."

I couldn't send the Men in because even if they remained hidden whilst causing a distraction, Elivorn would know something was up. I could go down there and warn Raphaël, but would he be able to see me? And if he could, he might say my name and stick me right in it. I could call the police, but they'd take too long. Nope, none of that would work. But maybe I was making this too complicated. After all, the chateau had a security guard.

I pulled a spear from the wall and glanced at Alice. "Stay here."

She nodded, looking pretty bewildered.

As quietly as I could, I headed out, ran down the steps and took the path.

From below, I caught Elivorn's voice. "Don't you know who I am?"

Grimmere ruled the goblin lands, which made Elivorn something of an overlord to Raphaël. I had to give it to Elivorn, he was playing the superiority card rather than ripping their throats out. Maybe he thought it was less trouble than having to deal with five of them.

"Who the hell cares who you are?" Raphaël hollered. Did he have a death wish?

I made it to the gatehouse. Shutting out the commotion, I peered through the office window. Opposite the bank of screens, Herbert was in front of a laptop watching Gandalf arrive at Helm's Deep. Shame I had to ruin the best bit.

I stepped back and hurled the spear at the office door.

Poor Herbert almost jumped out of his skin. As I disappeared into the shadows, he pulled the door open and ran a hand over his bald head. His jaw dropped as he noticed the spear imbedded in the wood. Then, as I'd hoped, he heard the row in the square.

Jeers and laughter came from the goblins, along with a few choice cusses.

Herbert jogged down the path, sprightly for his age. I peered over the wall, watching as he approached the old gate. It was too dark for him to notice the open padlock.

"What's going on?" he called. "Break it up or I'll call the police."

"I've been apprehended by these... boys," Elivorn replied smartly. "They won't leave me alone."

He wasn't lying. And the goblins were all dressed in loose T-shirts and scruffy jeans, the lot of them bristling, whereas Elivorn wore straight-backed confidence and a smart, human-realm shirt.

"I'm glad you're here," Elivorn added, managing to force

worry into his voice. "I wasn't sure what they were going to do."

"I can see that." Herbert's chest inflated. Even though he was who knew how old, something of his prize-fighter build remained, as did the self-assurance that he could deal with anything. "Get on your way, lads. I won't ask again."

It was unlikely any of them would want the police here. Elivorn because of the delay, and Raphaël because no matter Elivorn's involvement, reporting him would create more problems than it would solve, what with everything being connected to Fae.

"Thank you." Elivorn inclined his head to Herbert, then strode off along Rue de Rocher. Best guess, as soon as he rounded the corner, he would use some of that drac speed to get the hell out. He had his prize, and he would return to the omphalos ASAP.

The goblins muttered to themselves before taking the steps to Rue du Palais de Justice. No torn throats. Thank you, Herbert.

Now Alice and I had to get out.

I sprinted back to the tower. Alice was sitting on one of the tour guides' chairs.

"We have to go," I said, my breath heaving. "Follow me."

We ran down the steps and hid in the darkness behind the corner of the tower. I peeked out. Herbert was striding up the path, spear in hand. He knew where it had come from and was investigating. Mumbling under his breath, he climbed up to the tower.

"Give him a second to get inside," I whispered, "then we have to run. You up to it?"

"Completely." Her brow furrowed. "But I could've sworn that was Raph's voice. It couldn't have been, though—"

I grabbed her shoulders and fixed her in the eye. "Right now, we have to get out of here."

She shook herself. "Yeah, of course."

We pulled our hoods over our faces and darted down to the gate. Thankfully, Elivorn hadn't locked it, and there was no sign of him or the goblins. Alice had a new lease of life thanks to the potion. We shot across the square and took the steps onto Rue du Palais de Justice, then turned into a side street. Only then did we slow to a walk.

"That was way too close for me." I shimmied my shoulders down, my heart rate easing. We'd done it. Elivorn would be long gone by now, and Alice had escaped him in pretty much one piece. Roux was waiting in the SUV a little further up the street. Now I just had to get back to Grimmere.

"This is like that time in high school when we snuck into the cave replica in the Parc de la Préhistoire with Gilles and Xavier." Alice's bruises had almost vanished, and her spark had returned.

I laughed, releasing a whole lot of tension. "It would've been fine if you hadn't insisted on Xavier turning on the lighting."

"Hey, it wasn't as romantic in the dark. You couldn't see the cave paintings."

"I don't know about Xavier, but nothing was ever

romantic with Gilles. It was more gropy and proddy and... urgh. Best not remembered."

She grinned. "Well, we had ten minutes before the police got there, then we had to leg it over the back fence. That was as close as this. We only just got away—"

Five goblins darted out of a side alley and positioned themselves between us and Roux's SUV. At the centre was Raphaël. My heart sank into my trainers. This was the last thing we needed.

"Alice!" he cried. "I've been so worried. We all have." He stepped forward, his arms outstretched.

Alice gaped. She raised a hand before he could embrace her. "Uh, who are you?"

"Alice? It's me..." Those goblin wrinkles were crestfallen.

His friends exchanged confused glances, one shoving his clawed hands into his jeans, another sniffing nervously. Raphaël had said he'd seen Alice in Fae. Surely it wasn't going to take long for the penny to drop.

He narrowed his eyes at me as though I was the root of all his problems. But that meant he could see through my glamour. Maybe he wasn't my sworn enemy. "Camille, what's going on? Everyone's been frantic. The police have been hunting for Alice everywhere."

She turned to me, her jaw stiff, her mouth open. "You know this goblin? And why does he sound just like Raph? Camille, it's freaking me out."

"Goblin?" Raphaël said, his face aghast. "What did you do to her?"

"This is so not the time," I hissed at him. "Come on,

Alice, let's get back." The SUV was only a car away. I grabbed her sleeve and made to push past the goblins, but she stood her ground.

Roux got out of the car, followed by Gabe and Nora.

"Can I provide assistance, Camille?" Roux said.

"Thanks, but no." There was nothing he could do.

Alice switched her gaze between me and Raphaël. "Camille, you have to explain what the hell is going on." Her eyes pleaded.

I drew a breath. She had to know, and there wasn't a good way to put it. "Umm." I swallowed. "This *is* Raphaël. Raphaël is a goblin."

His lips parted as if he wanted to say something but couldn't find the words. The others gawked.

She laughed and shook her head. "Come on, Camille. The past few days have been hell. This isn't the time for a joke."

I needed to try harder. "You're seeing Raphaël as he really is. Look at him in your peripheral vision, or squint your eyes, and you'll see the glamour he projects in the human realm. The glamour all of them are projecting."

She snorted. "Don't be silly."

Raphaël managed to get a hold of himself. "You gave her verity," he growled. "What gives you the right—"

I wasn't interested. "Alice," I said softly. "There's a goblin standing before us who has Raphaël's voice. Could you just give it a go? Because after everything, we've got to get you back, and I have to return to Fae or all hell will break loose." I wasn't going to spell out the details in company.

Alice frowned, then turned her head and gazed at Raphaël from the corner of her eye. As usual, he was looking all boy-band cute, as were his friends.

His Adam's apple bobbed.

Alice stood stock still, her skin flushed, her only movement several large blinks. "Raph"—she gulped—"you lied to me."

"I... I... I couldn't tell you the truth. I wanted to, but how could I?"

Her jaw clenched. "Camille tried to tell me, and you denied it." He'd put his foot in it, there. But before Raphaël could reply, Alice said, "I want to go. Now."

I guided Alice past Raphaël and into the open rear door of the SUV. She clambered in and I followed. Nora joined us on the other side, Roux and Gabe in the front.

Roux fumbled with the ignition button. "Camille, we have to get you to the way marker. Tempus fugit."

"I know," I said. "Let's go."

Raphaël was attempting to peer in through the tinted window.

Roux pulled away. "Once we park up near the menhir, I'll neutralise your glamours. After you've gone, I'll drop off Gabe and Nora, then take Alice home. That's the plan."

"Sure." But I wasn't really listening.

Tears were running down Alice's cheeks as she craned her neck, gazing back at Raphaël.

CHAPTER 36

I PACED BACK AND FORTH ALONG THE LENGTH OF Lucas's main chamber. It had taken me less time than I'd expected to return. With the map of Stinkhorn, I'd navigated through the city quickly and easily, and the Ménac door hadn't been far from the Grimmere Castle door. There was a little while before midnight, when we were due to meet the Rouseaus in the courtyard.

I'd expected Lucas to be waiting for me, but there was no sign of him. I stiffened at the thought of being alone in the castle with Elivorn nearby, but as Alice had no further need for the amulet, it was now around my neck, tucked into my top. There was no need to worry.

The door swung open. I paused, expecting Lucas, but one of the servants entered. Head lowered, he skittered to the hearth and placed logs on the fire.

"Umm, would you happen to know where Lucas is?" I asked.

He rose and bowed. I was never going to get used to that. "Lord Rouseau is swimming in the lake."

Wortle had said Lucas enjoyed night swims, but the thought of what lurked out there in the darkness made the back of my skin creep.

"Thank you," I said.

I strode to the window and gazed down at the water. The full moon glinted off a rippling wake. There he was, swimming to the shore. He would be back in a few minutes, and then it was showtime. My stomach clenched as I paced up and down some more. Tonight was our chance to destroy the malum and stop the Rouseaus splitting the bounds.

After a while, still with no sign of Lucas, I slumped onto the couch. If he'd come here straight after his swim, he would've been back ages ago. Whatever, my nerves were roiling, and I couldn't wait around any longer. I'd go downstairs to meet him.

I headed out, leaving my blade behind to maintain the appearance that I was comfortable in this place. I made my way to the grand staircase and jogged down the steps, the glowing candelabras lighting my path. The place was deserted, as usual, the only sound my footfall.

I had no idea how Lucas would enter the castle from the lake, and there was no one around to ask. All I could do was head in the direction of the cove. I continued on through several grand reception halls, then entered a broad corridor. A little way along, a door opened and a head appeared. It vanished instantly, the door clicking shut. I strode over and pulled it open.

Poky stood there, trembling, a pile of towels in her hands. "Sorry, miss, I didn't realise anyone was about at this time or I would've made myself scarce." Clack. Clack.

She was actually worried that I'd berate her for crossing my path, which said plenty about how the Rouseaus treated their staff. And she'd called me miss, as if we hadn't met at the hole. Part of the subterfuge, I supposed.

"No problem." I smiled, but that just made her cringe. "Do you know if Lucas has come in from his swim yet?"

"Yes, miss. I mean, no, miss. He's still out there."

"Can you show me the way?"

She bobbed a curtsy. "Of course." Clack. Clack. Clack.

I followed her along a series of narrow corridors lit with lanterns, then we took a flight of stairs down several floors, passing kitchens, washrooms and workrooms, many of them filled with goblins despite the hour. Eventually, we passed the laundry. At the end was a small door. "That way, miss," she said. "I expect he'll be finished now. He's been out there a while." She bobbed again.

Outside, the stark moon glowed, providing good visibility, though the forest that edged the cove was dark. A few clouds skimmed the sky, driven by a raw wind. I couldn't see any sign of Lucas. Perhaps he was swimming out of sight further around the lake, although it was unnerving that he wasn't back yet with everything kicking off tonight.

I took the steps cut into the black bedrock, then crossed the sand for a better look. Halfway along, I paused. I had a clear view, but the water was still.

An eerie cry came from the forest, and the back of my

neck crawled. I wasn't alone. I scanned the trees. Where moonlight merged with darkness, ominous mist writhed in the trees. A maloumbro. Not good.

At the end of the cove, something lay near the edge of the water. It could've been a rock, but my tired and overworked mind imagined the angle of a shoulder and the line of a leg. I had to check.

As I neared, I caught more detail, a head, an outstretched arm. I sprinted over.

Lucas lay on the dark sand. He was naked, the lines of his jaw tight, the sinews of his body rigid. My heart hammering, I dove down and grabbed hold of him. He was cold... too cold, his chest still. I placed my hand over his mouth. No breath. Shit.

I shook him hard. "Lucas, wake the hell up." Nothing, and I could be doing more harm than good.

Then it struck me, my blood running cold... Mushum had said that Lucas's life was in danger. It was why I'd come here in the first place, but I'd become distracted with Alice and the malum and Lucas's family from hell. Lucas had played down my worries, and I'd allowed myself to be lulled into a false sense of security. Well, not security in this place, but it had become the least of my concerns. And I'd returned to the human realm, leaving Lucas here alone.

Shit. Shit. Shit.

But after everything we'd been through together, after everything in Grimmere, he wasn't bailing out on me. No fucking way.

I had to do something, but what? CPR...? Or, of course,

healing potion. Would the servants have any? If not, Lucas's pack was in his chambers. There was some inside.

The scant light dimmed as a cloud drew over the moon. A little way off, the maloumbro eased out of the trees, then recoiled as the cloud swept away and the moon shone bright. I couldn't leave Lucas to that thing, but the laundry wasn't far. I could ask the servants for help. By the looks of the sky, I had a few minutes before the next cloud covered the moon.

Adrenaline surging through my veins, I sprang up, charged back across the sand and raced up the steps. I burst into the laundry, startling Poky and a few others who were folding linen.

"I need healing potion," I managed through breaths. "Do you have any?"

"Umm, n-no, miss," a large-eared goblin said. "Lord Rouseau has some, and we keep a little in our holes—"

"Then I need Lucas's pack. It's in his chambers."

They stood there, wide-eyed.

"It's urgent. Lucas is sick. There's potion inside." The words tumbled out.

Still they stared at me.

"Now!" I yelled.

Poky threw down her sheet. "Yes, miss." She gathered her skirts and sped out the door.

Grabbing a lantern, I ran back outside, charged down the steps and sprinted across the cove. I could only hope the flame wouldn't go out as it would keep the maloumbro at bay. But before I could reach Lucas, a shape darted from the forest faster than humanly possible. Elivorn stood in my path.

"You..." I growled, my breath ragged, my heart thrashing. "You did this."

He laughed lightly, his hair and coat-tails shifting in the wind, his gaze dark with spite. "Of course I didn't. There are penalties in drac families for siblings harming or killing each other, and the Rouseau penalties are the worst of all." He shook his head. "No, my hands are clean. But what am I to do if one of my servants wheedled into Lucas's service? A very difficult task indeed, when my brother has so many loyal goblins. And what am I to do if that servant concealed a hefty dose of hemlock in his evening meal?" He tutted. "My staff do try to gain my favour. It really is quite terrible, the levels they stoop to."

"You absolute despicable, rotten bastard." He'd put Alice through so much, he'd forced himself on me, and now this. There was no end to the pain and suffering he was willing to cause.

The moon scudded behind a cloud and the maloumbro slunk out of the trees.

Elivorn smiled. "There's no need to be like that. Have some sympathy. Look at my poor brother. Though I doubt he's dead yet. Not quite. Dracs have strong metabolisms." He glanced at the seething mass that was edging toward Lucas. "Though the maloumbro should finish him off. It's terribly tragic."

Not dead yet. I still had a chance.

"And now, I can finally have you. This time while

watching my brother die. That will make it rather thrilling, don't you think?" He moved closer.

"You're sick, absolutely sick." Without thinking, I shifted back. He was a predator who knew no limits, and I was next.

He laughed. "Come now, Camille, don't step away. I like it so much when you play hard to get. Yesterday was the most fun I've had in a long time. Do try to escape again."

Try to escape? Had he deluded himself into forgetting that I'd left him with his trousers down? But how right he was—I didn't need to shrink from him. I had the amulet, and it was payback time. His gaze sank into me, alluring, mystifying, tantalising. The thumping of my heart grew slower, harder, firmer, each beat forceful, but the only thing it drove through my veins was wrath.

"Camille, come here." His voice was low and seductive.

I placed the lantern on the sand and obliged. We were almost touching, his noxious warmth seeping into me, his breath hot on my temple as he angled his head and drew in my scent. "There we go," he murmured. "You can't resist me."

I didn't doubt that so many others had been in this position, unable to defend themselves as he worked his charms. But I had to admit, he really was gorgeous, those sensuous lips, that heavy gaze. What a shame someone so beautiful had to be such an asshole. He raised his hand as if to cup the back of my head and draw me to him. Before he could touch me, I took a leaf out of Nora's book. With everything I possessed, I drove my knee into his groin. It was a classic move, and so appropriate.

He staggered back, releasing air with a strangulated groan as he clutched himself.

"What's the matter, Elivorn, not feeling it today? The boys a little uncomfortable?"

"What...? How...?" he spluttered.

I didn't wait for him to gather himself. I shifted onto my back leg, then thrust my heel into his jaw. He staggered sideways. That one was for Alice.

"Oh, dear. That looks painful." I was really quite impressed that he hadn't fallen over, though a trickle of blood ran from his mouth.

The maloumbro was almost upon Lucas. I needed to get over there, but Elivorn was strong. I wasn't sure the minor damage I'd inflicted would be enough to hold him at bay. I clenched my fist, drew back my arm, and channelled my anger into his face.

His head whipped to the side, and he dropped to his knees. That one was for Lucas.

I took a step back, gained momentum with a spin, then drove my foot into his gut. He fell onto his side, groaning. That one was purely for me.

"Honestly, in this day and age, Elivorn, you might want to get it through your thick skull that when someone says no, it means no."

I considered stamping on his head. The move would kill a human. But I had no idea if he'd conveyed the fake incantation to the mages. Anyway, the maloumbro was inches from Lucas. I grabbed the lantern, braced it before me and darted over. As the light touched the dark tendrils, the creature retreated, then slid back into the bushes. Poky burst out of the castle door and ran down the steps, the pack in her hand.

I dove to Lucas and grasped his shoulders. He was even colder now, I was sure of it, his sinews rock hard. "Stay with me," I rumbled.

There was nothing I could do but wait as Poky dashed over, gaping at Elivorn, who writhed on the sand. She thrust the bag at me and dropped to the ground.

I dove into the pack, drew out Lucas's leather potion case and unbuckled it. There had to be twenty vials inside. They weren't labelled, although some were different colours. "Which one is the healing potion?" I'd not taken much notice before.

Poky's eyes were wide. "I've no idea, miss."

There were a number of cerulean bottles. I was pretty sure it was them, and it made sense that he would bring plenty to Grimmere. I grabbed one and pulled out the cork. Cradling Lucas's head, I tipped it to his lips and poured it in. It pooled in his mouth.

"He can't swallow," I said. "How are we going to get it into him?"

"I'm not sure he has to drink it, miss. In my experience, some soaks in through the mouth." Behind Poky, Elivorn was groaning.

"Good. Good." I scoured Lucas's face for any hint that he might still be alive. The line of his mouth, the hollow of his cheeks and the soft sweep of his eyelashes drew me as always, even though he was so still. "Come on, Lucas," I growled. "After all the crap you've put me through, you're not going to give up on me now."

But nothing.

I glanced at Poky, who was aghast and doing her best not to clack. I had no idea how well she knew Lucas, but if he died, it would mean the end of everything Lucas's goblins had been working for.

"Shit." I grabbed another bottle, uncorked it, and tipped it into his mouth.

Still nothing.

I grabbed another. "Can he have too much?"

Poky shrugged. "I'm not sure you can make him worse than he is."

A good point. I tipped it in.

When Lucas and Elivorn had fought at Castle Rock, the drac caveat meant that Lucas's wounds wouldn't heal. He'd had to have something special. Was that the case now? But then, Elivorn hadn't hurt him directly, so surely that wouldn't apply.

For a moment, I thought I caught a slight moan, but it could've been something in the forest. Then Lucas's eyelids flickered. Poky and I exchanged glances, hope unfurling in my chest.

Lucas groaned and rolled onto his side, his knees up. The colour returned to his cheeks and his sinews softened. My breath left me. I could only stare as he clawed at his stomach and vomited.

I couldn't believe it. I damn well couldn't believe it. I grabbed Lucas's shoulders and shook him once more. "Don't you ever do that to me again." Probably not the best way of helping, but hey, I wasn't the doctor.

Poky closed her eyes and uttered a silent prayer of thanks, then released a volley of clacks.

"What happened?" He raised his head, taking in Poky and then Elivorn, who'd just fallen over after attempting to stand up.

Clack. Clack. Clack.

"You had hemlock for dinner, and Elivorn was about to let a maloumbro finish you off." My breath was still too shallow. I could barely believe that Lucas was moving, that the muscles of his lithe torso were playing under his skin, that a scowl creased his forehead.

Managing to sit up, he gazed at his brother. "But it looks like you got there first." He rubbed his head. "And you're back." His words were heavily weighted. With both Elivorn and myself here, it implied that things were going according to plan. I nodded and attempted a smile.

Clack. Clack. Clack.

"Urgh." Lucas brushed sand off his arms. "I haven't felt this sick in a long time. And what is that clicking sound?"

Poky thrust her hand over her mouth.

Elivorn was struggling to stand up again. His face was a bloody mess. A footman rushed across the cove toward us, gazing in horror at the spectacle. He paused between the brothers. "My lords, Lord Rouseau is wondering what has delayed his sons. He is waiting in the courtyard." He glared at Poky, who withered.

"I have to go, miss," she said. "I'm glad everything is alright."

I squeezed her hand. "Me too. Thank you."

She hurried away with the footman.

"We need to get to the ceremony," Lucas said.

We shoved the leather case and the vials into the pack. Lucas got up stiffly, clutching it before him to hide his modesty. Not at all like him. Elivorn had clambered to his feet. As we passed, he looked as though he wanted to tear me limb from limb. Let him try.

I smirked. "Oh dear, women can be such hard work."

"You..." he growled.

Lucas tittered. "Good effort, Elivorn. You haven't gotten that close to killing me since that time with the voodoo doll, the volcano and the porcupine, which I have to say was particularly well planned."

"I can see through you," he spat. "It's just a matter of time before I find out what you're up to."

"Just trying to help you and Father. What more could you want?" In no way was Lucas's innocence believable. It never was. He stared at Elivorn for a moment, his eyes narrowing, then took a step forward and thrust his foot into his brother's face, knocking him to the ground again.

"Better not keep Father waiting." The smile on Lucas's face was dark. Very dark indeed.

CHAPTER 37

WE STRODE ALONG THE CORRIDOR TO THE COURTYARD. Lucas had whipped on his clothes, and apart from appearing a little pale, he looked alright. He was lost in thought, though. For the third time since we left his chambers, he turned to me, his expression serious, his lips parted as if he wanted to say something. Then he shook his head and looked away. But I had to give him credit. He'd almost been dead minutes ago. If there was one thing that made a person pensive, it was death. Also, he was walking strangely, like he'd been horse-riding for days. Maybe it was a side effect of the hemlock.

Ignoring his cowboy impersonation, I drew in a shaky breath. Not only had I almost witnessed Lucas's demise, but we had no idea what was going to happen with the malum. The thought that we'd kept Lord Rouseau waiting did nothing to calm my nerves, either. Then it struck me. "Is your father going to mind that I just pulverised the heir to his rule?"

Lucas's lips quirked. "Not at all. Mates have the right to defend their partners."

"Well, that's something." But I couldn't ignore his walk any longer. "What the hell is the matter with you?"

His brow raised. "I'm doing fine, thank you very much, considering I was knocking at death's door a moment ago."

We headed down the stairs. "Your walk. You never walk like that."

He released a full laugh, the deep ring piercing my adrenaline rush and making me realise how overwhelmingly glad I was that he'd pulled through

"You really want to know?" The corner of his mouth turned up.

"Why wouldn't I?"

He shrugged. "One of the potions you gave me was for Monsieur Leclerc. I was going to drop it off on the way to Grimmere, but he wasn't in, and then I forgot it was in my pack. It was for his erectile dysfunction. You gave me a month's supply in one dose. I'm now... how to put it... rather swollen."

I laughed from the pit of my belly, resisting a glance down. That was why he'd been clutching his pack when we'd come back from the lake. "Oh well, it's better than being dead."

His eyes sparkled. "Not much."

As we arrived at the courtyard door, the seriousness returned to his face. "But, Camille... no matter what, trust me."

Without waiting for a reply, he pushed outside. Lord and

Lady Rouseau and Isarn stood by the menhir. Lucas took my hand and squeezed it as we headed over. I responded with a frown, needing clarification on his request. I knew he wanted me to trust him generally, but did he mean something more specific?

"Ah, good." Lord Rouseau placed one hand on Lucas's shoulder and the other on mine, a warm smile on his face. "Lucas, it's not like you to be tardy... or Elivorn, for that matter."

Lady Rouseau, dressed once again like an elegant pirate, squeezed my arm. I was surrounded by affection from a family that wanted to wipe out everything I loved. "All sorted in the human realm, I hope?" she asked.

"Absolutely," I replied.

"Any later and we would've gone without you," Isarn said. "And where the hell is—"

Elivorn hobbled in and glared at me as he tried to pull himself upright. Boy, was he a mess. One eye was so swollen he couldn't open it, and he was covered from head to foot in wet sand. He'd done his best to wash the blood off his face, but that was about it.

Lucas smirked.

"Speak of the devil," Isarn said. Never a truer word.

Lady Rouseau rolled her eyes. "This is why you boys were late. Fighting again. You do rub each other up the wrong way." Just an everyday occurrence, the two of them almost killing each other. But in this case, it hadn't been Lucas, it had been me—at least most of it. And as Elivorn's injuries hadn't started healing, it looked like he'd not had any potion, or perhaps the caveat extended to mates. Whatever, I hoped it hurt.

"Come now, Mireille," Lord Rouseau said. "Boys will be boys. And drac boys are the worst of all."

Elivorn adjusted his sandy cravat, attempting loftiness but by no means succeeding. "Let's get on with it, shall we?"

"Absolutely." Lord Rouseau wrapped his arm around his wife's shoulder. They stepped toward the way marker. Lucas and I followed, Elivorn and Isarn taking the rear.

We emerged onto the moonlit omphalos. The cloud encircling the peak writhed, tormented by the malum. I felt the torment too, despair saturating the air, seeping into me with every breath. We headed up to the crater, my hand in Lucas's. Once again, I had to fight the urge to turn tail, but Lucas's firm grip and encouraging glances rooted me. I could barely believe he'd almost died.

At the top, encircling the malum, numerous mages stood by as many menhirs, the way markers channelling desolation to lands beyond. I strove to hold my thoughts together as I gazed upon oblivion. A party was gathered a short distance around the crater. We headed toward it.

Lord and Lady Rouseau, Elivorn and Isarn greeted the dark elves like old friends. The elves took in Elivorn's state with curiosity. Lord Rouseau introduced us, then added, "It is a great pleasure that High Counsel Barduk and Lord Drikespur have been able to join us for such a momentous ceremony."

Barduk clasped my hand, her long hair and longer ropes whipping about in the wind. "Camille Amiel," she said, her voice melodious. "Conqueror of the hantaumo queen. We are honoured to meet you." There was my reputation again.

"Indeed we are," Lord Drikespur added with a solemn nod.

A mage approached, all beard and cloak. He bowed before Lord Rouseau. "The malum is strong and flowing forcefully to the bounds. The incantation has been prepared and we are ready to begin."

"Wonderful, Archmage." Lord Rouseau beamed at his family and the delegates. "Should the invocation boost the malum as we expect, this will be a fateful day indeed." He patted Elivorn on the back. "Well done for your meticulous research."

Elivorn nodded. "It gives me the greatest pleasure to aid in the destruction of all that hinders Fae. I live for it." My satisfaction at having pulverised him doubled.

Lord Rouseau turned to the archmage. "You may begin."

He bowed and hurried off.

Lady Rouseau smiled at her husband, pride and love glittering in her face.

Lucas met my gaze, communicating that I needed to be ready for anything. He stepped behind me and wrapped his arms around my waist, knotting his fingers over mine as we looked out upon the malum. This was our chance.

The archmage took position between two large menhirs further around the rim. He began chanting, a low and seeping tone. The mages joined with him and the incantation rose on the wind, discordant and grating.

The centre of the malum whirled, casting surges of darkness to the menhirs and the lands beyond. My breath grew shallow. The last thing the bounds needed was an outpouring of that gunk. Lord and Lady Rouseau and the delegates looked on avidly, Isarn watched with reserved interest, and Elivorn sucked in his cheek, his gaze boring into the swirling darkness.

The chanting soared, and with it, the malum spun faster, the surges more forceful, the sense of desolation horrendous. The incantation was having an effect, that was for sure. A grin curled across Elivorn's face, and his father nodded in satisfaction. Lucas clutched me tighter.

The wind built, gusting about, then it gained cohesion. For a moment it partnered the malum's whirl, then it spiralled into a frenzied hurricane. Lucas and I had to step apart to maintain our foothold. Elivorn's gaze narrowed. The others exchanged nervous glances. The mages struggled to hold their positions at the menhirs. Best guess, this was not in their plans.

The hurricane whipped up the malum, drawing it in on itself, shaping it into a vortex that pulled oblivion away from the menhirs and the rim, revealing the sheer cliffs of the immense crater. A pool of nothingness twisted far below, feeding the maelstrom.

The sense of desolation grew to almost unbearable proportions. The mountain rumbled, the ground shook, and the wind roared. All of us, mages included, retreated from the edge.

"What's going on?" Lord Rouseau cried above the commotion.

"I have no idea," Elivorn shouted. "This shouldn't be happening."

The malum soared upward, rotating faster, the ground undulating. Cracks grew in the rim of the crater, and rocks fell into the base of the vortex, taking one of the mages down, and then another. I had to give it to Roux, his faux incantation was doing its job. There was no doubt the place was crumbling.

"We need to get out of here," Lord Rouseau yelled.

We turned for the menhir to Grimmere, but the rock beneath my feet slid away, the ground disintegrating. My heart rose to my throat as I plummeted toward darkness.

"Camille!" Lucas cried.

Pain split through me as I slammed into a spur of rock a short way down. I scrambled up and clawed my fingers into crevices, gaining purchase, debris raining on me.

"Grab my hand." Lucas's voice rose above the chaos. I peered up through a shower of stones. He was lying over the edge, his eyes wild, his arm outstretched. He couldn't come down—the cliff was too unstable.

Behind me, the malum spouted into the heavens. Far, far below, oblivion swirled. I focussed. If I could just pull myself up... The rock disintegrated in my hand, revealing a new protrusion. I grabbed hold of it as the boulder beneath my feet crumbled. My arm burning, I hauled myself toward Lucas with everything I had. Our fingers met as my handhold broke away. Lucas gripped my wrist and dragged me up, then pulled me from the rim. We tumbled back onto jagged, undulating rock.

Only then did I realise the extent of the devastation. My jaw dropped, horror streaming through me. Elivorn had fallen part-way down the cliff and was attempting to clamber up. His father and mother were clinging desperately to the disintegrating rim. Isarn was on what remained of the edge, shouting instructions from above. Only a handful of mages and a couple of delegates remained, and they were on the ground.

"It's going to blow," Lucas yelled as he attempted to stand.

I steeled myself against the horror. Everything was going according to plan. The malum would be destroyed, and by the looks of it, the omphalos too. I glanced down to the way marker below. We just had to make a run for it, then stop anyone else from returning via the menhir, and that would be that. We'd done it. It was the end for the Rouseaus and their plans.

The shaking escalated, rattling my bones. Lucas had managed to get up and was stumbling about. He extended his hand. I took it and he pulled me to him.

"Let's go," I yelled.

He paused, his body too still amidst the turbulence. Something flickered in his gaze, wistfulness perhaps, then darkness, the corner of his mouth flickering up. "No, Camille. We have to help my family."

CHAPTER 38

Lucas wrenched me toward his parents.

I pulled my hand back. "What the hell?"

"Come on," he yelled. The ground lurched, and we struggled to stay upright.

He grabbed me again and yanked my arm. I fought against him, but he wouldn't let go. There was something in his gaze... a glimmer of arrogance... deviousness. Just like when he'd given me verity, or when he'd laughed at the destruction the Men had caused in my loft. He shook his head, then released me and sprinted over to his family.

Reality sank in, my thoughts spinning like the malum, my body trembling like the rock beneath. We were poised to end the Rouseaus' plans once and for all, but he was choosing to help them. He was on their side. He'd gone through the whole rigmarole of working with me and the goblins not to wipe out his family but so he could infiltrate the assembly. After all, when he hadn't known I was in

Grimmere, he'd ripped out Pierre's throat. He really had taken me for a ride. He was a goblin. No, he was the worst of goblins. He embodied all that was evil and odious in them. He was darker than night.

I fell to my knees, my chest raw. I'd been so stupid.

But so much didn't make sense. Why would he go to the trouble of destroying the malum if he was siding with his family? And this was the man who'd saved me from the black ward and Les Profondeurs, who'd thrust his sword into the hantaumo queen's side when I'd lost all hope. There were other things too. He took care of the townsfolk meticulously. He'd supported Gabe and Nora in acclimatising to the hidden world. He'd engendered the loyalty of a whole troop of small, wild Men. And despite his weirdness and trickery, he cared. He always pulled through. What's more, just before we'd taken the way, he'd asked me to trust him no matter what. There had to have been a reason for it.

Lucas barked orders for Isarn to support him as he clambered down toward his mother. He turned and met my gaze. "Camille, I need your help," he hollered.

Every part of me shook as he reached out for Lady Rouseau. Despite my fear, despite my misgivings, there was something within me that needed, that ached, for Lucas to be the real deal. I couldn't go on being split like this, mistrust fracturing everything.

Digdeep had said to trust my instincts. In the vulnerability of the night, when only my intuition had remained, I'd slept with Lucas's body encircling mine. His warmth and strength had felt so right. If I couldn't trust that, what could I trust?

And that meant if Lucas was rescuing his family after vowing to bring them down, there had to be a damned good explanation. Forcing uncertainty away, I drew a breath of fetid air and sprinted over to the Rouseaus.

Lucas grabbed his mother and helped her climb up the crumbling cliff. Isarn was nearby, dangling over the edge, his father's hand in his. Elivorn was hauling himself onto what was left of the rim a little further away. As I neared, a massive tremor tore through the rock, throwing me to the ground.

Pinning himself and Lady Rouseau between two stable boulders, Lucas managed to hold his position. Elivorn was knocked back down onto the ledge. Isarn was thrown forward. He released his father, grabbed a rock and swung from the edge. Lord Rouseau fell onto a ridge.

As the quake declined, the others climbed back up, making progress against the constant tumult of rock and noise and vibration, the malum spinning ever higher. But Lord Rouseau was struggling. The shelf on which he stood was breaking away. He groped for handholds as chunk by chunk the shelf tumbled into the swirling darkness. Several stable boulders protruded from the disintegrating cliff. At a push, I could jump down and reach him. The others were just about hanging on. There was no one else to help.

"Camille, get him," Lucas yelled. I didn't want anything to do with saving the man who'd killed Blisterch and so many others, the man intent on ripping the world apart. But Lucas had to be helping for a reason.

Before I could talk myself out of it, I sprang down onto the first boulder then leapt to the second, only just managing to balance on the undulating rock. Damn it. I was risking my life for a tyrant. I sprang onto the boulder nearest Lord Rouseau as he slid downward. Ramming one hand into a crevice to anchor myself, I reached out to him. He caught hold of my wrist as a huge chunk of mountain crumbled away beneath him.

My arm blazed with Lord Rouseau's weight, pain streaking across my shoulders to my hand wedged in the rock, my sinews tearing. He was too heavy for me.

Grim resolution marred Lord Rouseau's face as he swung back and forth, determined to reach a stable footing to his side. His hand was crushing my wrist, and with each swing, my shoulders felt as though they would dislocate. I cried out, pain consuming me, my fingers slipping from the crevice. For fuck's sake, the monster was going to pull me down with him. My fingers shifted a little more, then loosened. Everything slowed as I lost my hold, the malum a gaping mouth of nothingness below.

I was jerked upward. Isarn had climbed down onto a newly formed ledge and had hold of my belt, but Lord Rouseau still clung to my wrist. As Isarn hauled me up, the pain was unbearable. He managed to reach his father's hand. Lord Rouseau released me, and Isarn pulled us both onto the protrusion.

My shoulders screamed in agony as they attempted to

realign, the world tunnelling in. I fought to hold on to consciousness as our ledge shook. But then Lucas was there. He hoisted me over his back and climbed the rock face as Isarn helped Lord Rouseau. When we reached the top, Lady Rouseau hauled me from Lucas and Elivorn grabbed his father. As we staggered to our feet, a mammoth tremor ripped through the ground, the malum whirling in a frenzy, oblivion expanding.

"Let's get out of here," Lucas yelled. We pelted down to the way marker, self-preservation overriding my pain. The last thing I saw as we stepped into a shimmer of arched windows and black stone was the malum pulsing outward, darkness consuming the land.

CHAPTER 39

"WHAT THE HELL HAPPENED OUT THERE?" LORD
Rouseau bawled as he leant on his desk. The dull light of
dawn seeped through the arched window behind him,
making his black expression even darker. Lady Rouseau
stood at his side, her arms folded, her eyes glinting
dangerously.

Lucas, Elivorn and Isarn, standing with me, were
receiving the full brunt of the tirade. Only the desk
prevented Lord Rouseau from tearing them and possibly me
to shreds. He really was formidable, one of the most powerful
and ruthless creatures in Fae, and I would be lying if I said
my stomach wasn't swishing.

I was glad of the blade on my back. Not that it would do
me much good in this den of dracs, but it made me feel
better, as did having my pack with me, ready to go home.
Last night, after the malum had blown, Lord Rouseau had
been too angry to deal with the fallout immediately. By the

time Lucas had administered healing and fortifying potions and Wortle had fussed around us, it was almost morning.

Without the servants in place, we hadn't been able to discuss anything, so we'd sat on the couch nursing tea and staring into the fire. I'd been submerged by a deluge of thoughts and emotions, all of which were still with me now.

I was furious at the way Lord Rouseau had gripped me when I'd helped him. It had been clear that his priority was himself. If he'd gone down, he would've taken me too. Even now, with the healing potion, my arms and shoulders were sore.

But more than that, I was confused. We'd destroyed the malum. We'd stopped the Rouseaus from splitting the bounds, and yet I didn't understand why Lucas had insisted on saving his family. I was holding on to that trust I'd kindled last night. He must have a very good reason, but I needed answers.

Lord Rouseau paced up and down behind his desk. "All that effort. All the time we put into the malum," he growled. "Years of planning and gathering resources. All of it destroyed because of what?" He paused and fixed his gaze on Elivorn. "Because you didn't do your research properly."

Elivorn's hands were clasped behind his back, his shoulders square. He was still bruised from my thrashing, which meant the caveat must extend to mates, and I was glad he'd suffer a little longer. His spine straightened. "I did my research thoroughly. The number of dreary manuscripts I had to go through... They clearly indicated the scroll hidden in the Chateau de Foix. I don't understand it."

"What I don't understand," Lord Rouseau roared, "is how you got it so completely wrong." His pulse throbbed in his temples. He glanced at Lady Rouseau as though her presence alone was preventing him from ripping their sons' throats out. Although at this moment, she looked like she might do the ripping.

"One mage made it back," she said. "One of the *forty-nine* on duty, including the archmage. We lost High Counsel Barduk and Lord Drikespur. Only two of the delegates returned."

"The goodwill we formed with the dark elves is in ruins," Lord Rouseau added. "The experience of the mages in crafting the colludes..." His voice rose, flecks of saliva dotting his lips. "It's all gone!"

Even though Elivorn was doing a good job of withstanding his father's wrath, his admonishment was rather enjoyable. We'd put him right in it. His death and that of his family's would've been better, of course, but despite my confusion over Lucas's motives, I couldn't help a flutter of satisfaction that we'd scuppered Lord Rouseau's plans so completely. Lucas glanced at me, the gleam in his eye conveying that he was thinking the same thing.

Lord Rouseau drew a deep breath, then strode around the desk and paused before me. He was so intense and unyielding, radiating predator. I hated to think what he wanted.

"Camille." He met my gaze. I had to stop myself flinching. "You saved my life. You are already part of this family as Lucas's mate, a bond that I hope will grow from strength to strength, but you risked your life for me, and I am indebted to you."

"Uh." I didn't know what to say. He would've pulled me to my death. He was an evil monster and the last person on the planet I wanted indebted to me, but I had to act the part of the loyal mate. "Lucas's family is my family. I was honoured to help."

He nodded, satisfied.

"What's next," Isarn said. "Where do we go from here?"

I studied his impassive features. He'd saved me. He'd gotten to me before Lucas, and he'd stopped Lord Rouseau from pulling me into the malum. I still didn't have the measure of him, but I couldn't help feeling grateful. The sentiment was augmented because I hadn't seen his violent side, but who was I kidding? With a family like his, he had to be as lethal as the rest.

Lord Rouseau lowered his chin to his chest. "We have too many mages down, and the resources needed to reestablish the malum are immense, but..." He returned to his desk, drew open a drawer and pulled out a scroll.

Elivorn stepped forward. "Father, we agreed not to—"

The glare in Lord Rouseau's eyes stopped Elivorn in his tracks. "Enough. Your suspicion is dividing us. We need to be strong. I came to the decision yesterday, whilst Lucas and I were discussing tactics, to share everything with him. His and Camille's actions at the omphalos have only substantiated my decision."

Elivorn looked as though he'd combust.

Lord Rouseau unrolled the scroll across his desk. "This is

a timely moment for us to consider our plans once more, and to know that we are strong."

We stepped closer. The parchment was a map of Fae. On it, half of the territory was shaded.

Lord Rouseau's mouth drew into a tight smile. "The malum was only the beginning. A toe in the water. A highly effective toe, I have to admit, but if we discount the Fae lands that are inhabited by instinctual races, and those with no leadership, as you can see"—he swept his hand across the map—"with our allies, we constitute an unassailable force. The destruction of the malum was a minor setback. One way or another, the bounds will be split."

My jaw dropped, my heart flailing against my ribs. The implication was clear. Lord Rouseau didn't just have a few elves, dwarves and ogres in cahoots, he was supported by half of Fae.

He'd shared the information with Lucas yesterday while I'd been in the human realm, and Lucas hadn't been able to tell me. I shot him a side-eye. He was gazing at me steadily, willing me to understand why he'd saved his family. But it was all too clear. If we'd let them die, the leadership of this massive conspiracy would've transferred to another land, and Lucas would've lost his insider position. Now, the two of us were perfectly placed to bring the whole thing down.

CHAPTER 40

"I HAVE TO ADMIT," ALICE SAID, GAZING AT MAX, WHO sat at a table nearby, "I'd always known he was a troll. But I'm surprised he's quite so..."

"Meaty?" I asked, wrapping my hands around my cup and grinning. The two of us were leaning on the café counter, nursing cappuccinos. Today was just like that time Toulouse rugby team had stopped here on the way to Spain. Once they'd been served, we'd found a moment to drink coffee and ogle the muscle. This time, however, it was fae we were checking out, and there wasn't so much ogling, especially where Max was concerned.

Alice shifted her lips from side to side. "Yeah. 'Meaty' is kind of perfect."

I was so glad to be back. It was only this morning that we'd been standing in Lord Rouseau's study, receiving a rollicking, but it hadn't taken Lucas and me long to reach

Tarascon via the courtyard way. Once I'd been home and washed away all traces of Grimmere, I'd headed to the café. I'd desperately wanted to see Alice, and she'd returned to work, needing some normality. Thankfully, the afternoon was particularly quiet due to something going on at the town hall.

Alice had been with the police half the night, providing a statement and undergoing assessment by a doctor, not that it would do much good where Elivorn was concerned. Then she'd spent time with Inès, her mother, and the band of relatives who were overjoyed to have her back. Most people would've been exhausted, but ever since she'd taken the healing potion, she'd felt amazing.

I'd been worried that Elivorn might try something on Alice to ensure she didn't speak out about him, but Lucas had said that now he'd finished with her, it was highly unlikely he'd bother. Even so, he'd posted a guard of Men for the time being, and Roux was going to raise some protective wards around her house.

Max, aware of our scrutiny, shifted in his seat and glared at us as he stirred honey vigorously into his tea.

"And his head," Alice added. "It's kind of like a large bowling ball, but with layers of fat."

I studied him as he took a sip. "Yeah, I'd say that was a pretty good description."

Behind him, in the D&D nook, Félix looked startled, surveying the café with wide eyes. Actually, Zach and Hugo appeared bewildered too, and their D&D campaign wasn't even laid out on the table. Strange. Was this some kind of conflict with Gabe again? But Gabe sat in one of the armchairs, his back to everyone.

Nora was nursing an espresso at the table next to Max. She'd just come back from returning Shroom-Jean's cash and Madame Ballon's necklace. She'd fully admitted what she'd done. Apparently, they'd both reacted in similar ways, being shocked at first but then saying the important thing was that Nora had seen the error of her ways and had returned what she'd stolen. I couldn't help wondering if a little bit of aggro might have done more good, and I wasn't convinced that Nora had seen the error in anything. I had a sneaky suspicion that it had only been Lucas putting the fear of, well, him into her that made her return the loot. That aside, I appreciated that she'd not dropped me in it by mentioning me being in Elivorn's chamber, plus she'd admitted everything to Gabe. He was currently expressing just how pissed off he was by not acknowledging her existence.

Part of me had wanted to keep the amulet as protection against Elivorn, but we'd decided that it would be safe with Madame Ballon. She had no idea of its powers or of fae. It would continue to be an innocuous piece of treasured jewellery. And after all, it belonged to her, although if we ever needed it again, we could ask the Men to discretely borrow it.

Alice glanced into the kitchen. Mushum sat in the open window, licking his claws after having just finished off the massive fraisier cake I'd given him as a thank you. He hopped down and sprang over the back wall toward the sun-drenched buildings of fae Tarascon.

"Oh, and... I'd thought there were meadows and apple trees behind the café," Alice said, "but there appears to be a town. That was a surprise this morning, let me tell you."

"Uh, yeah. The apple trees are still there, just incorporated into the architecture. I wish I could've been with you to help you acclimatise." I studied her sweet face. Her bruises had healed, and she looked all clean and shiny. A far cry from the mess she'd been on the dungeon floor. Her forehead creased as she contemplated the fae town, and the despair I'd felt about not being able to share the hidden world with her welled up, tears pooling amidst my lashes. I leant my elbows on the counter and dabbed my eyes.

"Hey, Camille." She slid close, pressing her arm against mine. "Sweetie, what is it?"

I raised my head and laughed, blotting away the tears, a tumult of emotions coursing through me. "I should be the one supporting you, and here I am blubbering."

"But why?" She scanned my face, more concerned than she needed to be right now.

"I couldn't tell you about Fae, about any of it. It was so damned hard. I hated every minute, and I thought our friendship was finished. And now... I can't quite believe it." A wave of relief surged through me, my fingers trembling.

She put her arm around my shoulders and squeezed me tight. "I'm so glad we can get back to where we were."

"But I don't get it. I completely lost it when I found out

about Fae. And I hated the divide—some people knowing, some not knowing. It really screwed me up. Still does. You seem so relaxed."

She shrugged. "Things are as they are, and it's best to get on with life. Anyway, I think it's going to be more interesting with a few fae around. And as for not many folk knowing, well, we all have things we keep to ourselves or only talk about with our closest friends."

It was just like her to take it in her stride. I squeezed her back. Boy, did I need some of her levelheadedness.

Her gaze snapped to the open café doors. A BMW was pulling into the car park. "I haven't sorted everything out in my head yet, but there's one thing that's clear." She swallowed. "I have no problem dating a goblin per se, but without honesty… I don't know what our relationship is."

I felt for her and everything she would have to deal with. I'd been having similar thoughts. Lucas had shown me who and what he was, but I'd not been open with him about Elivorn. Perhaps with good reason, but it made me uncomfortable, my clothes too tight in all the wrong places.

Raphaël climbed out of the car and strode in, his wrinkles sagging, his ears drooped. Alice stood up stiffly and inclined her head, indicating for him to join her in the office. "We're going to need a moment."

My stomach turned. "Sure, hon. I'll keep an eye on things out here."

I served a customer that had followed Raphaël in, hoping Alice was okay. Lucas entered a minute later, looking much too good as always, his chin tilted arrogantly, his enigmatic gaze locked on mine. For a second, his work shirt and trousers took me aback. They were just so normal, yet he was a fae lord, a double agent, someone willing to carry out the worst of deeds, to risk his life for what was right. It confounded me.

His rigid form on the beach in Grimmere flashed in my mind's eye. We'd saved each other's lives multiple times, but seeing him there lifeless... I don't know. I was still reeling from it. The only consolation was that the servant who'd poisoned him had been dealt with.

He sauntered over and leant on the counter, his hair flopping messily over his forehead. "I have to say, it's good to be in the sun again."

I returned to the present. Lucas was here and he was alive. "Too right. Everything okay at work?" I started his noisette.

"The locum is finishing off today. I helped him with a couple of house calls, then I trawled through a million emails."

I released a laugh.

"What?" He arched an eyebrow.

"Emails... after Grimmere. So incongruous." I thought of Lord Rouseau and shivered. He was indebted to me, and it didn't sit well. "But your family trust us now. Even more so after their rescue—"

He raised a finger. "Slaughter."

The little guy popped up from behind a chair and saluted. "Yes, boss."

I grinned at him. He beamed back, his eyes sparkling. I

couldn't help but notice Félix's, Zach's and Hugo's expressions. They appeared to be gawking at Slaughter, but that was impossible, although there was a chance they were reimagining him as a small dog or something.

"Keep a lookout," Lucas said. "I don't want anyone listening in."

"Righto, boss." Slaughter vanished behind a chair.

The D&D guys flinched. Weird.

The machine had finished percolating. I passed Lucas his noisette, then cradled my cappuccino. Back to what I'd been going to say. "Your family trust us now—completely from the looks of it." Though I wasn't sure how comfortable I was with being a double agent—or was I a single agent?

He turned his cup in his hands. "It seems like it. But I'm sure my father hasn't revealed everything yet. I still don't understand how he thinks he can maintain Fae without the human realm, and he hasn't been clear about what he's planning next. Besides, there's not a hope in hell of Elivorn ever trusting me. But it's likely to be a while before my father recovers enough to make his next move."

When we'd returned from Fae this morning, we'd passed the bounds up on Coustarous. Now the malum was gone, the cracks had faded to almost nothing. We'd definitely bought ourselves some time. "And yet your father has so much more support than we thought." I took a mouthful of coffee.

He nodded. "We'll have to do something about it. And by 'we' I don't just mean you and me, but the assembly and all fae that have a shred of common sense."

I liked the idea that there were others out there on the

same wavelength as Wortle, Blisterch and the rest of Lucas's trusted goblins. "I have to say, this has opened my eyes to Fae. But it's also shown me how much I still don't know. I want to understand the place better, get a feel for the realm."

"The assembly is meeting soon, and I have to report back, not to mention I need to maintain the sham that I'll be there to gather information for my father. We'll go together."

"That works for me—"

Alice came out of the office with Raphaël, their faces grim. She saw him to the door, then headed back.

"Is there anything I can do?" I said.

She fiddled with her apron strap, her moist eyes blinking rapidly. "No, I'm fine. I'm going to take a minute in the office. I'll come out when I'm ready."

"Sure." I squeezed her arm. "I'm here if you need me."

I watched as she walked away, hating that Raphaël had done this to her. But she was strong. I'd always known that, and she'd proved it yet again with how she'd dealt with Elivorn and the whole fae reveal. I had to trust in that.

"I'm still open to breaking Raphaël's legs." Lucas swigged his coffee.

His words only half sank in. Max was itching the pointy tip of his troll ear, and Félix was watching, his eyes narrowed in confusion or possibly horror. On the opposite side of the table, Hugo was crying, and Zach appeared to be praying.

Lucas followed my gaze. "What's up with them?"

"I'm sure they can see fae." I headed around the counter and strode up to the nook. Collectively, they eased away from me. "What the hell is going on with you lot?" I said.

Lucas joined my side.

"Uh, what do you mean, Camille?" Félix said, stuttering. "There's absolutely nothing wrong with us. We're completely, totally, one hundred percent fine. No problem here." He was shaking.

I exchanged confused glances with Lucas. Gabe and Nora watched from opposite sides of the room, earwigging the conversation, unrestrained curiosity on their faces.

Max rose from his chair, his massive bulk blocking the light.

"Aaaaaaargh!" Félix cried.

"You can see Max, can't you?" I said. "As he truly is."

Lucas frowned. "That's not possible."

"Y... yes, of course we can see Max." Hugo's cheeks quaked. "Max the taxi driver. Max who likes to drink tea and sling abuse. Max who is most definitely a very large man."

Zach stopped praying. "That's right. Just normal old Max..."

Yeah, they could see his troll form, alright. But how...? "Oh, shit." The day I'd been thinking about giving Alice the verity, it had fallen out of my pocket. No. They couldn't have...

I fixed Félix in the eye, and he trembled some more. "A few days ago, you found a small vial on the floor. Before you passed it back to me, what did you do with it?"

All three of them cowered.

Lucas frowned. "I can't imagine you would've left verity lying around."

"Uh, the vial..." Félix said. "It didn't drop out of your

pocket. I... I, uh, saw it in there, sticking out, and I'd never normally do anything like that, but I just couldn't resist... I bumped into you and took it."

"You what?" I couldn't believe it, especially with Nora's pilfering too. Although Lucas said that humans were drawn to the stuff.

"We only took a drop each," Hugo said. "And then we started seeing things, like Max. But not only him, others too." His gaze flicked to a couple of goblins in conversation by the events room, then their eyes followed Max as he shuffled out. Gabe's and Nora's jaws had dropped.

"I don't like it, Camille," Zach said. "Help us."

I raised my hands. "Don't look at me."

"Make it stop, Doctor Rouseau," Félix pleaded.

Lucas shook his head, attempting to restrain a grin and not managing terribly well. "No can do. There's no going back after verity. You'll have to live with it. But I know two people who might be able to guide you through." He glanced at Gabe and Nora.

They exchanged massive grins, then rushed over and slid into the D&D seats, pushing the others along.

That, on top of everything else, was too much. "I need to sit down." I grabbed our coffees from the counter, took a large gulp of mine, then collapsed in Max's chair. Lucas sat down on the other side of the table.

"I don't ever want verity in my possession again," I said. "Keep me away from the stuff."

He laughed, watching the gang. "It'll be good for Gabe and Nora to have some company."

Gabe had taken off one of his silicone ear tips to reveal his real elf ear beneath. Félix was tugging at it, utterly dumbfounded.

"That lot plus fae equals trouble." I drummed my fingers on my cup. There was that restlessness again, that niggling that I needed to be completely open with Lucas, just as he'd been with me. But would he be able to handle the truth? Back at Castle Rock, he'd pulverised Elivorn, and we'd not even kissed. If I told Lucas and he lost it, everything would be ruined. But Lucas *had* trusted me when he'd smelt Elivorn on my skin. I scraped my teeth over my lip. I couldn't keep this from him.

"Uh... I need to tell you something."

"Oh?"

"I'm glad I know all about you and your family now, even if it is rather awful, because I don't think I would've managed to trust you with so much left in the dark."

He studied my face, the force of his gaze doing nothing to ease my tension.

"But I've not been completely open with you," I continued, "and I need you to promise that you won't overreact and blow everything."

"This sounds much too serious." He sipped his coffee.

"Promise," I said.

He raised his brow. "I promise."

"Alright." I sucked in a deep breath. "Back in Grimmere, when you smelt Elivorn on me—"

Every part of Lucas clenched—his jaw, the sinews in his neck, his arms, his fingers around his cup—all of him rigid. If his eyes had been closed, I might have thought he'd had another dose of hemlock.

I glared at him. "You promised."

From the D&D nook, I caught the word *Keepers*. The lot of them had their eyes on us.

"Just tell me," he managed through clenched teeth.

This was going to be fun. "Elivorn forced himself on me—"

His eyes grew wide, his chest rising and falling. Best I get the whole thing out as quickly as possible.

"He kissed me and bit my lip, which was why it was bleeding. Then later, before your father showed us the malum, he tried to go all the way, but he didn't get further than pulling down my trousers. Nora was there in the room for the papers. She managed to pass me the amulet, and I got out. Then when you'd been poisoned, he tried again. I had the amulet on that time and, well..." A smile tugged at my lips. "I paid him back."

Lucas turned purple, his nostrils flaring. Some of the clientele glanced our way. The lot in the nook gazed on in fascination as their doctor had a moment.

I raised a hand and fixed him with a firm gaze. "Elivorn was doing it on purpose, hoping to goad you to blow your cover."

Slowly, Lucas put his cup down and placed his hands on the table, his back arching, his face tightening until his skin was desiccated and hideous, his glower malevolent. His nails warped to black claws. I forced myself not to flinch. It really wasn't a good look. Ear-splitting screams emanated from Félix, Hugo and Zach as they bolted out of the café. Gabe and Nora glanced at each other, then followed, along with the rest of the fae in the place.

"I'm trying very hard not to return to Fae right now to rip Elivorn limb from limb." Lucas's claws scraped across the tabletop.

"Which is why I didn't tell you then and there. I'm not sure I did the right thing."

His expression softened just a little. "You made the right choice. With him so close, there was no way I could've stopped myself. And right now, I'm struggling."

I had to wonder why he was so possessive. A Keeper-partner thing, I supposed. I reached out and placed a hand on his, restraining a shudder at his leathery sinews. "He was trying to wind you up. Don't let him."

"I swear," he said, "I will kill him. I will bring my whole family down first, and then I will pulverise him."

I released a breath. We'd moved on from wanting to rip Elivorn apart then and there to planning to do it in the future. Progress.

He gritted his teeth, fighting to master himself. "What was it you said earlier?" he managed.

"About what?"

"You said something about being able to trust me." His eyes bored into mine, as though I was the only thing holding him here.

"Yes," I said. "I trust you. I trust you with my life."

Slowly, his inner drac retreated, his claws retracting, leaving deep scores in the tabletop. He gazed up at me from under his brow. "That means so much to me."

I was beginning to realise that it meant a great deal to me too.

GET FOLKLORIC FAE,
THE FOLKLORIC PREQUEL NOVELLA, FREE AT
www.karenzagrant.com

Perfect for reading at any point during the series

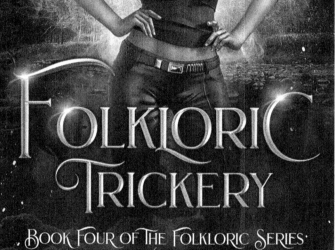

FOLKLORIC
TRICKERY

BOOK FOUR OF THE FOLKLORIC SERIES

KARENZA GRANT

Acknowledgments

At this point, halfway through the Folkloric series, I'd like to thank my readers for all their support. Folkloric would be nothing without you.

Particular thanks goes to my awesome ARC team, who have been unbelievably helpful in so many ways. Thank you, guys. You're incredible. With every book published, I appreciate you more.

As always, my gratitude goes out to Octavia Denning and Dorine Maine. A huge shout-out to my writing group: Viktoria Dahill, Katie Mouallek, Rachel Cooper and Abhivyakti Singh. Special thanks to Jack Barrow and P.M. Gilbert. Many thanks to Toby Selwyn, my super editor, and to Deranged Doctor Designs for the top-notch covers. Finally, Rillian Grant, you are the best beta reader EVER. You and Minerva Grant make it all worthwhile.

About the Author

Karenza Grant writes fun and feisty urban fantasy with plenty of humour and a little slow-burn romance.

Her early years in Cornwall were largely the source of her fascination with all things mysterious. She lived below a hill reputed to be the Cornish residence of the Unseelie Court, and the local myths got their claws in. Now she's inspired by a broad range of creators from Jim Henson, Arthur Rackham, and Olivier de Marliave, to a whole host of amazing authors on the urban fantasy scene. Currently, she's enjoying weaving her love of France into page-turning stories.

She has three black cats known as The Three Guardians, and a crazy lab x spaniel who is just about the only thing that can extract Karenza from her writing desk—if the pooch isn't walked, the legions of hell will be released.

CONNECT

There's nothing better than hearing from readers. Drop me a line or join me on social media. I hang around on Facebook on a daily basis and would love to see you there.

You can find all the links on my website:
www.karenzagrant.com

Printed in Great Britain
by Amazon

57557151R10202